AN ILL WIND

M K Turner

This book is dedicated to my husband Geoff and my dogs, Ted and Archie. All have been a little neglected during the writing of this book. Thank you for your patience, although I can't say it won't happen again.
And of course, YOU, the readers who encourage me to keep making stuff up.

Acknowledgements

Edited by Sharon Kelly & Jill Buss
Cover by: https://www.behance.net/lwpmarshala1e9
And, of course, my wonderful beta readers for all their invaluable input.

This edition published 2024 by 127 Publishing

Paperback ISBN **978-1-7394159-8-3**

Hardback ISBN **978-1-7394159-9-0**

Also by M K Turner

Meredith & Hodge Series

The Making of Meredith

Misplaced Loyalty

Ill Conceived

The Wrong Shoes

Tin Soldiers

One Secret Too Many

Mistaken Beliefs

Quite by Chance

Family Matters

Not If You Paid Me

A Measure of Guilt

Meredith & Hodge Bear Witness

Web of Deceit

Error of Judgement

Chance Encounters

Enough

Bearing Witness Series

Witness for Wendy

An Unexpected Gift

Terms of Affection

Meredith & Hodge Bear Witness

Little Compton Mysteries

The Murder

The Abduction

The Burglar

JJ Jenson Series

An Ill Wind

Others

Who Killed Charlie Birch?

The Cuban Conundrum

Murderous Mishaps

The Recruitment of Lucy James

Chapter One

THEY SAY IT'S AN ill wind that blows no good, and for Amber Wilton it was. But it went unnoticed because she was happy. She didn't know that the breeze lifting her hair from her face was an ill wind, and that as she laughed, her companion's hatred of her had reached the point of no return.

After an amusing evening socialising with friends, and aided by a little too much alcohol, she giggled as she struggled to climb onto the low stone parapet of the bridge. It took a while, her short stature and top-heavy figure hindered her, causing a few false starts. Once finally upright, she adjusted her clothes and embracing the breeze that lifted her tangled curls, she held her arms aloft.

"I'm so bloody happy," Amber yelled into the wind. "Oh, that's cooled me down. Told you I could do it. Be quick, I can't look down. I don't think I should have drunk so much." Amber saw the flash from the phone and leaned forward, her hand held out. "Thanks. One photo will do. Help me down before I go off the edge. I can jump down if you hold my hand." She giggled as her companion grunted disbelief and stepped closer. "Don't doubt me. I can do it. But brace yourself because I might make the earth move. I'm good at that," Amber warned, wiggling her eyebrows in jest.

Her merriment wasn't returned, and her laughter faltered before stopping abruptly, as the hand that should have helped her flew forward and banged hard into her thigh. It caused her to step back into the nothingness behind her. Amber's scream was short and shrill as she lunged forward to grab them, grab anything, but her efforts were futile. There was nothing to grasp.

Amber plummeted backwards towards the stream below. The fall might not have killed her if the water level had been higher, but it had been a dry June and the stream was little more than a trickle. Amber landed on a rocky relief in the centre of the scant stream, her skull cracking open as it met the edge of a rock. She was dead before the water could find its way into her trainers as it ebbed gently past her feet.

Her assailant didn't even bother to look, but hurried away into the shadows.

Chapter Two

JAMES JOHN JENSON WAVED goodbye to Jemma Freeman, owner of the Three Bells Inn, and headed towards the footpath that led through the woods.

"JJ, how much have you had? You live that way." Jemma jerked her thumb up the hill behind them.

"Not enough to be that daft. I'm going for some water shots at dusk. Don't hold me up, it'll be dark soon." JJ waved his camera and turned back to the footpath.

"You're mad. The wind's up. You haven't even got a jumper on," Jemma called, before stubbing her cigarette out in the overfull ashtray on the bench. Lifting the empty glasses surrounding it, she headed back to the warmth of the pub. Following a scorching hot day, the wind had picked up and there was now a definite chill in the air. Jemma guessed it was the fault of the jetstream the weather reporters blamed everything on, and said as much to her Uncle Sam, who was propping up one end of the bar.

JJ didn't think it was mad. He loved exploring the night with his camera. Loved the contrasts and shadows his lens revealed and his eyes never saw. Jemma had been right about the jumper. The breeze was chilly, and rather than waste time taking shots as he passed through the canopy of trees, he hastened towards the bridge. The moon was full, and the sun hadn't quite set. The effect on the water should be spectacular in the clearing by the bridge. A fox startled him as it ran across the path only feet away, causing JJ to curse because he hadn't had the camera ready. The fox was carrying something in its mouth but moving too fast for JJ to make out what. His camera would have found out.

Not wanting to miss any further opportunities, JJ lifted the camera. Every few steps, he aimed it at a different angle away from him, paused, took the shot and moved on. He knew he would delete most, but there would be a couple of gems that would otherwise have gone unnoticed. As he rounded the bend leading down to the stream, he paused and aimed the camera at the bridge. There was movement there. He was too far away to see what. The distance and shadows hindered his view, but his camera would find out. When doing night photography he had managed to get some wonderful shots of deer, foxes, and once the tail end of a badger. If he was lucky, one night he'd get a badger face on. Tonight might be the night. Focus, click, click, click. Walk on, pause, click, click... What was that? Lightning? That might be useful. Should get some thunder now too. Wearing only shorts and a T-shirt, he wasn't dressed for a storm, but he'd get some cracking photographs.

Seconds later, JJ stopped dead in his tracks because it wasn't thunder he heard next. It was a scream. He hit the replay button and looked at the last few shots.

In the first few frames, a figure stood on the parapet of the bridge, her arms upstretched, her midriff showing below her ample bosom. JJ swallowed as he zoomed in. It was a little out of focus, but it was definitely Amber Wilton. He flipped through the remaining shots until the last frame. Amber had disappeared.

Allowing the camera to fall suspended by its strap, he put his hand on it to stop it bouncing against his body as he ran towards the bridge. He slowed as he reached the final few yards and looked around. The long grasses at the edge of the bridge swayed in the stiff breeze, and a few older trees creaked with the effort of movement forced upon them. The stream, now only a trickle of water, made barely any noise on its way to join the river. There was no one there.

JJ raised his camera, and focusing it on the ground at his feet, walked forward as he clicked away. Once he was on the bridge, he looked over the parapet.

"Shit. I bloody knew it. Don't move, Amber, I'm coming down." JJ turned away and photographed the bank before he slid down to the stream bed. He took several more shots before hurrying to Amber. He doubted there was any evidence, but if there was, he had a record of it.

On reaching Amber, he dropped down and cursed again at the pain shooting through his knees as they hit the rocky ground. Amber's eyes were open, as was her mouth, which formed a perfect O. It was clear she was dead, but JJ still checked. Taking his fingers off her neck, he cursed some more before climbing the bank to make the call.

First, he called the emergency services, then he called Sharon, his partner. She knew he was going out with his camera, and she wouldn't be worried if he was late, but he needed the comfort of hearing her voice. Once over the shock, Sharon was full of concern, and despite his protests, insisted on meeting him with his jacket. He stopped arguing and ended the call. He looked back up the hill, the quickest route to the bridge when on foot. JJ wondered if an ambulance would come that way or enter further along the stream by the dog walkers' carpark, and then drive along the bank of the stream. It was wider there. He shrugged and supposed it all depended on where it was coming from.

Sitting on the parapet, he lifted his camera and looked at the sequence of fames in more detail. There. He cursed again as he realised what he was looking at. Amber didn't fall. Someone had pushed her. In one frame only, he'd captured what looked like someone's arm, a dark shadow with a flash of paler colour as it moved towards Amber. He enlarged the image. Yes, it looked like a hand on Amber's leg, but which sex it belonged to, he couldn't tell. The distance was too great as he'd focused on the parapet where he'd expected to find life. Instead, he'd captured Amber, moments from death.

Getting to his feet, JJ wandered back to the end of the bridge, where he had clambered down to Amber. The path which ran along that side of the stream was overgrown, and there was no sign that the grasses and brambles had been disturbed or trampled recently. He took several photographs. Whoever had pushed Amber off the bridge hadn't come past him and hadn't gone that way. He walked to the far side of the bridge and looked left. The passage of feet and paws had created an elephant path down to the disused watermill and beyond. He took several more shots. The dry ground was full of cracks revealing how long it had been since it had last rained. He turned to look the other way. It was much the same. The path was wider, and gravel had been put down a few years before to avoid a quagmire during the winter months, but the earth had absorbed most of it, while some had dispersed into the stream, and what remained did nothing to help walkers wanting to avoid being up to their ankles in mud by the time winter arrived. There would be no footprints that way. He took a few more shots before returning to his seat on the end of the parapet.

Sharon arrived first, waving his jacket as she approached. Dropping it to the ground, she pulled him into a hug.

"How are you doing? I'm so sorry, JJ," she murmured into his unruly mop of greying hair. Then, spotting Amber's body below, she stepped away. "Shit. Come and sit on this side." Lifting his jacket, she walked across the bridge and removed her own coat. "That wind might be chilly, but I've worked up a sweat running down here. Put yours on though, you must be freezing."

JJ walked over to join her, and sitting on the opposite parapet, pulled her down to join him. "Stop fussing. I'm fine. I told you I was fine. Adrenalin is pumping. She was in the pub, you know. Left about half an hour before I did. There was a group of them. They'd been to a keep fit class in the school hall and came in for a couple before heading home. Think it was someone's birthday. They made a right racket. Old Sam was cussing because he couldn't hear the football."

"Bums and Tums on a Tuesday. I knew I should have come with you, but I wanted to get that project set up ready for tomorrow. If I had come, you wouldn't have found her. I would have made you come home with me," Sharon told him as he wrapped his arm around her shoulder.

"But then someone else would have, maybe a child out with their dog. That wouldn't have been nice. I've seen far too many dead bodies. I'm used to it." JJ sighed. He'd been a police officer for almost twenty-five years, and he'd seen atrocities in Africa, so as dead bodies went, Amber Wilton's was a good one. If there could ever be such a thing as a good one, but Sharon was right, because each one was one too many.

"It's Wednesday tomorrow. Kids will be in school, they won't have time to...Oh God. What about Luke? Where is he? At his nan's or with a babysitter? I doubt Gary would come out here to babysit for an hour. Have you got his number?

Should we call him?" Sharon was not only young Luke's neighbour but also his teacher at the local primary school.

As though tempting fate, the sound of a muffled telephone ringing reached them. JJ walked to the other side of the bridge and looked down at Amber's body.

"It's hers. Probably someone wanting to know where she's got to," he said as he walked back to join Sharon.

"Aren't you going to answer it? Should we answer it?"

"No. The police will deal with that, just as they'll deal with Gary. It's not my place to call him. Don't worry, I'll tell them about Luke." JJ patted Sharon's knee as he sat next to her.

Sharon was worried, though. Luke hadn't taken his parents' separation well and had been uncooperative and disruptive in school. It had lasted about six months, and he'd only recently turned the corner. This would knock him back again. "But poor Luke. He's only just got straight. I'll have to speak to Connie in the morning, and Gary, of course. Luke will need counselling if we're to head this next crisis off at the pass. If that's even possible. He's had so much to deal with, and now this. Oh. I wonder if he'll stay at Frampton? Perhaps he'll live with Gary in Bristol."

JJ patted her knee again. "All in good time. And Connie Gerrard will do whatever suits her best. I'm sure she'll be on the phone before the post-mortem is finished, if it means more money coming in."

JJ didn't like the head of Frampton Down Primary school. He believed she expected too much from her staff. In his book, Connie Gerrard didn't care enough about anyone, including the children in her care. He also thought she was too opinionated on just about everything for her own good. He didn't need to say this again because Sharon had heard it many times before. They sat in silence for a few moments.

"Cavalry is coming." JJ pointed at the distant blue lights approaching through the trees. "I wondered if they'd come in that way, through the dog walkers' carpark." The flickering blue images tempted him to lift his camera and take a few photographs, but now wasn't the time, and he left the camera dangling from his neck.

The car stopped on the other side of the bridge, and a young female officer climbed out and waved acknowledgement. She held back, waiting for her superior to lead the way. A stocky man carrying too much weight clambered out of the driver's seat and slammed the door.

"Oh, save me! Of all the coppers in the world, they had to send him." JJ ran his fingers through his hair.

JJ remained where he was and watched DS Clive Evans lumber across the bridge. Evans' suit was crumpled, and a button on his shirt was missing, exposing his rotund, hairy belly. JJ didn't like Evans, and the feeling was mutual.

"I thought it was you, JJ. What you been up to now?" Evans chuckled and looked over the bridge at Amber's body. "I hear you know her. Were you with her? Did she jump or was she pushed?" Turning back, he looked Sharon up and down. "Threesome, was it?" Even his soft Welsh accent didn't soften the offence his words caused.

Evans held up his hands in surrender as JJ's expression and clenched fists revealed his disgust, and Sharon gasped.

"Just kidding, a bit of gallows humour, that's all. You know what it's like, JJ. You've got to, haven't you? That said, you never had a sense of humour, did you? Talk to me." Looking over his shoulder, he beckoned his colleague forward. "PC Sampson, you can take notes. We won't go down. Forensics and recovery are on their way."

"I used to like a Welsh accent before I met him. I just want to smash his face in every time he opens his mouth," JJ muttered to Sharon, before walking across to PC Sampson, his hand outstretched. "JJ Jenson. Sorry to meet you in these circumstances."

"Rachel Sampson, Rach. The guv told me all about you, JJ." She gave him a cheeky smile as she pulled her pen from her notebook. "Ready when you are."

"The guv? Not him, surely? Because that would be a pinch of salt stuff." JJ jerked his head towards Evans, who had walked around the bridge and was standing at the top of the bank that JJ had scrambled down.

"God no. Not the sarge. I zone him out if I can." Rachel grimaced. "DI Rowntree. He sends his regards and says he hopes to see you soon."

"Ah, Tom. That makes more sense. He wasn't working a night shift, surely?" JJ joked.

"No, we were out on something else. He got the call at home and called us. Told me if it was JJ, I was to listen up because you could teach me a lot. Said you went way back. So—"

"Okay, okay. Let's get on with it. In a nutshell, Jenson." Evans had dropped the familiar use of JJ. It didn't go unnoticed. "They'll be here in a moment."

"The deceased woman is Amber Wilton. She lived at number eight High View Terrace. She's separated from her husband Gary, who lives in Bristol. I've got his address at home. But, and here's the crucial bit, she should have been home a while ago. She's got a seven-year-old son called Luke. We don't know who was watching him while she was out. Could be with her mother Emma. She lives on Station Road. Don't know the number, but it's the station end, three doors up. I think sorting Luke out should be a priority. He's not had it easy the last year."

"You seem to know a lot about them. What were you doing down here?" Evans jerked his thumb over his shoulder.

"She's a...was a neighbour. Sharon teaches Luke at school. I'd been to the pub, and was coming down here to get some shots, I saw—"

"Of what? I heard you'd had a hard time, but drugs?" Evans tutted and shook his head. "How the mighty fall."

"Photographs." JJ held up his camera. "I saw a flash, no, no. First, I saw movement, thought I might be lucky and catch a badger. I took some shots, or for you, Evans, as you still think two plus two makes five, photographs, and I saw it was Amber. She was standing on the parapet, her arms in the air." JJ held up his own arms to demonstrate.

"Where were you when you were taking these photographs?" Evans looked around as though trying to pinpoint the spot.

JJ pointed up the hill. "Up there on the bend. As I was saying, I realised it was Amber, and—"

"How did you know it was her from right up there?"

"Because my camera has better eyesight than me. She was in the pub earlier, and I recognised her stripy top and her mop of curls. She had wild hair, you could always tell it was her from a distance. So, I was going to amble on down when there was a flash. I thought it was lightning at first, but then I heard the scream."

"So we're to believe you were doing wildlife photography in the dark?" Evans interrupted again. "Why?"

"No, I was coming down to photograph the water. It wasn't dark when I left. And I'll let you into a secret, shall I? There's a lot of nocturnal wildlife around here. Nocturnal means—"

"All right, smartass. So she fell off."

"No. I think someone pushed her. I'd have told you that ten minutes ago if you didn't keep interrupting. Look and listen."

JJ scrolled through the images and found the series of frames he wanted.

"Look here. I saw a movement and took some shots. Watch the sequence. She's climbing up on the parapet, arms up, and gone. I'll show you again. Climbing, arms up, flash, gone. And again. Climbing, arms up, flash, push. Look at this one." JJ halted the slide show. "This dark shadow, I reckon that's an arm, and this is a hand, pushing her here, on her thigh. I'll need to get it downloaded to see if I can enhance it."

"Looks like a shadow to me." Evans held his hand out. "I'll need the card. That's evidence now, that is."

"No kidding. He's good, Rachel. Bet you thanked your lucky stars when they paired you with him." JJ rolled his eyes. "I'll download my stuff and let you have it when you come up to the house."

"Why am I coming to your house?" Evans raised an eyebrow.

"Because you want her estranged husband's contact details. And because I live next door but one to Amber's house, and you have to make sure her child is safe. Just a guess, it's your case. Oh look, saved by the bell. They took the shortcut."

JJ stepped away from Evans and watched a car drive down the hill from the pub.

A grumpy-looking woman with grey hair pulled into a tight ponytail climbed out and collected a bag from the rear seat. Her younger colleague gave a nod in greeting, and reached into the boot, pulling out a couple of bagged overalls.

Opening one, she handed it to her colleague. The grumpy woman looked over as she slipped her shoes off, and her face lit up when she saw JJ.

"JJ, is that you? Come here and give me a hug. You can tell me what we've got." Placing the overall on her bag, she opened her arms. JJ obliged and walked into a hug. "Thank God. I thought I'd have to deal with Evans." Denise Thompson, the forensic pathologist, renowned for her loud, reverberating voice, slapped JJ's shoulder. Evans scowled as he approached.

"I'll tell you what we've got. He's not working any more, as well you know." Evans tapped his temple and raised his eyebrows.

JJ held a hand up to stop Sharon from giving a retort on his behalf. "Denise, it's a pleasure to see you, too. I'll leave you with Evans, who should now know as much as I do. Ask Rachel if you need more. She took notes. But I will tell you this, I think someone pushed her. Someone hit her on the left thigh when she was standing on the parapet." JJ looked past Evans to Rachel. "Number five, High View Terrace, when you need me. I'll have the card ready for you." JJ tapped his camera. "I've taken shots of all the surrounding terrain immediately after. Noticed nothing odd and didn't see anyone else. I'll leave you to it. I don't need to hang around for this. 'Bye, Denise, we'll have to have a get-together one of these days."

"I didn't say you could leave," Evans snapped, trying to gain control over the conversation.

"Why do you want me to stay?" JJ didn't hide his irritation and stood square on to Evans and looked down at him.

Sharon, who had pulled on her coat, was still sitting on the wall watching the interactions. She picked up JJ's coat and walked to him.

She squeezed his hand. "Let's go, JJ. He'll manage without you if he tries hard enough."

Evans flipped a dismissive hand. "Do as you're told. I'll catch you later. Don't leave the house until we've spoken to you."

JJ looked at Rachel Sampson. "Don't forget the child, Rachel, because he might."

Rachel nodded. JJ saluted, and pulling Sharon with him, squeezed past Denise's car to start the climb back up the hill.

Chapter Three

A car door slammed shut, and JJ opened his eyes. They hadn't closed the curtains properly so the sun shone through the gap, lighting up the bedroom. A lot of sun. Rolling onto his side, he looked at the clock. It was ten past nine. JJ rolled the other way to wake Sharon, but she had gone. He pressed his hands to his face and groaned as he remembered the events of the night before. Poor Amber, and poor Sharon, he'd woken her up shouting again last night. He hadn't had the nightmare for weeks. Probably brought on by the shock of what had happened to Amber.

Kicking off the duvet, he walked to the window and peeped through the curtain. Gary Wilton had parked his shiny BMW in front of JJ's old banger. Leaning forward, JJ pressed his head against the window to look further up the street. Amber's mother, Emma, was talking to Gary at the gate. They both looked as washed out as he felt. He'd not had much sleep, but he doubted they'd had any. They seemed to come to an agreement, as they nodded at each other before they walked into the house.

"They're going to tell Luke, the poor, poor buggers." Turning away, he went into the bathroom and turned on the shower. He set the temperature low and gasped as he stepped into what felt like the skin-shredding flow of water.

Down in the kitchen, he lifted the note from the table. Sharon hadn't wanted to wake him, and apologised for the lack of milk, but she'd needed plenty of caffeine to kick-start her brain. She'd be home for lunch. JJ opened the fridge to make sure she wasn't joking. She wasn't. Stomping back up the stairs, he pulled his tracksuit bottoms over his boxers and picked up his phone. He'd jog to the shop. Two birds and all that. He eyed his camera as he collected his wallet and keys.

No. Not today. He'd be glad not to see anything or anyone at all this morning. Shoving his keys and wallet to the bottom of his pocket, he left the house, head down. His hopes of not seeing anyone were shattered as he closed the gate behind him. A shout to his left caused him to pause. Luke Wilton flew out of his garden, his father not far behind. JJ stepped into Luke's path and scooped him up.

"It's okay, Luke, it's okay," he whispered into the wriggling body encased in his arms.

"Put me down," Luke screamed. "They said my mum fell off the bridge and has gone to heaven. She hasn't. I'm going to find her."

Gary tried to take Luke, but that made the boy kick and scream even more. Emma arrived, tears streaming and snot running.

"Luke, we're so sorry, love. Come on home, I'll make you some hot chocolate with the marshmallows you like. Then we can talk. Come on, my love."

"No. Go away. I hate you. You're liars. I'm never coming home again, not until my mum does." Luke buried his face in JJ's shoulder. "They're liars," he repeated, in case JJ hadn't understood. When he felt JJ move and try to pass him to his father, he kicked out again. "Don't give me back. I'll run away. You'll never find me."

"You can't do that, Luke. What would you eat? Where would you sleep? It wouldn't be safe. Do you want to come for a run with me? Just down to the pub and back. We'll see who's fastest, then we'll come back, and your nan can make us both a drink. Miss Elliott went to school after using all the milk. I haven't even had a cup of tea. What do you say?"

"S'pose." Luke didn't see his father nod permission, and he allowed JJ to lower him to the pavement.

"On your marks, GO!" JJ started jogging down the hill before Luke was ready.

"That's cheating. You never said get ready," Luke complained as he took off after JJ. The boy caught up with JJ, found another gear, and flew off down the hill.

"Bugger." JJ increased his pace, and by the time he'd caught up with Luke, sweat had stuck his T-shirt to his back, and his hair to his forehead. "This is killing me. I'm an old man, you know," he managed, between breaths.

Luke slowed down. "I know. I knew I'd beat you."

Luke had stopped crying, but his little tear-stained face looked determined. JJ wasn't convinced he wouldn't take off again.

"If you get to the bench before me, and you don't tell everyone how bad I was, I'll buy you a lemonade and a packet of crisps at the pub."

"Done." And off Luke went. JJ also increased his speed but slowed as Luke stopped at the bench and jogged thankfully to a halt. "I won. But the pub's closed." Luke gasped as he gulped in air.

"Not for us, it isn't. Watch this." JJ walked up to the door and banged on it with his fist.

"We're closed. Bugger off," Old Sam called from inside. "Come back at half eleven."

JJ banged again, and the door opened.

"Are you deaf?" Sam demanded, before looking from JJ to the boy. He jerked his head. "Oh, it's you. Come on in."

"Told you." JJ nudged Luke. "Go on, be quick, or he'll get in trouble for serving us."

Luke walked in wide-eyed. He'd only been in the pub a few times, and then only to use the toilet when they'd had a meal in the garden. His nose wrinkled as he looked around the traditional bar. The dark wood furniture, although battered and scratched, shone with the years of polishing, and the patterned rugs had all seen better days. "It smells in here."

Sam drew in a long draft of air. "Beautiful, that is. Be grateful they can't smoke in here any more. Mind you, I liked the smell then, too."

"Sounds disgusting." Luke's nose wrinkled some more. "JJ said I could have a coke and a packet of crisps, but I want Monster Munch. Have you got them?"

"Nope. We only sell the good stuff. You can have crisps, peanuts, pork scratchings or bacon bites." Sam opened the hatch and walked behind the bar. "What'll it be?"

"Um. Bacon bites, and a large coke," Luke replied, standing on tiptoe to make sure he got the right sized glass for his coke.

"Take a seat. I'll bring it over. What can I get you, JJ?"

"I don't suppose you could run to a cup of tea, could you?"

"I can today. We heard about last night. Police came in just as we were locking up." Sam nodded as JJ held up a finger to stop him speaking.

"We'll be in the corner. Luke, this way, it's my favourite table when it's too cold to sit outside. You can see the proper village." JJ walked to the table in the bay window and took a seat. "Look at that."

Luke knelt on the chair opposite and looked out of the window and shrugged. "What do you mean, the proper village? It always looks like that."

"How old do you reckon the houses are that you can see? And the shops down on Main Road? Go on, have a guess. I'll give you a clue. They're older than me."

Luke's eyebrows rose. "A hundred."

"Close. The oldest is three hundred years old, the newest one hundred and twenty odd. That was pretty much the village when I was your age, apart from a couple of streets they had added on after the war. Then I went away to work, and when I came back, they'd built those ugly modern things all around the edge. Hundreds and hundreds of them. But they'd also built a school to take all the kids from those ugly new houses, and I was glad about that because that's where Miss Elliott works."

Luke nodded. "So you stayed even though you thought they'd made it ugly because of her?"

"I did. Because Miss Elliott makes everything seem better. I was very sad. Sadder than I'd ever been, and she helped me get better. I'll never leave her."

Sam came over carrying a tray. It held a pot of tea, a pint of coke, a plate of packaged biscuits and two packets of bacon bites. "I brought you two bags in case you missed your breakfast. Is that a big enough glass for you?"

Luke nodded. "Thanks, Mr... I don't know your name."

"The polite ones call me Old Sam. My best friends just call me Sam. You can be a best friend."

Luke's eyebrows rose, and he nodded solemnly. "Thanks, Sam."

Sam saluted. "You're welcome, lad."

"My best friends call me Zed. You can call me Zed."

"Well, Zed, I'm honoured to be a best friend. Thank you." Grinning, Sam walked away and finished washing the glasses from the night before. The police had put a halt to their usual routine last night.

JJ laughed and leaned across the table. "Is that true? Do your best mates really call you Zed?"

"Yep." Luke almost smiled. "If not, I'll tell them to. You know, if they've forgotten." Luke used two hands to lift his glass to his lips and still it dribbled down his chin. Wiping it away with his forearm, he looked at JJ as he opened a packet of bacon bites. "What made you sad?"

"My dad died, and I loved him very much and I didn't get home in time to see him. Other things had gone wrong, and I didn't know what to do. Miss Elliott came to my rescue. Her and my sister. I didn't think it was possible, but I'm well now. It just takes time."

"They told me my mum's died and gone to heaven. She hasn't, has she?" It was almost a whisper.

JJ nodded as he leaned forward. "Was she good, your mum? Yes, she was. Did she love you more than anything? Yes, she did. Does she deserve the best? I reckon. So yes, Zed, that's where she is. And do you know what? I wish she wasn't there almost as much as you do. But here's the thing, if she can't be here, where else would you want her to be? Because heaven is where only the best people go, to be everything they ever wanted to be. She'll be waiting for you, and even though you'll be a very old man when you die, you'll be her boy once more. Her Zed." JJ forced a smile. "Was your mum allowed to call you Zed?"

Luke's bottom lip quivered. "She didn't know because I just made it up. I don't want my mum to be in heaven. I want her to come home. Anyway, I don't know where it is, and Kaleigh in school said her dad told her there's no such thing as God and he's supposed to be in heaven. So I don't know if heaven is real. But Ben and Hamza said there was a heaven, but their God was different and the best one. They nearly had a fight. What if Kaleigh was right? Or what if there are loads of Gods and I don't know which one my mum went to?"

JJ smiled and placed his palm face up on the table between them. Luke hesitated and then reluctantly placed his own hand on top of it. JJ's fingers, huge in comparison, closed around it. "Here's the thing, everyone believes different things. No one is right, no one is wrong, because we just don't know. We have to go with what's in here." JJ thumped his chest with his free hand. "I used to be a police officer. Did you know that? Well, it's true, and one day I met a wise man called Nizar. He was a Muslim, like your friend Hamza, and was telling the judge about what he'd seen, and he had to swear an oath to God that he would tell the truth. He placed his hand on the Bible. Do you know what the Bible is?"

Luke nodded solemnly. "It tells you all about God and Jesus, and the angels and stuff."

"Correct. The Bible is used by Christians whereas Muslims have a book called the Koran. It's much the same. They are both about what's right and what's wrong, and both teach kindness. Anyway, the judge stopped everything and asked Nizar if he was a Muslim. Nizar said yes, and the judge asked him how he could swear a true oath on the Bible, and do you know what Nizar said? I'll never forget it. It makes everything so simple, so clear."

Although Luke's eyes were still misty, the tears hadn't arrived, and he shook his head.

"Nizar looked the judge in the eye, and said, 'It would have been a true oath. I believe there is only one God. Some of us, the Christians, the Jews, the Muslims, simply believe different versions of what happened next. We are only human, but God is God. This is one of his books,' and he tapped the Bible."

JJ placed his free hand palm down on a beer mat. "So you see, it doesn't matter what you believe while you're here, heaven is heaven when you get there. You'll find your mum, no problem. But, and here's the most important thing, that's going to be a while yet, and in the meantime, you have to live your best life. Be kind, be thoughtful, and always choose to do the right thing, whatever you believe, because it all counts." He squeezed Luke's hand. "Does that help?"

"Sort of. Do you believe in God?"

JJ closed his eyes for a second. That was a question he wasn't expecting or wanting to consider today. When he opened them, he reached out for Luke's other hand, which was given more willingly this time. "Honestly? I struggle sometimes. But I want to, and I try to be a good person. So, on balance, I'd have to say yes. What about you?"

"On balance, I've got to say yes, then my mum will wait for me."

JJ laughed. "That was the best answer. Now, are you going to eat those bacon bites, or shall I have some?"

Luke pulled his hands free, and lifting the packet, he poured some of them into JJ's hand.

"Thanks, Zed. Not quite the bacon sandwich I thought I'd have for breakfast, but they nearly taste the same. Steady with that. It's fizzy." JJ warned as Luke emptied half his drink in one go.

Ten minutes later, more tears avoided, snacks eaten, and their drinks emptied, JJ stacked everything back on the tray.

"Are you ready to go home now? Your dad and your nan need you."

Luke nodded. "I'll win, you know."

"I'm sure you will. It's uphill. But I'll give it my best shot. Come on, then."

"I need to pee first. I can't run when I need to pee."

"Through that door." JJ pointed to a door in the corner. "Do you want me to come, the door is heavy?

"No, I'm seven. I can do it." Luke flexed his arm. "I've got muscles."

"Oh, yes. I forgot you were getting on. I'll pay Sam."

Luke went off to the gents alone, having to put his shoulder against the heavy wooden door to push it open. JJ carried the tray back to the bar, where Sam was reading a newspaper. Sam shook his head.

"It's not right, is it? The police came on closing time. I hear you were there. An obnoxious git wanted to know what time you'd left."

"Ah, Evans. He's a charmer, isn't he? And, yes, I found her."

"That's not what I'd call him. Why would she jump off that bridge? I mean it did the job, but that was a fifty- fifty chance. It's not very high, and she was happy as Larry in here." Sam waved his hand as JJ pulled his wallet from his pocket. "On the house."

"Thanks. Yes, she was happy and I don't think she jumped. Someone pushed her."

"What? That's not what the charmer said. He implied it was, you know, suicide. Asked for the names of the girls she was drinking with too." Sam drew his finger along his throat as Luke called from the other side of the door.

"I'll pop in later. Not a conversation for now. I'd better let him out." JJ walked to the door of the gents and pushed it open, smiling at Luke. "It's a heavy door, that. Are you ready for this race? I don't think I'll make it all the way to yours, though. Why don't we say the signpost halfway?"

"Okay. I'll still win."

"We'll see." JJ waved to Sam. "I'll catch you later. Keep your ears open for me."

"Will do, JJ. 'Bye, young 'un. Take care." Sam saluted as Luke waved.

Outside, JJ lifted his foot onto a bench and retied his laces. "Don't want to trip up or I'll gift it to you."

"You should have Velcro like me." Luke waved a foot in JJ's direction.

"I might try some. We'd better get going. Your dad will be worried. Are you ready?"

"Will I have to live with my dad now? I don't like his flat much. You never see anyone, and you can't have animals there. I'm not leaving Fluff behind. She's an old cat, she wouldn't like it," Luke shoved his hands in his pockets and scuffed the toe of his shoe on the ground.

"I don't know. Is it just the flat that's worrying you?"

"Yes. And leaving here. Will you ask him to come and live here with me? If not, I'll have to live with my nan. Then I won't have to change school and Miss Elliott can make me feel happy again, too."

JJ ruffled Luke's hair. "Bless you. I'll have a word. But you've got to remember your dad has a business to run. He's got to earn money to keep you in Velcro trainers. It might not work out."

"It will! He lived here before, he only moved there because him and Mum fell out. I thought he'd come back, but then she said she might get a new husband. I won't have to live with him, will I?"

JJ sat on the bench. "You certainly won't. I didn't know your mum was thinking about getting married again. Do you like him?" He watched Luke shrug and frowned. "But you've met him?"

"Not yet. Mum said she'd bring him round so I could meet him because if we were lucky, he'd pop the question. I didn't know what that meant, and she said it was about getting married."

"Ah, I see." JJ stood and raising his hands above his head, stretched from side to side. "Better warm up. Ready, steady, go!" He took off at a jog, leaving Luke shouting in protest, slowing as he approached the sign. Luke flew past.

"My house we said, keep going," Luke called with a grin.

JJ followed a little slower and when he reached the gate to the Wiltons' garden, he made a show of grabbing it and gasping for air. "You beat me good and proper. Go and knock."

A red-faced Luke nodded. "Can we race again? Not now, maybe tomorrow. You don't work, do you? Mum said you were an artist like her. But not with paint. I didn't know you could do art with photos. But if you can, it means you make stuff and don't have to go to work."

"Anytime I'm around, it would be a pleasure. Oh, here's your nan. Looks like she could do with a hug."

Luke ran to his grandmother. She hugged him tightly. His father appeared behind them and smiled at Luke as he patted his shoulder.

"Go on in, get that hot chocolate Nan promised you. I need a quick word with JJ and then I'll join you."

He walked over to the gate and waited until the pair had gone in before turning to JJ. He looked like JJ expected him to. There was no colour in his face, and the lines at the corner of his eyes had deepened. It was clear he'd been crying.

"How did you calm him down?" Gary's voice had a husky quality, as though it was an effort for him to speak.

"We had a theological discussion, and he accepted that if you wanted to believe there was a heaven, then that's where he'd find his mum when the time came. He's a good boy, and he's worried about what will happen to him now. I don't know what your plans are, but he says he wants you to come back here to live with him. He doesn't like your flat. If I was giving out advice, I'd suggest that's what you do to start with."

"That's pretty much what's going to happen. The police said you found her. Why do you think she did it?"

"I don't think anything at the moment. No one should until they've finished their investigation. When I saw her in the pub, she looked happy, not like someone about to throw herself off a twenty, twenty-five-foot high bridge? That wouldn't provide a guaranteed exit, if that's what someone wanted, and I don't think she did. The police may have jumped to conclusions. Who did you see? Evans?"

"Can't remember his name, Welsh chap. Called round at eight this morning. I panicked at first, I can tell you. Or I did until he told me they'd got Luke's nan to come and let the babysitter go home. I know we weren't together, but I'll miss Amber. I always thought...you know." His voice broke, and JJ patted his shoulder.

"Yes, I know. We all will. I didn't realise that getting back together was on the cards. I thought it was all over between you. That said, I didn't hear anything about her seeing anyone. She wasn't, was she?"

Gary Wilton's nose wrinkled. "She had a fling with that idiot Baxter. It didn't last long. Someone also mentioned Manton, but would she be that stupid? I don't know what the male equivalent of a slag is, but whatever it is he's one. Of course I asked her, didn't want Luke picking up Manton's habits, but she told me to mind my own business and stop listening to gossip. I took that as a no. I'd better get back to Luke. Thanks for looking after him."

"Anytime. Like I said, he's a good boy. I'm going down to the shop. Can I get you anything?" JJ asked.

"No thanks. I've got no idea what's in there." Gary nodded towards the cottage. "Cheers though."

Shaking his hand, JJ turned away. He could understand Gary's dislike of Sean Manton. If gossip was accurate, he'd been responsible for more than enough marital issues in the village. Who knows, he might even have been the reason for the Wiltons' breakup. But probably not, as that had been over a year ago. He wouldn't still be on the scene, surely? JJ started his jog down the hill towards the shops. He'd have to ask around because the last he'd heard Manton was loved up with the woman who lived above the post office. But then again, that was gossip, too. JJ had one of those brains that soaked up seemingly useless information, but some of it came in useful. Although JJ still wished his mind would have a day off now and again.

Chapter Four

SHARON ELLIOTT STOPPED OUTSIDE the head's door and yawned into her hand. It was only half ten, but it felt like midnight. It was going to be a long, long day. She tapped on the door and went in. As always, the room smelt of lemon polish, and other than the bare necessities, which included a wooden tray holding the coffeemaker, every surface was bare. It looked like it was waiting to be made comfortable.

"Morning, Connie, you wanted to see me? I need to speak to you, too." Sharon closed the door behind her.

Connie Gerrard removed her glasses and placed them on her desk. "Have a seat. If you don't mind me saying so, you look like shit. You were late this morning, and you yawned all the way through assembly. I thought you'd nodded off at one point. What's going on?"

"You haven't heard yet?" Sharon dropped onto the chair.

"Heard what?" Connie walked to the coffeemaker and held up a cup. "I'm guessing you want one."

"Please. Amber Wilton, Luke's mum, died last night. JJ found her. It was Luke I wanted to speak to you about."

The cup chinked on the saucer as Connie put it back down. "Dead? How? Where and what was JJ doing there? Did he see anything?"

"Photos. What else? She fell, or it seems more likely that someone pushed her off the bridge down by the watermill. We had to wait for the police to come down to the bridge, and when they'd done their thing, come up to the house for statements and Gary Wilton's contact details," Sharon explained. "Can you pour that coffee, please?"

Connie ignored the request. "Pushed? Did JJ see who did it? What does Gary Wilton have to do with it? He lives in Bristol. And when you say pushed, surely they don't think it's Gary, do they?"

"I don't know. I was in shock. JJ has given them his memory card. He saw movement, thought it was wildlife, and clicked away. Please pour me a coffee." Sharon wound her finger in circles to speed Connie up.

Filling the cup, Connie placed it in front of Sharon, who blew on the coffee before wincing as the hot liquid filled her mouth. She swallowed it slowly and sighed contentedly. "Thank you. Now what did you want, or shall we stick with the Wiltons?"

"Um, yes, carry on. I can't believe Gary would do such a thing. Can you?"

"I sincerely hope not. JJ knows him better than me. Who knows, though? What would happen to poor Luke if it was him? Doesn't bear thinking about. I mean, look what Luke was like before, and that was only because they'd split up. He's going to have a hard enough job dealing with the loss of one parent. Two is unimaginable. I think we need to get him a counsellor." Sharon shivered and finished her coffee. She considered asking for more, but didn't want to be refused, so she went to the machine and refilled her cup. "What do you think?"

"I think Gary is a good man, and an excellent chair of the PTA. I can't believe it of him. Are there no other suspects?" Connie leaned forward.

"I meant about a counsellor. I'm not getting dragged into gossip, Connie. This place is bad enough without any encouragement."

"So you do know something. I think you should tell me, Sharon. Gary Wilton is on the PTA. It wouldn't do to have a murder suspect in the PTA."

"Connie, I know nothing. We didn't discuss it. I was just hanging around, dealing with the police, passing out, and waking up late for school. The counsellor?"

Connie flipped her hand. "I'll look into it. I think the police have victim support, don't they?"

"I doubt that's what Luke needs. I thought you'd welcome the extra funding," Sharon suggested as she emptied the second cup. "Look into it, please."

"I will do my best. But no money, no can do. You know that."

A bell rang, and Sharon got to her feet. "PE for me now. Might teach them meditation. Do you think twenty-four seven-year-olds will lie quietly for me? See you...Oh, you never told me what you wanted."

"Not to worry. You'd better get on." Connie put her glasses on and lifted a file from her in-tray. "I now have more important things to worry about."

Sharon opened her mouth to ask what but decided to leave instead, while the going was good. As it was already going to be a long day, she didn't need to add more to it. She'd stay away from the staffroom at lunchtime. A sandwich in the stockroom sounded perfect. It almost was too, but fifteen minutes before class was due to start again, there was a knock on the door before it opened.

Jill Craig, the school secretary, winced and smoothed a hand over her already immaculate hair. It was bad news. Jill was never good at hiding things. Sharon sighed.

"What now?" Sharon asked, as Jill forced a smile.

"Sorry to disturb you, Sharon, but Tommy Hill has just got back from his appointment, and he's told everyone that Amber Wilton is dead. Someone called him a liar. There were fisticuffs and now half your class is in tears. I tried to help, but I think they need to come in early. Is that okay? Connie said you wouldn't be happy, but you don't mind giving up five minutes of your break, do you?"

"Yes, of course. How did he know? And it's fifteen minutes," Sharon complained as she put the lid on her sandwich box, brushed the crumbs from her lap, and wheeled her chair back into the classroom.

"Tommy said the police came round to see his mum, so he was late for his appointment. Connie isn't happy. She said, 'There's a time and a place for telling children things. The school playground isn't one of them' Then she did her cough." Jill mimicked her boss perfectly, as she held the door open for Sharon to pass her.

"Why the cough?"

"I don't know. Who knows what starts her off? She's talking about an emergency staff meeting after school today. Just for the record, I won't be there. I must have a dentist appointment or something."

"Yes, me too, or perhaps the police are coming back round? Something anyway. I'll work on it."

"The police? Are you serious? Why?"

"Connie didn't gossip, well that surprises me! It was JJ who found Amber. But I'm not discussing it, I've got some confused kids to sort out."

"Oh, my God. How is he? That must have been horrible. Are you worried about him? Was it suspicious? It must be if the police are coming back round. Oh no, was she murdered?" Jill's hands sat upon her ample bosom, her mouth open in shock.

Sharon pulled open the door to the playground, clapped her hands and yelled, "Year three, line up here. Now, please!" She watched as those closest stopped what they were doing and looked around before year three separated themselves and formed a line as required, the front half asking non-stop questions about why because the bell hadn't gone, the rest moaning because the bell hadn't gone.

"You didn't answer me. I'll take that as a yes." Jill's eyes were wide. "You should say, you know, if there's a killer on the ..." Jill stopped speaking as the second girl in the line gasped and burst into tears. "Damn. Sorry, I'll go." Turning on her too-high-for-school heels, Jill practically ran up the corridor. Probably to see who she could catch in the staffroom with the gossip before they went back to class.

"If you would," Sharon muttered, and put her arm around the shoulder of the weeping child. "Come on, Zara, you can help me today." They led the crocodile of chattering children back to the classroom. Sharon wondered if JJ was up yet, and if she should be worried about him. He had appeared to be fine, seemed to have everything in perspective, but JJ was good at masking his feelings.

Sharon had been right about Jill gossiping. As she entered the staffroom for the afternoon break, three of her colleagues made a beeline for her.

"Sharon, is it true? Luke Wilton's mum was murdered?"

"How did they kill her? There's been nothing on the news, I googled it."

"You must be so worried. JJ didn't need that. Have you seen Luke?"

The questions kept coming, and Sharon held a finger in the air. "Behave. What is wrong with you all?" she asked.

The entire room fell silent. Everyone waiting to hear what she had to say. Connie was there, too, that was unusual. Her lips pursed, and jutting out so far, she looked like someone on Instagram, showing off her new fillers.

"I'm not going to answer questions, because I don't know the answers. I'm going to tell you what I do know, as a fact, and not speculation, and then I'm going to have a coffee. Amber Wilton is dead. She fell from the bridge down by the watermill. The police are investigating it. JJ found her. Luke is going to have a tough time with it, whether it was an accident, intentional, or something more sinister. You should be asking how we can help Luke, not be after the salacious details about how his mother died, don't you think? That's it. That's all I know. Excuse me." Sharon headed straight to the kettle.

"Well said, Sharon." Connie said, heading towards the door, which would take her back to the sanctuary of her office. "Amber Wilton has always been odd, her artistic bent, I suppose. I'm sure the explanation of what happened will not include someone pushing her off the bridge. Enough gossip for one day, I think." Nodding curtly, she left the room.

Jill sidled up to Sharon and held out the almost empty biscuit tin. "Pushed off the bridge? There's a Hobnob left. She's such a hypocrite. But we knew that."

"Who is?" Sharon took the Hobnob and a custard cream.

"Connie, of course. She's going to see Mr Wilton after school. What for, if not to get more details?" Patting her chest, Jill asked, "Have you heard from JJ?"

"Yes, he texted me. He's making curry tonight. He makes a good curry, as you know. I can't wait, I'm starving. Did you get that copying done for me? I'll grab it once I've eaten these." Sharon couldn't help herself, and asked, "Why is Connie going to see Gary Wilton?"

"First-hand gossip. Then she'll have one over on us. She likes that. Your copying is in your cubbyhole."

Three thirty finally arrived, and Sharon winced at the scraping of chairs being pushed back and forth as her class collected their things. She couldn't wait to get home and collapse. "Line up quietly, please." When the children had lined up by the door, she nodded. "Perfect. Luke Wilton is going to be very sad for quite some time. We need to help him. If you see him, be kind. Don't ask lots of questions because he won't want to talk about it. Yes, Tommy?" Sharon looked at the chubby boy at the end of the line with his hand up.

"Does he get extra holiday because his mum's dead, or will he come back tomorrow? He's got my blue fast racer."

"Luke will have some time off, yes. But it won't be a holiday. He'll be sad, he won't be having fun. I'm sure he'll keep your fast racer safe until you see him again. Now quietly along the corridor."

As she pulled open the door to the playground, she saw Zack Dent's mum crush her cigarette under her flip-flop, and bet that if she could be bothered to check, Sara Dent's car would be parked on the zigzags outside the gates. Normal rules didn't apply to Sara. It was at times like this she was grateful that Connie seemed to revel in confrontation. She hid her smirk as Connie barrelled towards Sara. But before there was a confrontation about school rules, Zara Peters broke rank and ran to her mother.

"Mummy, you're safe. There's a killer out there. He got Luke's mum." And then she burst into tears.

Connie pulled her head back as Sara Dent jabbed a finger at her. "Who told them that? Why are these kids coming out of school talking about killers? I know it's true, but that's for us to tell them, not you. Zack! Over here." When her son arrived, she put an arm around his shoulder. "Are you okay, son? Don't you be thinking about killers. He won't be after kids. I expect he's long gone."

"Mrs Dent, please lower your voice. No one, I repeat, no one, knows what happened to Mrs Wilton. Gossip will do no one any favours." Connie used her best head teacher voice and looked around at the other parents, making sure they were taking note.

Sara Dent shook her head with a smirk and jabbed her finger towards Sharon. "She knows. Her old man found her. And Old Sam in the Three Bells said it was murder because Amber was in there last night, so he's had the police in. So, no, not gossip, thank you very much. There was a murder in Frampton Down, there is a killer on the loose, and it's about time the police told us what was going on. Alright? Get your facts straight before you go pulling people up. Ha!"

Pulling her son with her, Sara did her best to turn her bulk in a dignified manner before marching towards her car, which she had, yet again, parked on the zigzags. Connie looked at the cigarette butt and shook her head. Stooping to pick it up, she waved it at Sara's back.

"No smoking on school premises! And if you're parked on the zigzags again, the camera will have picked it up! That's a fine on its way to you."

Sara's head drooped a little. She'd forgotten about the new camera. Recovering, she put her nose in the air and held up her middle finger as she marched on, wondering where she'd find the money.

With her last pupil safely collected by a parent, Sharon walked back into school. There was still a large huddle of parents, their children within hearing distance, discussing Amber's demise. She doubted there would be a single resident of Frampton Down who believed Amber hadn't been murdered before the six o'clock news came on. Sighing, she pulled the door closed behind her.

"Oh no. Not tonight, Connie, I'm going home. I worked until gone ten last night, and I'm not staying for another meeting. What would it achieve?" She waved a finger as a red-faced Connie marched towards her.

"I never said there was a meeting. Did I say that? Why do people insist on knowing what I'm going to say? I have things to do."

"Oh, sorry. It's just that Jill said...Oh it doesn't matter. Why are you going to see Gary? Don't you think you should leave it a couple of days?"

"And why do they give me unwanted bloody advice? I'm going to tell him he has the full support of the school. Is that okay with you? Go home, Sharon. I expect you in on time in the morning. No doubt they'll have organised a kangaroo court. They blame the bloody school for everything." Jerking her thumb towards the huddle in the playground, Connie left Sharon standing in the corridor.

"Why would they blame the school? Connie, calm down." Sharon called before Connie disappeared.

Connie turned and almost lost her balance. "Calm down? Did you just tell me to calm down? I've had that fat slob insulting me in front of everyone, and now you're telling me what and when, and to calm down! No, Sharon butter-wouldn't-melt Elliott. I won't calm down, because I'll do as I please. Including going to see Gary."

Sharon's mouth fell open and her hands hit her hips, but seeing the look on Connie's face she simply raised her eyebrows, nodded, and turned away.

Chapter Five

JJ STOOD ON THE steps of the pub and looked down at the village. It was still called a village, but it was more like a small town now. It was ten times the size of the village he'd left at eighteen. They even had an out-of-town supermarket behind the Treetops estate. He didn't resent it. He didn't want to look at it, but he didn't resent it because it was necessary. All those people had to live somewhere, and unlike some villages, Frampton Down had no holiday homes standing empty for half the year. Only families looking to build a life. Growth brought services. They still had a regular bus service into Bristol and elsewhere. There was a health centre, a gym, two churches, three pubs, and of course, the primary school. Without growth, there wouldn't have been enough kids to keep the drafty old building he'd attended open. Even if the new bit didn't excite his camera lens, it was still a good place to live. Or it had been. It might be a bumpy ride for the next few months. He'd not heard of any sort of murder in Frampton Down before, and Jemma and Old Sam had had the busiest Wednesday lunchtime on record because of the drama of it all.

Curling back his tongue with his fingers, he gave a whistle that could have shattered glass and waved at Sharon as she started up the hill. He walked over to meet her.

"I know I said I'd only take the car when the weather was terrible, but I think I'm getting too old for this hill. How are you, JJ? How's your day been?" She placed a palm on his cheek and looked into his eyes. He'd been a wreck the night before, and she wished he would tell her about his nightmares. It might help exorcise them if he spoke about them.

“I’m fine, stop fussing, and my day has been interesting. I’ll tell you once we’re in. I’m guessing yours wasn’t ideal. You only moan about the hill when you’ve had a bad day. How’s Connie?” He took her hand, unable to hide his smirk.

“Do you know what she called me?” Sharon stopped walking, one hand on her hip.

“I could make suggestions, but then I’d be in your bad books, too.” JJ feigned injury as she elbowed him.

“Sharon butter-won’t-melt. What does that mean? I know what it means, so I don’t want a literal translation. But why, I’m not a goody-two-shoes, am I? What do you think she was getting at?”

JJ chuckled and stepped out of elbow range. “I’d take that as a compliment. Compared to Connie, you’re positively saintlike.”

“I suppose, but I don’t know what’s got into her. I know Amber’s death has us all a little on edge, but it was ridiculous, and I don’t know how I didn’t laugh when Sara Dent gave her the finger.”

“To her face? That I would like to have seen.” JJ’s grin broadened.

“Yep, and in front of all the parents in the playground. Everyone is saying there’s a killer on the loose. Some kids are terrified by it, and a few think it’s the best thing that could have happened. Have you heard anything more?” She placed her hand on his forearm as he opened the gate for her.

“Only bits of gossip. Not seen a copper for dust. So unless they did the door to door when I was in the pub with Luke, I—”

“In the pub with Luke? Luke Wilton? Open that door. You’ve got some explaining to do.” Stepping into the house, Sharon sniffed. “Mmm. That smells good. Lamb or chicken?”

“Chicken. What first, cup of tea, glass of wine, or a bath?”

“Bath with wine, and you can tell me what’s been going on.”

JJ sat on the bathroom floor, rolled up a towel, and used it as a backrest, his long legs forcing his feet to rest against the side of the bath. He told Sharon about his encounter with Luke Wilton.

"... So given the circumstances, it went as well as it could have. Gary's probably going to move back here, but I don't know for how long. And like I said, I think it would really help if you go and see Luke when you have a minute."

"Yes, I will. Not sure if you should hold me up as the bringer of peace of mind, though. I might fail miserably."

"You healed me." JJ held her gaze. "Without you, who knows?"

"Yes, but that was because of the sex as much as anything else. Not sure homework will have quite the same effect." Sharon grinned at him. "Seriously, JJ, how are you? I have been worried, but I employed self-control and didn't call every time I thought about you. Tell me honestly."

"Honestly, it's scary, and I'm still shell-shocked by what I feel about it. But you'll prise it out of me, anyway. From the little I've heard, Evans is a bigger wanker than I thought he was. He's treating this as misadventure, but hinting it was suicide. It wasn't. So, I've been asking questions, and in my humble opinion, Amber was meeting someone after the pub. I haven't found out who or why, but I want to. Hence, I'm shocked." JJ grimaced. "It's scary wanting to investigate a murder again. And here's the weird thing, it's not because I want to get one over on Evans, although I do, of course, because I'm a petty individual. But more importantly it's because I was enjoying it."

Sharon sipped her wine as she considered this. "Two things, first, you don't do humble opinions. Not in these circumstances, you do kind but forceful, and second, Evans is the biggest wanker that ever walked the earth. You could never think too lowly of him. Fact." She pointed a finger dripping with bubbles at him. "I suppose the real question is, even if you carry on asking questions, how would you make *him* listen to you?"

"I'll speak to Tom Rowntree. You know I would never talk this over with Evans. My marbles might roll about a bit, but I've not lost them yet." JJ rubbed the side of his head.

"Glad to hear it. Pass me a towel. My fingers look like prunes." Sharon accepted the towel pulled from behind JJ's back. "Thank you. Now, slave, you may proceed to the kitchen and put the rice on. I'm starving, and then it's an early night for us."

JJ raised his eyebrows. "Are you planning on extra healing?"

"I'd love to, but if I'm honest, no. Nothing could be further from my mind. I just want a warm body to snuggle up to while I sleep, and yes, probably snore because I'm knackered."

"Oh. In which case I might withhold the peshwari naan, and I'm going to use the microwave rice." Pulling a face, he left the bathroom.

Sharon appeared in the kitchen a few minutes later and smiled. "Oh lovely, a tray. You know me so well. Do you need a hand?"

"No. Madam may make herself comfortable in the sitting room. I'll bring it through. More wine?" JJ held the bottle up and pointed it at her.

"But of course, I'll even pour it myself. Are you joining me?"

"No thanks, water will be fine."

They settled on either end of the couch, and when Sharon had eaten a few mouthfuls, she pointed her fork at JJ. "Go on. Who said what that's got you interested?"

"Oh, before we get to that, and I need to ask you who was Amber seeing? I heard something I wasn't expecting, and I know you lot chat about more than books on the boozy nights at the book club."

"Ah. What have you heard?" Sharon's dimples appeared despite trying to hold back the smile.

"No. I went first. You tell me what you know. And then I'll tell you why I asked."

"Well, and starting with the proviso that this is gossip, and not directly from Amber. I was told she had an on-and-off relationship with Sean Manton. And to be honest, if you weren't looking for a long-term partner, who could blame her?"

"I beg your pardon, should I be worried?" JJ's fork hit his tray with a clatter. "I can't believe you told me that." JJ's already rugged face crumpled into a pout, but his eyes revealed his amusement.

"JJ, I love you. I live with you. I'm not looking for love or anything else, anywhere else. But if I was single, and I wasn't looking for love, but just for a bit of healing, he wouldn't be at the bottom of the list. But then, nor would George

Clooney etcetera. As I'm not looking, they're on standby, and you can get rid of that smacked-arsed look. Your turn. What did you hear?"

"Luke said his mother was going to introduce him to someone who might pop the question." JJ smirked as Sharon's eyes widened. "You didn't know that. I asked Gary if she'd been seeing anyone, and he told me she'd had a fling with Mark Baxter that didn't last long. She also sort of denied having anything to do with Sean Manton. When I saw Karen Baxter in the shop, she said, and I quote, 'It's not for me to gossip, but I hope you've got an excellent memory for all the names you'll get asking that question.' I asked her to explain, and she waved her finger, and said no because she didn't gossip." Laughing at Sharon's expression, he added, "Do you have anything concrete to add?"

"Marry her? Not Sean Manton, then. And miserable Mark? Why? How? But more importantly, why? Amber was fun. The only time she wasn't laughing was when she was painting. What on earth would she have in common with Mark? I've never met anyone with such a negative view of everything. She must have been seeing someone else. Even if one of those two proposed, Amber would never accept. No, never. There has to be someone else. Do you think Karen knows they had a fling?"

JJ shrugged. "Who knows? Karen wouldn't tell me that, even if she knew. Who would you say Amber would be most likely to confide in?"

"I suppose that depends on what it was she needed to confide. Her mother, for most things, Amber and Emma were very close. But confiding about lovers, probably not with your mum. But that said, if she thought someone might pop...What the hell?" Sharon stopped speaking and looked over her shoulder towards the hall where someone was hammering on the front door. "Have you upset someone?"

JJ put his tray on the coffee table and went to answer the door. "Why is it always my fault? It might be for you." Yanking the door open, he stepped out onto the step without looking at the caller and jabbed his finger on the doorbell. The opening bars of Mozart's fifth symphony echoed in the hall. "Yep. Thought so. The bell works, and ..." JJ lifted the brass acorn knocker and tapped it against the plate behind, "the knocker still works, too. Was there a reason you tried to damage my front door, Evans?"

Still on the doorstep, JJ towered over the squat form of DS Clive Evans.

"I was in a hurry. I want a word." Evans was blushing like a sixteen-year-old but pulled his shoulders back and pointed into the house. "Can I?"

JJ would have loved to have embarrassed Evans further by refusing, but he wanted to talk to him, so he pursed his lips and tapped his foot a few times. "If you ask properly, yes. I don't think the force has dispensed with manners, have they?"

"Fuck off, JJ. Let me in. You've caused me enough bother for one day. Saying please isn't—"

"You see. How hard was that? Yes, Evans, you may come in. Go through to the kitchen. Sharon's eating in the sitting room and she thinks you're a wanker too, so she'll get heartburn or something."

As Evans squeezed past, JJ asked, "I see Rach is in the car. Is she not coming in?"

"PC Sampson won't be needed. This won't take long."

JJ heard the scrape of a chair being pulled from under the table, and leaving the door ajar, went to join Evans. "But she's the note-taker, and you're obviously stopping because you've taken a seat."

"JJ, can we just get on with this, please?"

"Another please. You're getting there, Evans. What's bothering you?" JJ pulled out the opposite chair and folded his arms, resting them on the table.

Evans lived on the third floor of a modern block of flats in town. His kitchen was white and functional, but tiny. He looked around JJ's spacious kitchen. Aga, Belfast sink, slate floor, farmhouse table and chairs, and old. On balance preferred his box to the picturesque cottage. He turned his attention back to JJ.

"I've come here to warn, no, wrong word, ask you to stop telling everyone that someone murdered Amber Wilton. The locals have inundated the station with calls, mainly parents, but also the media. We've had several 999 calls too. It's causing chaos for no good reason. Everyone thinks there's a murderer on the loose. Not sure what you're hoping to gain, other than giving the force a royal headache, but it needs to stop. The PM has only just started. No one knows, if we ever will, why Amber Wilton went off that bridge."

"And I'd warn, no, wrong word, ask you in return, to stop insinuating that Amber killed herself. She didn't. And if you don't know that, perhaps you're in the wrong job." JJ watched Evans grind his teeth and clasp his hands together to hold back his temper.

"Clever, JJ. Brilliant, in fact, but you don't know it's murder. Why are you spreading that around? Tom Rowntree isn't happy."

"Does Tom have all the facts? Don't answer, I'll call him. And for the record, although this isn't being recorded, I've not said it was murder. I simply said I don't think she jumped. Although I do think it was murder, or manslaughter at the very least, I haven't voiced that outside of this house. If Denise is doing the PM now, we'll have her opinion soon enough."

"We? Since when did you get copied in on PM results? Back off, JJ, just because you found her, it doesn't mean you can go poking your nose in and causing a shit storm." Evans got to his feet. "Back off. You left the force, your choice, and from what I hear, before they pushed you. Stick with playing with your camera."

JJ followed Evans to the door. "I'll do what's right, and Evans, all joking aside, so should you." Closing the door, he went into the sitting room and dropped onto the end of the couch. "Did you hear all that?" he asked, as he made himself comfortable.

"Most of it. And by the way, thanks for sharing my opinion of him. It's weird when you talk to him or even speak about him. Generally, you're always so gentle, but you get all macho 'don't mess with me' when he's around."

"He brings out the worst in me. That's what it takes to survive on the force, you know. Broad shoulders, thick skin, attitude. Getting out, albeit reluctantly, was like having a weight lifted. It's why I feel so uncomfortable not feeling uncomfortable about getting involved in Amber's death. Bloody hell, I can't even talk straight." JJ shook his head, as he drummed his fingers on his knees and fell silent.

Eventually, Sharon brought him back into the room. "What are you going to do?"

"Not sure. Denise will be a few hours if she's only just started, and Tom knows Evans' limitations. I might wander up to the pub and see who's saying what, as you're after an early night."

"What about my healing powers? I ... who's that?" A movement outside caught her attention, and Sharon went to look out of the window. "Blimey, I think the press has arrived. Look."

Looking over Sharon's shoulder, JJ watched someone from the village place a bunch of flowers up against the fence of number eight. A man in a crumpled shirt stepped forward and took a photograph, before shoving a phone towards them. Little was said, and the well-wisher hurried away. The man rolled his eyes, crossed the road, sat on a wall, and lit a cigarette. His lined face seemed to cave in on itself as his congested lungs tried to produce enough effort to take a drag. What remained of his lungs filled with smoke, and he looked up at the sky and blew it out slowly.

"Why do they do it, JJ? What makes them think badgering a bereaved family is a good thing to do?" Sharon looked up at JJ. "It's so cruel."

"I don't know. It's a shame Evans had already gone. He would've had a word. Probably one of the few things we agree about, the press. Ooh! Look who's trying to park." JJ pointed further down the road to where a red Corsa was making a meal of parallel parking. The car ended up with one back wheel on the pavement, and its nose sticking out into the road.

"Connie? She'd better not be coming here because my butter is well and truly melted," JJ stated.

They watched Connie march up the road carrying a large, highly decorated tin. As she drew level, she didn't even glance towards their home.

"Must be going to see Gary and Luke. I stand corrected. The ice queen has a heart. Do you think she's baked a cake?" JJ asked.

"Connie? No. She once invited me to lunch, said it would be beans on toast or toast on beans, whichever was ready first. I declined, and we went to the Italian. This should be interesting, he's just taken a...oh, she's noticed."

Connie had stopped walking and turned to look at the man on the wall, who lowered his phone. JJ leaned around Sharon and opened the window.

"Did you just take a photograph of me?" Connie used her best headteacher voice. "If so, why? I take that as a violation, an assault of my being. Who are you?"

"The name's Davie George, *Daily News*. Are you related to the family?"

"Working for that rag, and you admit it? Whatever happened to pride? What family? Oh, I see, you mean the poor Wilton family. No. No relative, I'm here for...silly me, I've come too far. Get that phone out of my face, you horrible little man. If I find out you've even looked at that photograph again, I'll sue you. You do not have my permission. Do you understand?"

Connie didn't wait for an answer, instead she turned and hurried up the path of number five, as JJ and Sharon jumped away from the window. Mozart announced she'd found the doorbell.

"I'm definitely going to the pub. I'll hang around to see what she's going to say first, though."

Sharon pointed a finger at him. "And if I can't get rid of her, we'll be coming with you." Twitching a smile, she opened the door.

Connie stepped inside and slammed the door shut. "Thank you! I thought for one horrible moment you might be out." She looked Sharon up and down. "Did I get you out of bed?"

"Not quite. I had a bath, ate dinner, and was about to go to bed. As you know I didn't get much sleep last night and I don't want to be late for school again, so you'll be keeping me from it if you stay. What can we do for you?" Sharon didn't invite her further than the hall.

"Just give me a moment to catch my breath. Do you know there's a bloody reporter out there from *The Daily News*?" Connie fanned her face with her hand. "It's warm again tonight. I almost wish that wind would return."

"Is that for me?" Sharon nodded at the tin Connie was carrying.

"No. Gary and Luke. I told you I'd pop round and offer support if needed, and I didn't want to come empty-handed. Flowers never seem right for a man."

"You baked something? Have you had lessons?" Sharon pulled her best shocked face.

"Don't be ridiculous. I popped into Waitrose and picked up a selection of goodies. I put them in here because, well, arriving with a carrier bag didn't seem appropriate either." Connie shoved the tin into Sharon's hands. "You can pop it in for me. I told the reporter I wasn't going there, so now I can't."

"Will do. Now, if that was all, I'll let you get off." Sharon tried to reach around Connie to open the door.

"Are you trying to get rid of me? I was going to ask if you'd heard anything else."

"Yes, and no."

Connie caught a movement behind the door to the sitting room. "Is that JJ? I'll have a quick word with him as I'm here. You go on. I'll see you in the morning." Leaving Sharon standing in the hall holding the tin, Connie walked into the sitting room and looked at JJ.

"JJ."

"Connie." JJ mirrored the curt greeting and said no more.

Connie's chest rose as she drew in a calming breath. "Sharon was telling me you don't believe that Amber's death was accidental."

"No, I don't."

"Do you think it's wise to spread rumours?" Connie sat on the arm of the chair opposite JJ.

"I don't. I think it's reckless." JJ wondered how long it would take Connie to lose her temper, as he offered only brief answers to her closed questions.

"But isn't it also reckless to suggest it wasn't an accident?"

"Depends on the circumstances, and in these circumstances, I'd say no."

"Circumstances? What circumstances?"

"Can't say I'm afraid. The evidence is with the police." JJ got to his feet. "Now, if you'll excuse me, I'm off to the pub."

"So there's evidence it wasn't an accident, I didn't realise that. What evidence?" Connie tried again.

"There is. But I can't discuss it. Shall I show you out? I think Sharon's gone to bed." JJ held back his smile as he heard Sharon scuttle down the hall to the kitchen.

"Hint taken." With a roll of her eyes, Connie followed JJ into the hallway and paused as he opened the front door. "Do me a favour, make sure that idiot doesn't bother me." She jerked her head up the street before stepping out of the house.

JJ followed her and looked at the reporter who had returned to his perch on the wall opposite the Wiltons' house. "You go down to your car. I'll have a word. 'Bye, Connie."

Connie was tempted to stay and watch, but knowing JJ wouldn't even raise his voice, she headed for her car. JJ walked over to the reporter.

"Evening, can I help? Only I see you've been here a while." JJ looked over the wall, wishing he'd brought his camera. The shadows cast by the rows of runner beans in the allotments behind it would produce some interesting shots.

"Do you live here?" Davie George slid off the wall. "Do you know the Wiltons?"

"I've just walked out of that house, and I'm barefoot." JJ jerked his thumb back towards his cottage. "An educated man would guess that I'm a neighbour."

"Yes, I guessed that. I was just checking. It doesn't mean you know them, though, does it? So do you?"

JJ caught the movement of Davie's hand and knew his phone was recording.

"I do. It's such a shame. They are distraught, as you would imagine. Why are you hanging around? What was it you were hoping for?" JJ leaned against the wall.

"To know what happened to her, of course. When it came in, the report said it was misadventure. Then I get a call from someone saying she was pushed, and then another asking if we're covering the murder. I was after a quote, and if I was being cheeky, some detail." Davie winked.

JJ's eyes narrowed, and he inclined his head. The man looked familiar. "From the family? You thought they might discuss the loss of a dear family member with a hack?"

"That's not nice, I prefer journalist. But to answer your question, not necessarily the family, the police, although that's a long shot. A friend, maybe even a neighbour. What's your name, sir?"

"JJ but I'm not going to talk to you. Go home and find something useful to do."

Davie George was frowning. JJ knew what was coming next, and he braced himself for the slew of questions. A sigh escaped as Davie's frown disappeared to be replaced with a crooked smile.

"I knew I knew you. JJ bloody Jenson. You don't remember me, do you?"

"Should I?" JJ still wasn't sure, but the man looked vaguely like one of the press who used to hang around outside the station, but he wouldn't make it easy for him. "What did you say your name was?"

"You should do. I saw you nearly every day when I covered the Daniel Boyd case. Nasty business." Davie shook his head as he shivered. "So you're back. I heard you found God and went off ..." Davie searched for the right description. He could see the mention of Daniel Boyd hit a nerve. If he was to get a story out of this, he needed to tread carefully. "Went off to do good. It's me. Davie George." He took a step back. "How are you?"

The question didn't sound sincere coming from Davie's lips, mainly because it wasn't. But the mention of Daniel Boyd hadn't gone down well, and he needed to earn a few brownie points. He certainly didn't want to discuss Daniel Boyd. Davie spent his days avoiding thinking about him.

"Davie George?" JJ was still struggling with who the man was. "I'm fine. What are you doing out in the sticks?"

"But you do remember me, yes? We got pissed after the bastard walked. You remember that, surely? I even took you home and stayed with you."

JJ's brow furrowed. Other than arriving back in Frampton Down and hearing he'd come home too late to see his father, it had been the worst day of his life when Bryn Jenkins had walked out of that court. Taking a closer look at the man grinning at him, he shrugged and shook his head. "No. Apologies. I'm drawing a blank."

"Davie George. Come on, JJ, two days I stayed with you to stop you from doing anything stupid." Davie looked JJ up and down. "Mind you, I didn't recognise you straight off. It's the hair, it's long and you're going grey, but we're all getting old, and I've never seen you with a beard. You were always so smart back in the day. I see you're going for the casual look now."

As Davie pointed at JJ's shapeless shorts and baggy T-shirt, JJ realised who the man was. He studied him for a while before responding.

"Davie, I'd say it was nice to see you but it's not. You're still trading on people's misery. Don't want to be rude but have you been ill? You've lost a lot of weight and I remember you with hair."

"Not was, I am. Terminal. Hence the cue-ball appearance and being half the man I used to be. Still, you can't let it stop you." Davie rubbed his head, where only a few wisps of hair had grown back. "Not going to sit round feeling sorry for myself."

"I'm sorry to hear that, and although I like your attitude, I can highly recommend empathy for others. And I'd also recommend giving up those things." JJ pointed at the pile of dog ends at the base of the wall. "Do some good, Davie. The bloke I remember was a kind but misguided man. I thought you'd seen the light after helping me out. I'm sorry to see you back doing this."

Davie gave a mirthless laugh. "I don't think God has a place for me, JJ, do you? The thing is, I have to do something. I'm not going to just sit in a chair waiting to die. Having someone else wipe my arse and shovel food into me? No thanks. This is the better alternative."

"No, it's not." From the corner of his eye, JJ saw the curtains twitch in Luke's bedroom. "I was going for a pint. Just the one. Do you fancy joining me and leaving these people to their grief?"

"The other thing I heard was that you'd gone teetotal. My sources are crap. Yes, I'll have a drink with you. I'd like that." Davie held up his hands. "I'll have to find alternative sources."

"The Three Bells." JJ pointed down the hill. "Sit outside if there's room. No air flow in the bar. I'll get some shoes on and see you there. I'll have a Guinness."

JJ watched Davie walk towards the pub and wondered if he'd been wise. It removed Davie from outside the Wiltons' home, but at what cost to himself? The chances of avoiding a conversation about Bryn Jenkins and his heinous crimes were slim to non-existent. Davie George had been the only person JJ had spoken to about Jenkins since the case collapsed. Only Davie. He wasn't sure he was ready for this. JJ glanced down into the village, at the church, as he walked to collect his shoes Only Davie and God. Neither had helped.

Chapter Six

JJ SIPPED HIS PINT and licked the thick white froth from his upper lip before using his hand to wipe his mouth. Davie's choice of table surprised him. The Davie he remembered liked to be in the thick of it, picking up snippets of gossip, and joining in conversations uninvited. This evening, Davie had chosen the table at the far end of what the Three Bells laughingly called the garden. It was little more than a strip of concrete with some benches and a few half barrels filled with bedding plants. Perhaps Davie wanted to talk.

"So, you say it's terminal. If you don't mind talking about it, how long have you got?" JJ's voice was gentle, and he kept his eyes on Davie.

Davie's shoulder twitched. "Don't know. A couple of years. Maybe. I don't want to talk about it. What's the point?"

"Is that what you said to the doctor when he told you to give up smoking?" JJ eyed the packet of cigarettes sitting on the table.

Davie laughed and rapped on the table. "Exactly, JJ, exactly. Word for word. And I meant it. What's the point of going through all the grief of giving up when it's already too late? What do I want a couple of extra months for? No, no, no. I don't think slow and lingering is for me. I reckon I'll just keel over and have done with it."

"What about your family? They might like you to stick around as long as possible."

Davie rolled his eyes. "Like you, JJ, I've got no kids, and the wife buggered off years ago while you were off doing God stuff. I don't think my brother is going to come down from Yorkshire to mop my brow."

"You don't have anyone else?"

"Nope. Nor do I want them. Anyway, look at me, JJ." Davie held his arms wide. "Who'd be interested in this bag of doodoo?"

JJ laughed. "Doodoo? Doodoo? Since when did you curb your language? Anyway, they say there's someone for everyone. Perhaps if you packed in smoking, wore a pair of clean jeans, and pressed your shirt, you might have half a chance."

"Oh really? Advice from the man in green flip-flops, who's found the only outfit that looks older than he is. Even if I was interested, which I'm not, where would I find this shortsighted woman?" Davie held up his hand. "Don't answer that. It wasn't a serious question. I'm fine, JJ. Not happy, per se, how could I be? My numbered days are flying by, but I don't want more than I've got, except perhaps a little more money. I've made my peace with it. Now change the subject before you try to get me into that church down there. Talking of which, tell me about that. The JJ I knew was a good man, irritatingly so, but he wasn't religious. What happened?"

"I needed some peace. Too much crap, too many horrors. I was looking for some good in life. The church provided it ... for a while. It's not that complicated, Davie. I was in a bad place, you know that. The church rescued me. Sort of."

"I heard you'd become a minister, or a priest, or something." Davie sipped his pint. "And if I'm honest, it didn't seem that odd."

"I just did some missionary work. South Africa first, then Kenya."

"Explain. Aren't all the religions already established there now?"

"I wasn't converting the natives, Davie. Get a grip. In South Africa, I worked in an orphanage for kids with AIDS, and in Kenya, I helped build and open some schools. It's rewarding work. It's tough, and often it's sad, and from your point of view, it might seem pointless. You know what missionary work is. Why did you ask?"

"Just getting the measure of the man I'm drinking with. People change, and I wanted to know how much. That's all. No agenda on this side of the table. Did you marry again?"

"No. But I am living with a rather remarkable woman. Her name's Sharon. Why do you ask?"

"Just wondered if you became an old cynic like me."

JJ didn't know how to answer that. He'd survived too many years of not believing there was any good to be found in the world. But there was. Most people were in too much of a hurry to notice it while they were dealing with the overwhelming bad.

"There's good to be found, Davie. You have to look for it, granted, but it's there." JJ grinned as he pointed at Davie. "Now there's a challenge for you. Don't write about the crap that's going on around us. Leave the victims in peace and go in search of what good people are doing. You'll find it, and you'll appreciate it. Far more fulfilling, I promise you."

"Give me a break, JJ. No one pays for good news. Do you think I want to be sitting on a wall in the middle of nowhere? Although, as fate would have it, I've found you. You're one of the few I'd want to say goodbye to. Weird how things work out. After seeing the state you were in and keeping you alive that weekend, I really thought I'd be attending your funeral. That the next time I saw you, you'd be in a box, not the other way around. You look well, in body, anyway. But you still have that look in your eye."

"I don't have a look. Behave yourself. Do you want a top up?" JJ hadn't finished his own drink, but when he'd said one, he meant it. Drinking made him sleep too heavily. If he slept, he dreamed. That was never good.

"Haunted. That's what it is. Hardly surprising, though, not with the jobs we did. Just a half. I'm driving." Davie passed his empty glass across the table.

JJ nodded acceptance. As he went into the bar, he pondered Davie linking writing about the awful things that happened to actually seeing them in all their technicolour horror, and then having to deal with the people responsible. Evil was still evil, whichever way you looked at it. A hand appeared in front of his face, and he blinked as his neck jerked back. Jemma clicked her fingers again.

"Blimey, JJ, what planet were you on then? What can I get you?" Jemma waved an empty glass at him.

"Half of Guinness, please. Sorry, Jem, lost in thought."

"You can say that again. Just the one? Does your companion not want one?"

"This is for him. I'm not drinking tonight. Well, not after the one I've got, anyway." JJ looked around the bar. "Busy again tonight."

"Yep. Won't last long. Once they've picked up the latest gossip, only the regulars will be here. Isn't that right, Sam?"

Old Sam wandered down the bar. "Yep. Who's that you're drinking with, JJ? I've not seen him around before."

"Someone I sort of used to work with. We bumped into each other. What's the latest?" JJ placed an elbow on the bar and leaned forward.

"Are you suggesting I listen to gossip?" Jemma took the note in JJ's hand. "Or were you asking him? In which case, sit down, he's not stopped circling all night. Love a good tale, don't you, Sam?"

Old Sam winked at JJ. "I'll bring it out when it's ready."

JJ nodded and went back to Davie. "They'll bring it out. Can I ask you a favour?"

"Another one? Thought it was you who owed me a favour. Isn't that the way it's supposed to work when you've saved someone's life?" Davie grinned. "Go on then. I'm making no promises."

"How badly do you need the money from selling this story?"

"That's not a favour, that's an intrusive question. But everyone needs money, JJ. I've got no police pension like you. All I've got is me. And don't go suggesting I should claim benefits. Not how I work, anyway a dog couldn't survive on that, let alone someone with bills to pay and a car to run. Things are tight, always have been, always will be. I need stories, JJ, and the more exciting, the better."

"I'm going to ask you a favour, and I want an honest answer." JJ looked stern, and Davie gave agreement with a nod.

"Will you stop hounding the Wiltons? Luke, he's Amber's son, has already had a tough year, and this is going to be hard enough on him without kids telling him about the lurid stories their parents have read. Would you do that for me?"

"But—"

"It's a yes or no answer, Davie."

"Oh, for God's sake, yes but, and there is a but, you're going to have to find me something else to write about."

"I have your word?" JJ searched Davie's face for any hint that he might be lying. He found none.

"I said, didn't I? Don't like you questioning my word, JJ. I've never lied to you, not when it matters. Why does this matter so much?"

"I'll tell you in a minute. Here comes your drink. Listen and say nothing, okay?"

"Oh, the plot thickens. I like this." Davie reached for his cigarettes, but JJ got there first and covered them with his hand.

"You also need to cut back on these. For me. I know I can't save you, but I can keep hold of you for a few more days. I care, Davie." JJ looked up at Old Sam as Davie rolled his eyes. "Take a seat, Sam. This is Davie. We used to work the same cases."

Sam passed Davie his drink, placed his own on the table, and perched on the edge of the bench. His knees wouldn't cope with lifting them over, and he held out a hand. "Nice to meet you, Davie. Any friend of JJ's."

"Likewise."

"Anything new?" JJ asked.

"Two of the girls who were with Amber came in. One of them, Shelly, was telling our Jemma what a shame it was. Said she couldn't believe it because Amber was so happy. She'd got another exhibition agreed. Out at the castle. That's good, as you know. And Amber told Shelly she didn't want to jinx it, but her love life was looking up, too. That idiot, Evans, came back in and asked if we had any CCTV. I waved me arm around the bar and asked if he saw any. Then the cheeky bugger thought he might not have to pay for his pint. He paid. But that's it, JJ. He was tight-lipped other than that. The rest is just people looking for gossip, not delivering it."

"Are we talking about Clive Evans?" Davie's nose wrinkled.

"Yep. I see you're a member of his fan club, too." Sam laughed before taking a sip of his pint. "Do you also think someone pushed Amber off that bridge?"

Davie's eyes widened. "Evans thinks someone pushed her?"

"Not that I know. That would only be JJ."

"Well, in my experience, if JJ says it was murder, he's probably right. Never made many bad calls, did you, old chap?" Davie grinned at JJ.

"How long have you two known each other?" Sam asked.

Davie blew out a breath as he shook his head. "Ten years, maybe more. What do you reckon, JJ?"

"Too long. First time I came across you was just after I came out of uniform. Found you hanging on the back of the door in The Cedars." JJ laughed.

"It wasn't funny. That bastard Finlay had no need. An hour I was hanging there. My jacket had torn through the skin under my arms. The nurse said she'd seen nothing like it."

"Or smelt probably." JJ checked the time. "I need to get back, finish your drink, and I'll walk with you. Sam, let me know if anything interesting gets said." Picking up his inch of warm Guinness, JJ emptied his glass and pushed it towards Sam.

"Will do. Oh, Sean Manton doesn't look happy. I heard—"

"Yes, so did I." JJ glanced at Manton, who was walking into the pub as he got to his feet. "Let me know what's upsetting him. But tomorrow. I need to sleep tonight."

Sam saluted and made two failed attempts to get to his feet. JJ took his elbow and helped him up.

"Getting old is a bastard, boys. I don't recommend it." Sam arched his back with a grunt. "Everything stops working properly."

JJ watched the emotion flit across Davie's face before he joked, "In which case, I'll give it a miss. 'Night, Sam. Nice to meet you." Picking up his drink, Davie took a last sip. "You do a good pint, Sam. I'll be back, I'm sure. JJ, I'm all yours."

As they walked back up the hill towards JJ's home and Davie's car, the two men discussed the case. JJ explained what he'd seen, or more accurately what his camera had captured, and Evans' apparent indifference to the fact that Amber's death was no accident.

"And it's wrong, Davie. She was a lovely woman, a talented artist, and a brilliant mum. I have never regretted, or only a little anyway, leaving the force. Never missed it. Didn't like the circumstances of how it happened, and you know that as well as anyone, but I've never wanted to go back. But this, I can't walk away from this."

"No, I can see you're all fired up. But why make me promise to back off, then drop that bombshell in my lap? Unfair, JJ. If there's anything dodgy to find out, I'm the man people talk to. Not the coppers. I'm pissed off, if I'm honest."

"Don't be. I only asked you not to harass the family. I never said don't ask questions, and now Old Sam thinks you're ex-job, you've gained extra trust that, let's be totally honest, a hack from *The Daily* would never get. But you can't write about it. Not yet. Let's see the case through to its conclusion, then, Davie, you can go to town. You might even find that more reputable papers are interested."

"That's fine in theory, and I'm up for it, but what do I live on in the meantime? Can't eat fresh air, JJ." Davie shook his head and sucked in a breath, like a builder pricing a job. "That's a big ask."

"What have you got so far? Nothing. Yes, you could break your word and run a story on my theories, but then what? And I'll deny it. Say you've been misquoting me. But it won't come to that. Come on, Davie. We're old men...nearly. Wouldn't you like to do something worthwhile? Wouldn't you like to get one over on Evans? I would, but that's just a bonus for me."

"Have you got a spare room?"

"Yes, but—"

"Then we have a deal, JJ. Won't be your fault if I go broke, but as I can't afford to put petrol in the car for going back and forward every day already, it's a win-win. I was going to sleep in the car tonight if it was necessary. I've got a change of clothes." Davie rubbed his hands together. "And just think, I'll be around if you try to do anything stupid, too. Going to be like old times." Davie slapped JJ on the back. Then paused for breath. "That bloody hill might finish me off before the cancer does. This is yours, I believe. Do you need a word with her indoors before I get my gear?"

"Sharon will be in bed. I'll tell her once we've got you settled. Keep it down." JJ watched Davie grab a large holdall out of his boot. He covered his face with his hand as Davie walked towards him.

"Oh God, I'm going to regret this, aren't I?" JJ looked at the bag. "That's a big bag for someone who was planning one night in the car."

"He can't help you now, JJ. Do I need my sleeping bag?" Davie didn't wait for an answer but walked up JJ's path with a spring in his step.

Davie crept up the stairs behind JJ, approved of his room, and whispered that he'd wait until the morning to shower, because he didn't want to wake Sharon. He was unbuttoning his shirt before JJ had closed the door. Pulling back the covers, he climbed into bed and smiled. What a turn up. Somewhere to die in peace. He had almost nodded off when he heard Sharon shout.

"You've done what?"

"Charm offensive needed in the morning," he mumbled, before turning over and savouring the feel of a mattress caressing his aching bones.

Chapter Seven

SHARON PLACED HER MUG down on the table and looked at the ceiling. The sound of someone singing off-key in the bathroom shattered her normally peaceful breakfast habits.

"Okay, he seems a nice bloke, and yes, he's having a tough time of it. And yes, I noticed he put his dishes in the dishwasher, and he asked if I'd mind if he used the shower, but how long is he staying?"

"I don't know. A couple of days, maybe a week." JJ placed his hand over Sharon's. "He's helping me out."

"That's the other thing. He implied he'd helped you out before. How did a reporter from one of the tackiest publications help a straighter-than-straight JJ Jenson? When he mentioned it, you looked uncomfortable. Is there something I should know?" Sharon inclined her head, knowing from JJ's expression he didn't want to talk about it.

"Loads. But not now. I promise we'll get there, but not today." JJ squeezed her hand. "It was another black tunnel moment, and Davie helped me through it."

"I like him a little better. So how is he helping you now? You told me you were okay." Sharon held his gaze. "I'm here."

"And I'm not looking for that type of help. It's Amber's murder. I've decided I'm going to investigate it, with Davie's help, because despite all his flaws he has the ability to get people talking. Then if Evans doesn't shape up, I'll have something to take to Tom."

"Okay, I think. What will this investigation involve? Whatever the outcome, we still have to live here. It wouldn't be good if you or our new house guest upset anyone." Sharon got to her feet and cleared the table. "I'm not saying don't do it. Just be careful how you go about it."

"I know what you meant. It's why I need Davie because he can ask the questions that would be offensive or inappropriate coming from me. And I have a list of questions I know Evans probably won't ask. I'll work through it, then if the police don't start making the right noises, I'll go and see Tom."

"I'm going to agree with you because you seem focused. Focused is good. A couple of days, you reckon?" Sharon looked at the ceiling again.

"About, yes. I can always ask him to stop singing." JJ tried to keep a straight face.

Sharon walked over to him and took his face in her hands. "It's not just the singing. I have to remember to get dressed before I leave the bedroom. I don't like sharing because I have to be considerate. He could be the nicest man on earth, and I still wouldn't want him here. Day one. Now give me a kiss and I'll escape to work."

JJ kissed her goodbye and even saw her out. She was one of the most considerate people he knew, but he understood what she meant. He was concerned that Davie hadn't told him the whole truth because that bag held at least a month's worth of clothes. What if Davie was living in his car? How could they ask him to leave then? Add living in a car with a terminal cancer diagnosis, and it would be impossible, whatever happened with the investigation into Amber's death. JJ resolved to ask bluntly. Then at least he could tell Sharon the truth and they'd have to take it from there.

He filled the kettle and listened to Davie whistle his way across the landing to the spare bedroom. In JJ's experience, it was better to clear the air as soon as the opportunity presented itself, and that would be in five minutes. He drummed his fingers on the table while he waited.

"Alright, JJ? Is it okay if I chuck this lot in the washing machine? I'll look like you want me to then. Where do you keep the powder?"

"Um. Yes. Under the sink. Which brings me neatly to a question I'd like an honest answer to."

Davie found the washing tabs and threw one into the machine. "Another honest answer. You're going to ruin my reputation. Bloody hell, what's that?"

Mozart rang out in the hall, and JJ got to his feet. "The doorbell. Stay where you are."

"Saved by the bell," Davie muttered, and shoved his washing into the machine. He shook his head at the digital display, and not understanding what he was agreeing to, he pushed the start button with the fingers on his other hand crossed.

JJ called something to him but with the machine gearing up, Davie didn't hear and went to find out what he wanted. When he got to the door, JJ had disappeared, and a young boy stood there staring at him.

"Who are you?" Luke asked.

"I'm JJ's friend. My name's Davie. Who are you?"

"Same. My name's Luke but my friends call me Zed," Luke explained, and smiled when Davie didn't look shocked.

"Nice to meet you, Zed. Any friend of JJ's is a friend of mine." Davie shook Luke's hand. "Where is JJ?"

"Gone to get his trainers. We're going running. Do you want to come? I'm fast."

"I'd love to. But I'm a tad poorly at the moment, don't think I could run if I tried, and I've got work to do. But if I'm here when you get back, I'll make you a cold drink. It's warm today. I saw some Ribena in the fridge."

JJ came down the stairs and looked at Davie. "I see you've met L...Zed. We're going running. I'll be about half an hour."

"So he tells me. Catch you later."

"No, you'll catch me in half an hour. Be here."

Davie saluted, and as he closed the door behind them, he heard Luke tell JJ that his dad had let him have cheese on toast for breakfast. Glancing at the clock, Davie opened the door to the cupboard under the stairs.

"Bingo. First time."

Davie pulled out the ironing board and set it up in the kitchen before going back upstairs and getting his last clean shirt. His jeans would have to do until the washing had finished. Shirt ironed, he went back upstairs and threw his T-shirt into the corner of the room. He went to the bathroom and helped himself to JJ's toiletries. Smelling like the fragrance section of a department store, he went back downstairs and looked around. The dishwasher stood open, and he added a couple of mugs before switching it on and wiping the crumbs from the kitchen table. If he was going to stick around, he'd better make himself useful. He checked the time. Ten minutes to avoid giving another honest answer.

Rubbing a sheet of wet kitchen towel over his shoes, he checked his appearance in the hall mirror.

"The lad scrubs up well." He smiled at his reflection, counted the change in his pocket, and made sure he'd shut the door properly before heading for the pub. It was another week before he'd see any money. He set off down the hill, and was nearly at the pub when he realised it wouldn't be open yet. "Losing it, Davie. Get a grip." He paused, pondering an alternative. There was a row of shops on the main road, but would he make it back up the hill? Deciding it was better to try than run out of petrol, he continued his walk.

Ten minutes later, a little pink in the face, he entered the budget supermarket. Based in a row of Victorian houses, which had been knocked through to provide more space, it was still tiny compared to the average city supermarket. But to his surprise, it really was a budget shop. He wandered the three aisles, smiling when he saw the greeting card display with a sign telling him they were all less than a pound.

Selecting the card he wanted, he ambled along the aisle leading to the checkout, listening to the conversation at the till. He stood behind the two women who were talking to the man behind the counter, tapping the card against his leg.

"Yes, sir, what can I get you? You'll be standing there a long time waiting for these two to stop chatting. They drop the kids off at school, then gossip until they've got to pick 'em up again."

Davie handed him the 'In Sympathy' card. "Just this. Such a shame."

One woman peered at it before it went into the paper bag.

"Ah. Is that for Gary Wilton?" She placed a hand on her chest.

"Yes, poor old Gary. And poor little Luke. I'm glad he's got JJ to help him."

"How is JJ helping him?" Sara Dent asked. "Thought it would have been enough for JJ finding Amber like that. Are the police admitting it's a murder yet?"

Inside, Davie was dancing a jig. But, ever the professional, he gave a deep sigh. "I don't know. I only arrived last night. Like I said to JJ over breakfast, the police need to get their fingers out. If it was murder, the culprit needs to be locked up, not wandering free in a picturesque village. But Luke needed to get out of the house. He needs something to take his mind off it. JJ takes him running. I'm sure Gary needs some respite, too, you know, to grieve."

Sara's eyebrows rose as she considered this information. "You're staying with JJ and Sharon Elliott then? Are you related?"

"No, although we worked together for so long, it feels like it."

"Ah." Sara nodded. "Work. The church? No, you mean the police, don't you?"

"Yes. I admire what the church does, but I'm not JJ Jenson, and I certainly couldn't do missionary work. I'd get too angry."

Sara laughed. "No turning the other cheek for you...sorry, I didn't catch your name."

"Davie. Did you know Amber well? From what I hear, she was very popular, and very active in village life."

"Yes, Amber was lovely, arty farty, but that comes with being an artist. But she liked a laugh, and she didn't deserve to be pushed off that bridge. How's Gary coping?" Sara took a step closer, but her bulk got in the way, so she leaned forward. "You know they weren't together, don't you? Split about nine months ago, might even have been a year. I think Gary wanted to come back, but Amber had other fish to fry, if you know what I mean."

"Yes, I knew that, but I didn't realise Amber had met someone else. Was it serious? I'm not being nosy, but if it was serious, he should be told. Sounds to me like the police aren't doing much of anything."

Sara patted his arm. "Don't worry, love. News travels like it's got a rocket up its arse in this place. He'll know."

"Ah, he was local. Must have been a nasty way to find out. Tittle-tattle. No time to compose yourself."

Sara opened her mouth to say more, but her friend waved a finger. "That's enough, Sara. Don't start trouble for anyone."

"Alright, Jo. I'm not about to give him his address, or the...anything else. Look at the time. I'd better get going. Nice to meet you, Davie."

Jo Harris picked up her shopping bag and looked at Davie. "Tell Gary we're thinking of him. We put some flowers by the gate last night."

Davie assured her he would and watched the women leave. Turning to the man behind the till, he rolled his eyes. "I take it Amber's love interest was married."

"Correct. She seemed to prefer them taken. I heard it was miserable Mark before Steve. Then again, there aren't many single blokes around here. They all move to somewhere with a bit more life, and a lot more women."

"And who can blame them? Did you know Amber well?" Davie leaned his elbow on the counter.

"No. And don't let the wife hear you ask that!" The man chuckled. "Just kidding. And no more than the average customer. She came in for bits and bobs sometimes. The wife knew her better. Book club mates. She's really upset."

"I'm sure. And do you think Steve will know?" Davie asked, winging it.

"Hush. Keep your voice down, Mary's just come in. Yes, of course he'll know," the shopkeeper whispered, flapping his hand. Then, raising his voice, he looked past Davie. "Give me a shout if you need anything from the top shelf, Mary."

Davie glanced at the elderly woman scanning the tinned goods behind him and lifted the bagged card from the counter. "Understood. I'll see you later, no doubt. Nice meeting you." Davie left the shop carrying the card he hadn't paid for.

Wandering along the street, Davie wondered if JJ would know who Steve was. Spotting a café on the other side of the road, he crossed over. There were only three people in there, but one of them was the woman named Jo, who had been in the supermarket. He went in.

"Oh hello." He waved and she smiled. "We meet again. It's Jo, isn't it?" He waved at her and she smiled.

"Morning. What can I get you?" A tiny woman with a ruddy complexion and frizzy bleached hair walked back behind the counter, leaving the tray she was carrying on a table in the corner. The badge on her overall told Davie her name was Teresa.

His eyes quickly scanned the chalkboard behind her. "Morning, Teresa, just a tea, please."

"Take a seat. I'll bring it over." Teresa held out a hand, and Davie counted the correct number of coins into it. "Thanks. If you'd have wanted a full English, I might have refused. I think it's even hotter today than it was yesterday."

"Glad I didn't. I might have taken offence." Davie winked at her, adding, "But you're right, it's going to be a scorcher." He took a seat on the table next to Jo. "I thought you had somewhere to be?"

"That was Sara, not me. I'm working the afternoon shift. Thought I'd treat myself before I went home and pretended I wanted to do the housework." Jo pointed at the empty plate in front of her. "If you're peckish, I can recommend the toasted teacakes."

"No, I'm good. I'm just having a nose around the village. I've not been here before. When I last saw JJ he was living in Bristol," Davie replied. "Do you know JJ?"

"Yes. Not that well. I know Lynn, his sister, and Miss Elliot better. Or Sharon, I should say. Habit. She teaches my daughter. How is JJ? Is he fully recovered?"

Davie grimaced and waggled his hand from side to side. "He's getting there."

"My mum knew his dad. Both gone now, but Mr Jenson was very proud of JJ. I think it was almost a blessing JJ didn't get back in time."

"Why do you say that?" Davie asked.

"Dementia is a cruel illness. He probably wouldn't have known who JJ was. Saw Lynn in the pub one night. She said it was an awful situation, what with him not knowing who she was and he'd even gone as far as chucking her out of the cottage, accusing her of stealing from him. All she was doing was looking for his chess set because he'd said he fancied a game. So sad."

"Yep. My old mum was much the same. Kept telling me she had a son called Davie, but he was probably at school. Does Lynn live locally?"

"No. She was clever too, like JJ. Went away to university, came back with a posh husband." Jo grinned. "He's a looker. They've got four kids. Four! I can't cope with two. I don't know how she copes. Although he's a psychologist, so he probably knows how to reason with them, and I don't think she works, so that will help. How long are you staying?"

"As long as it takes." Davie replied, hoping to add mystery to the conversation.

"What's that?" Jo settled back in her chair after ordering another cup of tea.

"You could have said before I brought his over," Teresa complained as she placed Davie's tea on the table.

"I wasn't stopping, but we're chatting. You should be grateful." Jo rubbed her fingers together.

"Oh, I am. Ever so. Might get to retire on the profit from an extra cup of tea. But I'd be more so if your timing was better. Who are you then?" Teresa looked at Davie.

"JJ's friend. He's staying with him. They used to work together," Jo answered for Davie, who nodded agreement.

"Police or church?" Teresa asked.

"Police work. Can't remember the last time I was in a church, and the next time I'll probably be in a box." Davie sipped his tea. "That's an excellent brew, Teresa."

"So it should be. I make it properly. No teabags on bits of string in here." She flicked a cloth over the adjacent table, before turning away. "One more tea coming up."

Jo tapped the table. "You were telling me why you were here. Said you were staying as long as it takes. As long as what takes?"

Davie pursed his lips, then sighed, and then tutted. Not sure what else to do to show his reticence, he leaned towards her. "Me and my big mouth. Can you keep a secret?"

Jo nodded. "Of course. It's Sara that's the gossip, not me. Go on."

"Well, JJ told me all about finding Amber, what he saw, what the police are saying, and neither of us like it. JJ is certain Amber didn't jump off that bridge. He said she was happy that night. He'd seen her in the pub."

"She was. She was. I was there. In the pub, I mean, not at the bridge." Jo's head was now nodding continually. "So, what are you going to do about it?"

"Calm down, Jo. You'll get me in trouble. We're just making sure that justice is done. It seems the police don't even know about miserable Mark or Steve." Davie bared his teeth and groaned. "Damn, have I said too much? You knew, didn't you?"

"Of course. But I thought it was a secret. How do you two know?" Jo looked around to make sure no one else had entered the café. "Mark Baxter was a nothing thing. They got drunk and had a fumble. Karen is far too sharp to allow anything to develop. Not that it would have. I mean Mark, have you met him?"

"No. But everyone calls him miserable, so that gives me the idea that he wouldn't be at the top of my Christmas card list. Did his wife find out about the fumble, if it was a fumble?"

Jo hooted out a laugh. "Yes. She found them round the back of the pub. They'd gone out for a sneaky ciggy, and one thing led to another. I wasn't there that night, but there was a right old barney. Steve's different."

"Why's that?" Davie asked, before sipping his tea.

Jo waited until Teresa had placed her tea down before replying. "Their marriage has always been dodgy. She left the village for six months. No comment on where she'd been or why she was back. She's not a mixer. But they don't have kids, so that makes it easier."

"Amber was keen, was she?" Davie kept the questions coming. He didn't know who these people were, but JJ would, and it might help their investigation.

"She said nothing was going on. But I'd seen them. All innocent if you weren't looking properly, a conversation here, a wave there. And I know it sounds like nothing, but you don't kick Sean Manton to the curb unless you've replaced him."

"Sean Manton? I've not come across him." Davie frowned because the name rang a bell.

"Mr Muscle, we call him. Likes to keep himself trim and isn't too shabby to look at either. They had a thing going. Although I think he liked her more than she liked him. She told me he was a pain in the arse. Kept coming round when Luke was there, so she finished it."

"I know who you mean. He came into the Three Bells last night, and he didn't look happy. It seems like Amber was quite active on the romantic front." Davie knew what he'd be writing about if he hadn't made a promise to JJ. This was a story that would sell.

"Now, hang on a minute, Amber was single, Sean is single...ish. He's always got someone on the go. Nothing happened with Mark Baxter, and Steve was all speculation. Amber said nothing was going on. Don't put too much store in gossip. Don't ruin her name based on it." Jo wagged her finger at him.

"But you believe it? Or why tell me?" Davie resisted the urge to roll his eyes.

"Because this is a village. It's what we do. Nothing happens here. The odd drunk, a small lottery win, and when things really get going, a slanging match in public. What's not known we make up. Do you see?"

"I do. But there's a saying about no smoke without fire. So, you can see it gets things moving up here." Davie tapped his temple.

Jo emptied her cup and stood up. "I feel guilty now. I've said stuff I shouldn't have. You tell JJ it's pinch of salt stuff. I liked Amber, and if anyone pushed her off that bridge, I want them to pay for it, but I don't want people thinking she was putting it about. She wasn't. I'd better go before I cause any trouble."

"You haven't. This conversation goes no further than JJ, I promise." Davie gave what he hoped was a sincere smile. For once, he was telling the truth. As Jo left, he took their empty cups back up to the counter where Teresa was buttering a mountain of bread. "Thanks, I'll be back."

"You're welcome. Don't want to take a sandwich for your lunch, do you?"

"Not today, love. Thanks."

When Davie got outside, he paused. It was so quiet in Frampton Down; it was spooky. He couldn't even hear a lawnmower. Nor was there any sign of life. Not knowing where else to go without direction from JJ, he knew he'd have to tackle the hill and consider another honest answer.

He stopped halfway up and sat on a wall surrounding a neat little bungalow. His breathing was laboured, and his bald head glistened with sweat. It was just as well he had access to a washing machine because he could feel his shirt sticking to his back.

A car drove past, the driver rubbernecking him. He waved to confuse them.

"Are you okay?"

Davie turned to see an old woman shuffling towards him, carrying a glass of water.

"I'm okay. Just not used to physical exercise," Davie replied. "I've been ill, and I'm way past my prime."

Dorothy Williams chuckled. "Like me, then. Here, have this. You look like you could do with it."

Davie thanked her and drank the water. "Is everyone as friendly as you in Frampton Down?" he asked, handing her back the empty glass.

"Most. We've got a few miseries around, but generally I'd say yes. I've not seen you around before. Are you lost? You went down the hill at half nine, and it's almost half ten now. I hope you haven't been going round in circles."

"No, not lost. I'm staying with JJ Jenson. He's out, Sharon's at work, so I thought I'd have a look around. I bet you could tell me a story or two, nothing seems to get past you." Davie realised too late that he was implying that the woman was a curtain twitcher, which she was. Not only had she noticed him going out, she had also timed him. Luckily, she didn't notice.

"I could, indeed. Starting with James John Jenson. I used to teach him, you know. In the old school, they made that into two houses when they built the new one. I don't much like it. No character. Tell JJ that Mrs Williams said hello and he should pop in and see me."

"Will do. I bet JJ was a model pupil." Davie stood and stretched his back.

"Not far off. He was a good boy, still got into more than enough scrapes, though. But no malice in him. When everyone was gossiping about him, shocked he was going off to Africa, it didn't surprise me. I told them he had been a good boy, and he's a good man. Of course, James senior was still with us then. They didn't dare gossip when he was around. Known for his straight-talking was James Jenson senior. Shame James' mind betrayed him. I saw JJ earlier running down the hill with the Wilton boy. Poor lad. Jackie, she's my cleaner, says there's a rumour going around that Amber was murdered. What's JJ got to say about that? He found her, and with his experience he should know."

"Let's just say that he doesn't think the police should pass it off as misadventure, and I agree. I used to work with him. What else did your cleaner tell you? We'd be interested in hearing what people are saying."

Mrs Williams folded her arms across her chest. "I'm not one for gossip. I thought I'd told you that. Of course I listen to it, I've got little choice most of the time, but I don't go spreading things around. If I did that, we'd have a village full of divorcees. The police would be here all the time if half of it was true, and many people would be too ashamed to show their face in public. Why would you be interested?"

Davie took a step towards Mrs Williams and beckoned her to lean in closer, so only the low wall separated them. "Can you keep a secret?"

Mrs Williams' hands flew to her hips. "Isn't that what I've been telling you? Spit it out. Whatever it is, no one will hear it from me."

"JJ and I don't think the police are keen enough to find out what really happened, So we're investigating Amber's death. But unofficially. Don't want to get ourselves in trouble. Having said that, if you hear anything you think we should know, please give us a shout."

"Oh. I see. Well, there was...No, let me think about it. I'll need to sort the fact from the fiction. Tell JJ to pop in and see me this afternoon. About two would suit. You can join us if you like."

"I'm not sure what he's got on, but if nothing else, I'll be here. Nice to meet you, Mrs Williams."

"I'm sure. Now I know you said you had been ill, past tense, but you don't look well now, present tense. You should probably see a doctor."

To Davie's surprise, she winked at him before shuffling back towards her bungalow, muttering to herself.

Davie looked up the hill. The Three Bells was beckoning. It would be a good place to break the rest of the journey before he found out what JJ wanted to ask him, although he had a good idea. Still, he could afford a quick pint before that, and hopefully find out more about the Manton bloke.

"Morning, Davie, you're early. Only just opened up. Pint of Guinness?" Sam greeted him as he pushed open the door.

"Bit heavy for this time of day, Sam, I'll have a San Miguel and pretend I'm on the Costas." Davie climbed onto the bar stool. "How's business?"

"Good enough. But that's about it. We're never going to get rich. Poor Amber has raised the profile, though." Sam put the glass in front of Davie, who pulled the change from his pocket.

"How much do I owe you?"

"First one's on the house. How's the investigation going?"

"It's off and running, picked up a few snippets today I need to discuss with JJ."

"Yes, he asked if I'd seen you, stopped for a drink with young Luke. Poor lad. They'd been running again."

"Did you tell JJ what you'd found out about Sean Manton? His name came up a couple of times earlier."

"Not much to tell. Manton wasn't in a talkative mood. Sat in the window, drank more than a man should be able to in the time he was here, and left again. Never spoke to anyone. Even his mate, whose name escapes me, got told to sling his hook when he tried to sit with him. Word was he's fallen out with his latest."

"Oh dear. Who might that be?" Davie asked.

"Ha! Pick a name and you could be right. Could be anyone. I heard he'd finished with the girl above the post office a while back. Who knows with him, though? I know he's a good-looking bloke, but you'd think they'd have more sense. Never understood women, probably why the wife disappeared." Sam grinned. "That and the fact I couldn't stand her. You married?"

"Not anymore. She didn't like my line of work, nor the hours it demanded, and just got fed up nagging me about it in the end, and found someone to keep her company. Was a relief for both of us when she left. Last I heard, she was living on a Greek island somewhere, shacked up with a waiter, doing a Shirley Valentine. So, given there's not many people out and about, where's the best place to bump into people, other than the pub?" Davie asked.

"If it's gossip you're after, the pub, the café, and the health centre, don't get ill around here if you want it kept a secret, JJ can vouch for that, and I suppose the school playground. Although a bloke hanging around there might look shifty.

That's the old village. On the new estate, I couldn't say. They have the gym but never been inside, so no idea what you'd find there."

"The health centre? I can understand the others, but that's a stretch of the imagination."

"You'd think, wouldn't you? But all those people sitting around waiting to be called chat. That chat is disguised gossip. When I went for my rheumatism, I found out that Dr Bentley was in a strop because his wife had gone to stay with her mother, and that Sadie was pregnant again. It's her fifth, and Keith, her bloke, still doesn't have a job. The reason she keeps getting up the duff I reckon." Sam chuckled. "And that our Jemma was on HRT."

"Interesting. Who's Sadie, anyone I should know?" Davie asked.

"Local councillor's daughter. He was expecting great things of Sadie. Straight-A student, degree in something from Exeter University, and then she met Keith. Mind you, he's besotted with the kids, just not with their father. Oh, look who's here. Morning, Frank. You're early. The usual? Excuse me."

Sam walked to serve the customer who had entered as Jemma appeared from the door behind the bar.

"Morning all. Frank, you're early, it's not midday yet." Jemma smiled as Frank gave her a quick wave.

"Well, I was meant to see the doctor and have my bloods done, but it's chaos down at the health centre. Dr Bentley hasn't turned up, and I can't sit in there listening to that lot moaning and groaning. Like I said to Kerry Snell, it's not good enough. They should have called and cancelled some of us, but apparently the little blonde one, you know, with the cross eye, has got Covid. Thought it was a cold and still came in. They packed her off, and they're all back in masks again. Poor Dr Singh, he was rushed off his feet. Looked proper stressed. So, as I had my clean shirt and tidy trousers on, I thought what's the point of listening to the missus chat to the telly? I'll pop into the Three Bells. Do you want me to come back later?"

"Don't be daft. Take a pew, I'll bring it over. What's wrong with Dr Bentley?" Jemma took the beer that Sam had pulled and followed Frank to his usual seat in the corner.

"I don't know. I asked but Kerry had her bossy head on, and when one of the girls was about to answer me, she fairly ran me out. Gave the girl a look that could kill, then grabbed my elbow, and said if I wouldn't wait she'd see me out. She was in a bit of a flap. Not like Kerry at all. She's always in control, got an answer for everything, as you know, but she didn't this morning. She wasn't herself at all. I wondered if it was because of that poor girl that died. They were friends, weren't they?" Frank settled himself and lifting his drink, took a long draft. "That's better."

"They were friends, yes. Kerry was in here with Amber that night. It's not nice for anyone having a death in the village like that, although I'm not sure how close they were. You might be right. I'll bring your change over." Jemma took the note Frank had pulled from his wallet.

At the bar, Sam tapped Davie on the arm. "Told you. Shame you're not registered there. Sounds like there's a full house."

Davie finished his drink and grinned at Sam. "I could get registered though, couldn't I? Or pretend to. Where is it?"

A few minutes later, he was on his way back down the hill. He'd not made it to the bottom when a car pulled over and JJ got out and leaned on the top of the car.

"If I didn't know better, Davie, I'd say you were avoiding me. What have you been up to?"

"Why would I be avoiding you, JJ? Give me a lift to the health centre and I'll tell you." Davie pulled open the door and climbed in the car. "I thought my car was old until I climbed in here. Is it a classic?"

"If any of the parts were genuine, it might be. She's reliable, and when she's not, there's a garage as you come into the village, Buley & Sons, who sort her out. What have you found out?" JJ started the engine.

On the drive there. Davie told JJ about the bits and pieces he'd picked up.

"So, the first thing we need to do is find out who Steve is, unless you know that already. Do you?" Davie asked.

"No. Not sure if I even know of a Steve around here. I'll have a think and ask Sharon. Why are we going to the health centre?"

"Because Sam at the Three Bells told me gossip was rife there. Then Frank came in and said Dr Bentley hadn't shown up, and one of their girls came in with Covid, and it's chaos there. Good time to find things out, a chaotic period. Why are you looking at me like that?"

"You've settled in quickly. And already been to the pub. What's your excuse for hanging around an already busy surgery?"

"I'm going to say I want to register. I'll have to sit down and fill in a form."

"But you're not registering, are you? In your condition, you don't want to confuse the NHS about where you are living and who's taking care of your medical...which brings—"

"The thing is, I'm nearly out of my meds, so I'll need to speak to a doctor to get a prescription. Once I've done that, I won't need to bother them further. I wouldn't have thought so anyway."

"You could just phone your own doctor and ask for the prescription to be sent to the chemist here. No need for charades, is there?" JJ gave a wave to a man as he stopped to allow him to walk across the carpark.

"Blimey, this is bigger than I thought it would be. Very nice. I don't know how long I'll be. Better give me your number, JJ." Davie released his seatbelt and opened the door.

"Hang on a minute. We've got things to...you bugger." JJ cursed, but spotting a space at the end of the row, hurried to park the car.

By the time JJ entered the surgery waiting room, Davie was at the reception desk in conversation with a masked woman whom JJ recognised as Kerry Snell. He leaned against the wall by the entrance and watched the interaction. Davie kept holding out his hands and Kerry was doing a lot of headshaking. Eventually, Davie wore her down, and with a smile, accepted the clipboard and pen Kerry handed him, then took one of the few empty seats in the centre of the waiting area. Davie nudged the woman sitting next to him, causing her to smile and nod in agreement. JJ was about to ask for a word when Kerry appeared at his side.

"JJ, isn't it? I don't know if you remember me, Kerry, Kerry Snell, we've met a few times but never really spoken." Kerry lifted the mask away from her face for a few seconds, revealing her immaculate make up. "May I have a word?"

"Of course. What's it about?" JJ guessed he already knew the answer.

Kerry looked around, too many eyes were now on them, and she pointed at a door to the left of the nurses' treatment rooms. "In here, I think." She led the way into a room barely larger than a cupboard containing a small desk and two chairs. She saw JJ look around. "We use it for flu clinics. You know, in, jab, and out again. It means we can get through more patients in a timely fashion. Now, I know this might seem odd, and I wouldn't normally do this, but...I feel bad asking, but could you just confirm what your lodger has just claimed?"

"My ..." JJ considered his words. "My friend, you mean, Davie George?"

"Ah, okay. That's confirmed. I'm sorry, JJ, and please don't tell him I asked, but he didn't come across as genuine. I only saw Sharon the other day, and she didn't mention a lodger, so I thought he might be trying it on, and I had heard that the press was sniffing around. Vultures."

"Oh yes. He's staying with us for a while, last-minute thing. He's got cancer and his meds are running out."

"Well, he could have just got his own doctor to send a prescription to the pharmacy. I'd better tell him." Kerry's hand was on the door handle.

"I think there's something else wrong that he's not told me. You know lots of things are better kept for conversations with the doctor. Some people like to keep things private."

"Yes, well, I understand that but we're up against it in here today. If he's not time wasting that's fine, but he's going to have a long wait."

"I heard a doctor hadn't come in, and one of your girls has Covid, and I can see from the waiting room you've got your work cut out. Perhaps I can persuade him to leave it until tomorrow. Would that help?"

"No. Thank you, JJ, but I pride myself on our efficiency, and getting those that need to be seen, seen. Half of those only need to see a nurse, not the doctor. I'll have it cleared by lunchtime. Or soon after, anyway." Kerry offered a smile, which remained hidden behind her mask. "Chin up, shoulders back, we'll get there. Sorry to bother you, and again, I'd be grateful if you didn't mention I questioned his story."

"My lips are sealed."

"How's Amber's family? It's an awful time for them. I saw you running with her son earlier. Dr Bentley was worried about Luke."

"Holding it together, I think, just. I hear you were with Amber that night. Must be tough for you, too." JJ's smile was kind. "Sometimes people only concentrate on the immediate family. They forget about the ripple effect a death causes."

"I'm coping. Shocked and saddened, of course. Amber was...special. I'll miss her. But work keeps me occupied. Especially today. Talking of which, I'd better get on with it. I'll see if I can get your friend up the queue a little. We've got enough sitting out there just to pass the time. They won't notice." Nodding decisively, Kerry pulled open the door. "I take it you're waiting for him. I doubt he'd manage to walk back to yours."

Kerry had walked away before JJ could answer. Davie was deep in conversation with the woman sitting next to him, and deciding to leave him to it, JJ took a seat at the back of the waiting room. He busied himself taking photographs of the large potted fern, and the shadows it cast as the breeze from the open window caused the fronds to sway. Within an hour, Davie had been in to see the doctor and was walking towards JJ with a smile on his face. He glanced at the clock as he approached.

"I've got to come back tomorrow, first thing. My records should be sorted then. We've just got time to grab something to eat before our next appointment."

"Our next what? What have you roped me into Davie?" JJ asked as Davie led the way to the car. "I don't have appointments."

"Well, you do now. We're going to see your old schoolteacher. I didn't catch her name. Shall we go to the café? We can walk from here."

Chapter Eight

JJ SMILED AS HE placed their order. Davie was going nowhere. He was sitting at the table in the window, his chest heaving as he caught his breath after the short walk. Now JJ might get some answers.

Lunch loaded on a tray, JJ went to confront him. "I got you a glass of water. Thought you needed it, although you look a bit better now."

"I'm fine. I'll let you know when I'm not. Now, before you say anything, I've got a confession to make." Davie waved his finger back and forth as JJ opened his mouth. "Hang on, I said before you say anything."

JJ waited a few seconds and when Davie didn't speak, said, "Go on then."

"I was composing it. Stop interrupting my thoughts." Davie bit into his sandwich, and his head nodded as he chewed.

"Okay, while you compose, I'll ask some questions, and you never know, you might not have to compose anything other than truthful answers, of course," JJ retorted.

"Wait. I'll just shoot from the hip because I didn't do what you asked. I told the doctor I was a permanent lodger, although like I told him, that's not a word I could ever use. But I needed him to keep busy and not shoo me off to call my doctor. Who's Sandy Bentley?"

"You did what? What's Sandy Bentley got to do with anything?" JJ threw his hands into the air.

"She's the reason the doctor isn't in." Davie took another bite.

"And we care about that, why?" JJ asked.

"We care because when I said I thought I'd be seeing the other chap, couldn't remember his name, Dr Singh said, 'Sorry about that. You can blame Sandy Bentley, who will probably blame Amber Wilton'. Now, why would he say that?"

JJ was frowning. "I don't know. How odd. I'm surprised you didn't ask."

"I would have but he then started throwing questions at me about my condition and the treatments etcetera. Then he tells me to come back tomorrow and collect the prescription. He was on his feet with the door open before I could open my mouth. Well, I knew they were pushed, and you were waiting like the good mate you are, so I left. Worth looking into, though, don't you think?"

"Possibly. But to get to the point, are you telling me you've moved your doctor's surgery to Frampton Down? Specifically, to my address. Is that what you're telling me? Isn't that daft because you'll have to unravel it all when you leave?" JJ tapped his spoon on his cup as he spoke. "Why did you do that?"

"Two reasons, first to get my meds sorted, I wasn't lying when I said I was low. Second, because we need people to believe I'm your lodger and working with you, and third, who knows how long I've got." Davie picked up his mug of tea and used it to hide his face.

"You said two things. That was three, and the third was to tug at my heartstrings but I don't know why that's necessary. Listen, Davie, I know you're in a horrible position, but me and Sharon have a nice, quiet, no-nonsense life going. Sharon wants to whip across to the bathroom naked, and she wants to eat her breakfast and do the crossword without listening to you mangle some song. I want a very quiet life. I want to come and go as I please, and not be looking over my shoulder. It's not personal. I hadn't seen you for years less than twenty-four hours ago. So answer me honestly, are you living in your car?"

"Yes, and that's not ideal, is it? Not with being about to pop my clogs and what have you. So, if it's only Sharon that's the problem, leave her to me. I'll speak to her because you won't find me a problem at all. Happy days, all sorted." Davie rubbed his hands together and looked at the half-eaten sandwich on JJ's plate. "Eat up. We might get a detention if we're late."

"We're going nowhere until you explain what 'leave Sharon to me' means. Why didn't you tell me you were living in your car?" JJ lifted his sandwich but changed his mind and put it back on his plate. "I've lost my appetite."

"Calm down, JJ. I'll just explain how the land lies and take it from there. It wasn't her I saved, it was you. If she says sling your hook, I will. Why would I tell you I was living in my car? When did that become relevant? It is now, I'll agree. But until now, it wasn't, was it? Look at it from my point of view. I'm dying with no idea how long I've got. But I won't drag it out. A bloke I saved from...well saved, offered me a bed for the night, and asked me not to do the day job, but to help him solve a murder instead. Not only am I doing you a favour, but apparently, you're saving me from myself. A win-win. I haven't got to shiver my nights away on the back seat with my feet hanging out of the window, and you get someone who people tell things to. Wrap that sandwich in a napkin. We'd better make a move." Davie emptied his mug, wiped his mouth with the back of his hand, and got to his feet. "I've got to get back and get that washing out before the lovely Sharon gets home. Dishwasher needs emptying, too."

JJ blinked. He should counter that but he didn't know how. He smirked as he went back to the car. Sharon could do it. Or not. He suspected the latter, and his smirk fell away.

"Mrs Williams, how are you?" JJ sat in the chair she had pointed to.

"Same as I was on Monday when you saw me in the post office. But you, I hear, have had some sort of epiphany."

JJ frowned. "I have?" He glanced at Davie, who had already scored points by offering to take his shoes off. Davie winked at him.

"Davie tells me you're going to solve the murder of Amber Wilton. You gave up detecting a while ago. The fact that you're jumping in feet first with him tells me you know you still have something to give. I know the church didn't work out for you but doing good is ingrained in you. You've realised that now. Or did I get the wrong end of the stick?" Mrs Williams turned to look at Davie. "Did you get in here under false pretences because ill or not, you can leave."

Davie slapped his hand on his chest. "I did not. JJ and I are investigating the murder of Amber. He'll tell you. He doesn't lie. It's all very fresh. We only started this morning but we're getting somewhere, and hopefully will be even further along when you've shared what your cleaner had to say." Seeing the doubt on her face, Davie added, "Tell her, JJ."

"It's true. Sort of. But there was no epiphany. Simply an irritation with a less than competent police officer. In my humble opinion, that is. As soon as we have something more concrete than a blurred photo, we'll hand it over, and they can do the rest. Who cleans for you these days?"

Mrs Williams sat in her armchair. The one that sat in the small bay and overlooked the road. JJ noticed the notebook and pen on the table next to it and hid his smile with a scratch of his nose.

"Jackie Oston. Never stops gossiping. Usually, I let it go in one ear and out the other but she had a lot to say about Amber. Before the event, I might add. I've not seen her since. She's due tomorrow, so you might want to pay another visit. She wouldn't speak openly to you, not with her husband...you know."

JJ nodded, but Davie had to ask.

"What about her husband? Is he a copper?"

Mrs Williams found this hilarious, and it was several minutes before she brought her wheezing under control. She waved her handkerchief at JJ. "Did you hear that? Of course you did. Mr Oston is serving three years at Her Majesty's pleas...Oh, what will it be? His Majesty, or hers? It was hers when he went in, so I wonder if that changed straight away or if they need some act of parliament to make it official? Anyway, he's in prison. Nothing nasty unless you work for the Treasury. Tax evasion. Poor Jackie is not used to working, and not qualified to do anything except be a housewife. I'm lucky to have her, she cleans properly. Right into the corners. Look at those windows. Anyway, I think that because everyone had a field day when the hubby went to prison, she now gets her own back by gossiping herself. Not that I'd ever repeat it to anyone. Present company excepted, but I'm sure others do. You see?"

JJ nodded, and Davie asked. "What did she say about Amber? It could hold the vital clue for JJ to solve this."

"I'll tell you. I wrote down everything I could remember before you came." Mrs Williams patted the notebook. "But first, I'm forgetting my manners. May I offer you some refreshments?"

"Not for me, Mrs Williams. We came straight from the café. We're good," JJ replied.

"I never asked if you were good. Since when did you use Americanisms? You've been watching too much television. When someone asks you how you are, you're poorly, been better, or well. You are not good. When someone asks you if you want some refreshments, you do, or you don't. You can add a reason, of course, but you do not need to tell them how you behave. Nor do you answer for other people. Davie, may I interest you in a cup of tea and a slice of homemade Battenburg?"

"Oh, now you're tempting me. But JJ is right, I couldn't eat another thing at the moment but because I'm cheeky, I might ask you to wrap some up in a napkin to take home with me," Davie said with a grin.

Nodding in agreement, Mrs Williams picked up her notepad. "As best I can, I've put Jackie's snippets into a rough chronological order. I thought that would help. So, back in January, Jackie saw Amber kissing Sean Manton. Her umbrella had blown away, and he rescued it, and as he handed it back, he pulled her in close and kissed her. My understanding was it wasn't a kiss on the cheek."

"Yes, we heard about Manton but we're told that was all over, and that Amber might have been seeing someone else. Did Jackie hear that?" JJ asked.

"She did. Never witnessed it herself but there was an almighty row in the pub because someone caught Amber in a compromising position with Mark Baxter, of all people. When she told me I have to say my first, and very uncharitable thought, was why? I mean the man is so dour he could curdle cream. Amber was so cheerful and bubbly. If true, what was the attraction? That's one of hers. Charming, don't you think?"

JJ swivelled in the chair to look over his shoulder at the painting Mrs Williams was pointing at, and he sighed. It was a painting of the bridge. The bridge where her life ended, and yet in the picture it was full of life, depicting a typical spring morning. He turned back and nodded agreement.

"Exactly how I felt. I thought of taking it down but decided against it. I thought it would be like pretending it hadn't happened when it had."

JJ's eyes glanced around the room. There were several classical prints and a few photographs but nothing similar to Amber's painting. "Not a style I'd associate with you. I don't know why. Was there a reason you bought it?"

"First, it's where the late Mr Williams proposed. And it was for charity. Fifty percent of the proceeds went to Cancer Research, and that's a charity dear to my heart, given how I lost Mr Williams. Now, where were we? After Manton and before Baxter, there was the row with Sandy. You know, Dr Bentley's wife. It appeared to be something and nothing, Jackie told me, although Sandy banged her basket down on the counter and left the supermarket without buying anything. Apparently, she went back later and purchased what she needed."

"Was Jackie there for both events?" Davie asked with a twinkle in his eye.

"No, I was there on the return visit. Sandy was still quite grumpy, even then. She spoke, of course. She's too well-mannered not to, but she clearly wasn't happy." Licking the tip of her finger, Mrs Williams flipped the page. "Then, and I witnessed this myself, only a week or so ago, Amber put two fingers up to Kerry Snell. Bold as brass in the middle of the street. I was in the garden, and asked if she was all right, as one would. She said never better and thanked me for buying the painting. We got to chatting, and she invited me to an exhibition she was having in Bristol. Said she'd drive me if I wanted to go. I thought that was very sweet, far too strenuous a bus journey for me these days. Anyway, I never got to the bottom of why she'd done that to Kerry."

"I was speaking to Kerry earlier. She seemed upset by Amber's death. Perhaps I'll ask Kerry what it was about." JJ looked at the pad. "Anything else?"

"Yes. But I don't know how relevant it is. Amber was quite bohemian in both her outlook and style of dress. I'm sure you'll agree. She would rather sit on the grass in a tie-dye dress than she would in something smart on a chair. She walks...Oh dear, I should say walked. Too young, JJ, too young to die." Pulling her handkerchief from her pocket, Mrs Williams dabbed her eyes. "Amber would walk young Luke to school most mornings, and normally walk to pick him up too but over the last few months something changed. Nothing drastic, you understand, but her hair was a little tidier, not so wild, and her clothes had toned down a little. Still bright and noticeable but not...wild, is the best word I can come up with. We often exchanged a few words. She loved my roses. I used to give her a bunch now and then." Mrs Williams glanced out of the window at her garden and fell silent.

"That's interesting, Mrs Williams. It might seem irrelevant now but once we start to build a picture, it will all fall into place. I'm not sure how well you knew her, but if asked, who would you say was Amber's closest friend?"

"That's easy. Her mother. Amber and Emma were very close. But other than that, she seemed to be friends with everyone. Even Kerry Snell until that day." The pad closed and Mrs Williams shrugged. "I hope a little of that might be of some use to you."

"Me too. We've taken up enough of your time, and Davie has washing he needs to hang out, so we'll be off. Thank you for your time."

"Most welcome, dear boy. You were always a favourite I wasn't allowed to have. Now let me get you that cake. Davie has been ill. He needs building up. I'm glad he has you and Sharon to help him."

Davie gave JJ an 'I told you so' look as he followed Mrs Williams to the kitchen.

"Not like that. By the waist. Let me do it." JJ pushed Davie to one side and after hanging his jeans from the waist, he pegged out the rest of his washing.

"Thanks, JJ, now I'll empty that dishwasher. What else can I do? Got to get in the good books. Can I do anything for dinner?"

"Fish pie tonight. Peel the potatoes. I'll get the herbs once I've done this. And bring a bowl out with you. There are tomatoes in there that need picking." JJ jerked his thumb towards the greenhouse.

Leaving JJ in the garden trying to start the lawn mower, Davie went back inside and located the vacuum. Once he'd done that, he dusted the sitting room. By the time Sharon walked in, he was exhausted, and she was shocked as she saw the tremor in his hand as he wiped his cloth across the coffee table.

"Davie, isn't it? Are you okay? You don't look well." Sharon dropped her bag and went to join him. "Sit down." Looking around, she smiled. "Did you do this?"

Davie dropped into the armchair, and with the back of his hand dabbed away the perspiration on his brow.

"I'm told I don't look well a dozen times a day. And this," he waved his hand around the room, "was the least I could do. Sharon, can I have a quick word before JJ comes in? He's sorting the garden out."

"Of course. What's it about?"

"JJ is a good man but you'll know that, hence he offered me a bed last night rather than the back seat of my car. He knows my days are numbered, and I think he's going to offer me a bed until...well, you know. The way he looks at it, is I did him a big favour once, and now he's got the chance to return it. Add the fact that he's got his teeth into finding out who killed Amber Wilton, and I've been a lot of use to him on that today. So, I'm pretty sure he's going to ask you if that's okay. You know, to make sure I've got a roof over my head that isn't attached to a car, but being a good bloke, he will let you decide. After all, it's your home too. You don't know me from Adam, and I've never stopped you from...anyway I've said enough." Davie raised his eyebrows.

"Um, not really, no," Sharon replied, with a shrug. "All you've told me is that JJ might ask me if it's alright for you to stay until...because he thinks he owes you a favour. You haven't said why you're telling me."

"Didn't I? Not like me. I'm good with words. To the point. The reason I told you is because you must say no." Davie folded his arms across his chest.

That hadn't been what Sharon expected. "No?"

"Absolutely no. I can see why he thinks he owes me, and I'd feel the same given the circumstances, but once we solve this case, and we will solve it, I'll move on. You won't want me hanging around, however useful I am to JJ. You'll want to do what you want, when you want, without worrying if I'm going to pop my clogs on any given day. Do you see?" Davie didn't pause for an answer. "So, if he brings it up, the answer is no. Now that's sorted, one other thing, he needs this. Encourage him to take it up." Davie leaned back in his chair and closed his eyes with a sigh. "So glad we had this chat, wasn't sure I'd get the opportunity to sort it all out. What a relief."

Sharon gave a sigh of her own. "Encourage him to ask me? Sorry, Davie, for a man who thinks he's good with words, I think you should work on rearranging them to make a little more sense."

Davie's eyes opened, and he pushed himself forward. "Sorry. Encourage him to keep on investigating. It's what he does, it's what makes him tick. When we've solved this one, he should look for more. Do you see?"

"No. How and why would he do that?" Sharon glanced at the door. Where was JJ when you needed him? The sound of the mower reached her. He wouldn't come to her rescue anytime soon.

"It's probably because I'm so tired. I try to have long nights and short days, no stamina anymore. Let me try again. JJ was a copper. A bloody good one, too. The cockups with Daniel Boyd affected us all. It was just the worst, but for obvious reasons, it took JJ out. So, he jacked it all in and came home. Then he found God, or whatever happened there. We need to sort that out, and then what? He tells me he's a freelance photographer, and yes, he's got a camera or two, but I've not seen him use them. But I have seen him do what he does best. Work stuff out. Detect. Care about people and what happens to them, and—"

"Davie, can I ask you to get to the point? I'm dying for a pee and the lawnmower has stopped. He'll be in soon."

"And I've got to mash that potato. Look, the religion thing isn't what he does now, is the photography? I don't know, I've only just arrived. But before you ask him anything else, ask him what's new on Amber. Watch his eyes light up. That's it. I've said enough. You get where I'm coming from, I'm sure. You sort yourself out. I'll mash the potato."

Sharon nodded and went upstairs. Her mind was working overtime. Who was Daniel Boyd? And what had Davie saved JJ from? JJ didn't earn a substantial sum of money from his photography, but that's not why he did it. He had his pension. They had no mortgage, and she worked. They didn't need it to be profitable. JJ was happy being a photographer, wasn't he? Did he need something more? What did Davie mean, carry on investigating? Investigating what? This was Frampton Down, not crime central. She jumped in the shower to ponder it all. When she came down, the pie was in the oven, and the two men were sitting in the middle of the lawn on deck chairs. She went to join them.

"Where have you been?" JJ asked as she placed a kiss on the top of his head. "Not even a peck on the cheek when you got home."

"Sorry, JJ, thought I'd take advantage while you two were busy. Now we have someone staying, I didn't want to get stuck in a queue for the bathroom. I've showered the day away." Sharon pulled a chair into the shade and looked at JJ. "How's your day been?"

"Good. We're making progress on Amber's case. I don't think she was as sweet and innocent as we thought. Not saying she's done anything wrong, just that she had stuff going on we were unaware of. Or I was anyway. I'm going to pick your brains on some of that over dinner. Me and Davie were just discussing our plan of attack for tomorrow. Do you know I never saw one police officer today? Not one. How can you look into a suspicious death without someone on the ground? It's not right, Sharon, it's criminal. But I'll sort it."

Sharon shot a glance at Davie, who raised his eyebrows and smiled. Davie was right. The weariness usually found in JJ's expression wasn't there. He was animated and his hands had a life of their own.

"But we'll deal with that over dinner. How's your day been?" JJ asked.

"Boring and predictable. Connie has been a pain in the proverbial. All day. I don't want to talk about it. What is it that you want to know? I'd rather speak about that, horrible though it is."

"Blimey, I wasn't expecting that. I thought you'd be telling me to back off. Connie must have reached a new height of horribleness today. Is that a word? Don't answer, I don't care. Let me get dinner sorted, we'll eat in the garden, and we'll talk then."

Chapter Nine

SHARON'S EYES WERE WIDE, and she gave herself a shake. "And Mrs Williams told you all this?"

"As good as. So do you know anything about any of it? The rows with Sandy Bentley or Kerry Snell, I mean?" JJ asked.

"I don't. But you need to go back and speak to Jo. She was friends with Kerry and Amber. She's the one most likely to know. But what I want to know now is who Steve is. Any ideas?" Sharon was enjoying receiving what she considered to be guilt-free gossip.

"None. But I'll get Davie on to Jo again tomorrow. She likes him." JJ pointed across the table and laughed as Davie threw his hands into the air.

"I never said that. I said she was relaxed with me. But if it will get us some info, I'm happy to give it a go. Do either of you know Sandy whatsit and or Kerry Snell well?" Davie looked genuinely confused.

"I know both of them, but not enough to ask personal questions about Amber. And definitely not without them asking me a ton of questions I probably couldn't or wouldn't want to answer," Sharon told him. "What do you think, JJ? Do you want me to? I mean, what's the worst that can happen? They tell me to mind my own. I've no problem with that. But if I do, I doubt it will take long for everyone to know you're investigating Amber's murder, and then you could have that idiot Evans knocking the door down again."

JJ's brow furrowed, and he reached across the table and took her hand. "I can deal with Evans but, and I'm not complaining because I've got my teeth stuck in now. You seem to be encouraging me. Why?"

"I'd have thought that was bleeding obvious," Davie answered quickly. "Because it's what you do, JJ. It's what you do best. I can see that, and Sharon can see that. Blimey mate, it's obvious to anyone with any sense, which is probably why Evans doesn't like you. He didn't back then, and he definitely doesn't now. You show him up. Now, can we please come up with a plan because it's been a very long day, and I'd like to turn in. I know the night is young, but I'm not used to all this running around. Actually, hold that thought, I need a pee. I'll be back." Davie pushed himself to his feet and headed into the house.

When he'd disappeared inside, JJ squeezed Sharon's hand. "While he's gone, I need a word. Now's as good a time as any. He's ill. Terminal. He's living in his car, and I...I well, I don't think that's right, so—"

"Yes." Sharon nodded.

"You don't know what I'm going to say."

"I do, and yes he can. We'll have to have some ground rules. I reckon he's on his best behaviour at the moment. I don't want him to do the cleaning. He's not strong enough. But he can clean up behind himself and not take liberties. He strikes me as a liberty taker. I'm surprised you haven't already offered."

JJ got to his feet and leaned across the table to place a kiss on her head. "You're a remarkable woman, do you know that?"

"I do. He's coming back. I'll let you do the honours while I clear the table and disappear because I've got a few bits and bobs to do for sports day." Sharon piled the crockery onto a tray and smiled at Davie as he collapsed onto his chair, pale-faced. "You look exhausted. No wonder you want to go to bed. I've got some work to do. I'll leave you two to it. If you want me to speak to anyone, write down what you want me to ask, and how much I can tell them. Might be the weekend before I get the chance, though."

JJ and Davie spent the next thirty minutes going through a task list. But they kept coming back to Amber's secret boyfriend. Steve.

"That's the first thing we need to find out, JJ. He could be the key to this whole thing." Davie covered his face with his hands and yawned. "I'm knackered. I reckon we should be upfront and blunt. You know, tell 'em we think she was murdered. 'We're investigating it. Who's Steve?'. What do you reckon?"

"I reckon I need to think about it all, carefully. I don't mind doing this, and legally we're not doing anything wrong, but I don't want to wind anyone up for the sake of it. Not even Evans. So, let's call it a day, and talk again in the morning. I've got some stuff I need to do for...I forgot about Gary. I don't even know if the exhibition is still on. I'll take him the gift from Connie, I can find out about the exhibition, and see what else is news. You get on to bed. No idea how long I might be."

"What's Gary got to do with an exhibition?" Davie asked.

"He owns an art gallery in town. He's organising an exhibition and wants me to take part. You carry on."

Davie needed no further encouragement and left JJ in the garden. After mulling over what and how he might approach the subject of Steve, JJ collected the tin Connie Gerrard had left and headed for the Wiltons' house. He'd play it by ear. Luke answered the door in Spiderman pyjamas.

"Evening, Zed. I thought you'd be in bed. Is your dad around?"

"Yeah. Nan's just telling him how to use the microwave properly. She isn't happy." Luke grinned, and for the first time since his mother died, he looked relaxed.

JJ returned the smile. "And that's more important than you being in bed on time?"

Luke shrugged. "I haven't got school, so it doesn't matter. Dad was making me warm milk, but Nan said if I'd drunk it, it would have boiled my kidneys."

There was a shout from behind him, and the sound of breaking crockery. Luke flinched and JJ watched Luke's body jerk as he tried not to look over his shoulder.

"Talking of school. Miss Elliott is trying to sort some stuff out for sports day. Why don't you go down and see if you can help her?" JJ pointed towards the kitchen. "I'll help them clear up whatever got broke."

"I'm wearing my PJs. Someone might see me." Luke looked horrified at the thought.

"No they won't. Who's around to see? Go on, she'll be glad of the help."

The harsh whispers coming from the kitchen were all the encouragement Luke needed. He nodded and took off without another word. JJ sent a text, warning

Sharon to expect him. She opened the door as Luke shot up the path. Content Luke was safe, JJ banged on the door again, and headed for the kitchen.

Emma Reed was sitting at the kitchen table, her arms folded across her chest. Gary had his fingers linked on the top of his head and was pacing towards the back door. When JJ spoke, Gary spun around to face him, clearly shocked at his presence.

"Sorry, I did knock. Everything okay?" JJ looked at the puddle of milk and the broken mug in the middle of the floor, which neither had attempted to clean up. "This is for you from Connie Gerrard, the headteacher." Handing the tin to Emma, JJ dropped to one knee and started collecting the shards of china.

"Connie? Really? That's surprising. Very kind of her. Did Luke let you in?" Gary asked as he grabbed a tea towel and dropped it onto the puddle, pushing it around with his foot. "Leave that, I'll do it. It's one of the many things I've got wrong again today." There was a slight edge to his voice despite the smile.

"All I said was—" Emma's arms were now akimbo, and two red dots burned in the centre of her pale cheeks, competing with the dark smudges under her eyes.

"And you were right. I got it wrong. What if he'd tried to pick it up? I'm just so bloody tired." Gary cleared his throat. "But he didn't. So, I'll have to do better tomorrow. Where is Luke?"

"Gone up to see Sharon. The sound of the mug breaking and you two having words...I told him she needed some help." JJ walked to the bin and dropped the pieces in. "Is there anything I can do to help?"

"Tell him," Emma snapped. "You won't tell the police, so tell him. I hear he's been asking questions, so he'll want to know, and then he can explain why he's poking around." Emma pointed at the table. "Sit. If our Luke is okay, let's sort this out. Now, or none of us will sleep again tonight."

JJ had mixed emotions as he joined Emma at the table. It was awful that these two were at loggerheads given what they were coping with, but it gave him the opportunity to question them both by invitation. He waited for Gary to join them at the table.

"I have been asking questions, because I'm not convinced Amber killed herself. The police decided it was suicide far too quickly. I've also got a few questions for you, if you are happy to answer them, but first, tell me what it is that you won't tell the police." JJ looked from one to the other. "I know how much you both loved her, and I know it will be hard, but whoever killed her took away something precious from all of you. They shouldn't be walking free without a care in the world. Tell me, please."

Gary cleared his throat. "I got a card. Not posted, just shoved through the letterbox. Emma found it when she arrived to cook Luke's tea. It wasn't nice, and to add insult to injury it was one of Amber's. It's from a pack of the cards she sells. I mean sold. That's taking the piss, so I got mad and tore it up. Emma says I should give it to the police, but I don't know, JJ. I really don't. I don't want everyone thinking bad of her when she can't defend herself."

"Can I see it?" JJ held out his hand.

"He put it in the bin. I'll get it. I told him not to, but he's not thinking straight." Emma threw a challenging glance at Gary as she got to her feet. He merely shrugged, so she pulled the liner from the bin, and lifted it into the sink before rummaging through the contents.

JJ jumped up. "Gloves, Emma, gloves."

Emma was about to tell him she wasn't squeamish when she caught on and lifted the bright yellow gloves from the caddy on the drainer. JJ looked around, and not finding anything more suitable, he unwound some kitchen roll and laid it on the table. Emma placed the four sections on the kitchen roll. Following JJ's direction, she put the two sections of the envelope together. Sealed on receipt, Gary had sliced it open neatly. Addressed simply 'TO GARY'.

JJ nodded his approval. "That's good. Hand-delivered so there may well be fingerprints, and the lab might get DNA if they licked the seal. That might be a long shot, but they've managed it before." He looked at the watercolour image on the front of the card, it was of a bouquet of lily of the valley. Amber's signature, painted in fine strokes at an angle, was at the bottom of the image. "So pretty. Sharon has a pack of these at home. Amber was good with flowers. Open it please, Emma."

Emma opened the two halves and placed them together as best she could, then held them open for JJ to read the content.

"Whoever wrote that really hated our Amber, JJ. But I mean, even if you hated someone, why would you bother sending this once they were dead? What would they gain?"

JJ nodded agreement as he read the message. It had been written in blue biro in capital letters.

DON'T WEEP FOR HER SHE'S NOT WORTH IT. GOOD RIDDANCE. THE WORLD IS NOW A BETTER PLACE AND YOU ARE WELL RID OF HER. LIFE WILL BE BETTER FOR EVERYONE NOW. EVEN LUKE. YOU BOTH DERSERVE BETTER.

"What do you think, JJ? Should he take it to the police? Stupid question, if you're suggesting they could do DNA and stuff, and as you've been poking around with your mate why don't you tell us what you think is going on?" Emma asked when JJ didn't speak.

JJ raised his head and looked at her. His smile was brief.

"There's no easy way to say this, so I'll just come out with it. As you know, I found Amber, and I don't think she had an accident, and I certainly don't think she jumped. I think someone pushed her. I don't believe the police treating this as a crime and possibly murder. Evans is too keen to wrap it up as non-suspicious, so that's why I've been poking around. I've got a few questions I wouldn't mind asking if you're happy for me to continue interfering." JJ tried another smile, but it failed.

Gary's mouth had fallen open, and he didn't speak, but Emma was nodding, and she tapped the table as she spoke.

"I knew it. Not that someone killed her, but that something wasn't right. Start at the beginning, JJ, we'll answer any questions we can. Won't we Gary?"

"But why? Why would someone kill Amber? Why would someone write this? Amber was loving and kind and fun. Do you know why, JJ?" Gary blinked away his tears.

"Of course he doesn't. If he knew, he wouldn't be asking questions. Get a grip, Gary. JJ, ignore him, just keep talking, he'll catch up." Emma reached across the table and patted Gary's hand.

"Okay, I'll keep this as brief as I can, then ask the questions."

JJ explained what his camera had captured and that he'd handed the SD card over to the police. Since then, not happy with the lack of police activity, he'd been asking questions with the help of a friend. He decided against telling them Davie was gutter press.

"Now, this is where it gets a little delicate, so apologies Gary, but we've found that Amber has had several romantic relationships, which may not have ended amicably or caused someone grief, and that she has had a couple of fallouts with locals. Now, and I must stress this, none of that may be relevant to Amber's death, but it needs looking into." JJ held up his hands. "I'm happy to back off if you think I'm overstepping the mark, but I will go to my old boss and get him to give what we've found out the once-over." JJ's hands fell into his lap, and he looked at Emma, who he believed would be more likely to give him an honest opinion.

"We don't want you to back off. Do we, Gary? I don't know what this Davie bloke is like, but you're respected around here, JJ. People will trust you with their secrets."

JJ and Emma both turned to Gary. His foot was tapping, his cheeks flushed, and he seemed to be composing himself before he raised his head.

"How many romantic relationships?" he asked.

"Now, Gary, don't get wound up by that. Finding out what happened to our Amber is more important. You had separated. You weren't together, and don't tell me you've been living like a monk. Now, put that jealousy away, and let JJ ask his questions."

"But...Oh, just get on with it, JJ. What do you want to know?"

"Let's start with some general questions that might answer some of the others. I've already asked Gary this, so Emma, do you know if Amber was involved with anyone at the time of her death?"

"I know that she might have been because I came to babysit Luke, a couple of weeks back, and she was dressed up, you know, more than just going to the pub for a drink with the girls. So, I mentioned it, and she just laughed and said she'd tell me when there was anything to know. So I left it. She went into Bristol though. She messaged me when she was leaving." Emma shrugged and avoided looking at Gary.

"Do you think, whoever it was wasn't a local?" Gary sounded a little relieved.

"I never said that. What I said was she went to Bristol. I don't know who with or where they lived. Next question, JJ."

"Do either of you know if she'd had a run-in with anyone, however minor it might have seemed?"

Gary shook his head, but Emma was frowning.

"Emma?" JJ prompted.

"No. But she was mad about something, I'm trying to remember when it was. In the last couple of weeks. She'd been on the phone to the people who do the tea towels for her, and then the phone rang, and she huffed, answered it, and told whoever it was to sod off. I asked her who it was, and she said someone about energy efficiency. I'd had a couple of those calls myself, so I didn't question it further. Can we check her phone records? That might help. It would tell you who called after the tea towel people."

"It would help but I don't have the authority to access those. Although, do you know if she had an online account, might be able to find out from her statements. I know I can download mine, but I don't know if it shows incoming."

"Stay right there." Emma jumped to her feet but JJ held his hand up to stop her.

"Where are you going?"

"To get her laptop. She did all her business stuff online. Everyone does these days, don't they? You can take it and have a poke around, and . . ." Emma paused and looked at Gary. "That's okay with you, isn't it? There's no reason JJ shouldn't have it, is there?"

Gary shook his head. "None. No. If someone murdered Amber and the police are doing nothing about it, then JJ can. But I'll tell you this, JJ, I'm going to make an official complaint. It's not bloody good enough. It's bad enough they haven't got enough staff to investigate burglaries and the like, but to ignore a murder! A murder with photographic evidence, that's not acceptable." Gary ran out of steam and sighed. "Next question."

"But what about the...don't worry. I'll get it before you go." Emma sat back down.

Knowing he had their full cooperation, JJ steeled himself to ask what he would have asked if he was still a police officer.

"That's great. Thank you. If I have your blessing to look into this further, there's another thing I need to do, something the police should have done, and that's look at Amber's personal possessions. Go through her papers, her room, everything really. I'm not saying tonight, it's getting late, and Luke might come home, but have a think about it, and let me know tomorrow."

"What is it you hope to find?" Garry asked.

"Clues, Gary, clues. Don't you watch the telly? When someone is murdered or goes missing, the first thing they do is search their rooms. Of course you can, JJ. Whenever suits you." Emma leaned back in her chair. "Do you have any more questions?"

"I know Amber had some sort of relationship, however serious or fleeting, with both Sean Manton and Mark Baxter. Do either of you know anything about them?"

"Sorry, Gary, you can leave the room if you don't want to hear this. Look, JJ, you know what Sean Manton is like and so did Amber. It wasn't serious, it was a bit of fun. Women have needs too and he fulfilled them for a while. I'm not saying I approved. But I am saying they were both young, single, yes, Gary, single, and so why the hell not?" Emma paused to see if she was going to be challenged. When neither man spoke, she added, "As for Mark Baxter, well, even that flummoxed me. But she'd had a drink or two, and they had a snog. She was mortified. Came to see me the next day to see how fast the gossip had travelled. Swore she'd never drink again. So, yes, there was a connection with both, but nothing serious. Next question before Gary throws up."

"Someone mentioned someone called Steve. I don't know of a Steve locally. Did Davie get that wrong?"

"Steve?" Gary's brow furrowed, and he shook his head. "I don't know a Steve, do you Emma?"

"Plenty, but none Amber would have been involved with. Not even if she'd drunk the Three Bells dry. Are you sure it was a Steve, JJ?"

"Nope. Like I said, Davie may have misheard. However, and Emma will be best placed to answer this, who was she seeing currently? The girls seemed to think there was someone, but didn't know more than that."

"No one. Not that I knew, and why would she keep it a secret from me." Emma caught JJ's sigh and the drop of his shoulders. "What? What have you heard?"

"When I went for a run that first morning with Luke, he told me he wanted his dad to move back here, and wanted assurance that he wouldn't have to live with his mum's intended husband. I don't know the details, but Amber told him she'd introduce them soon, and that with a bit of luck, the man would pop the question. She had to explain to Luke what that meant, so I don't think he got it wrong." JJ raised his eyebrows at Emma, and he patted Gary's shoulder as he groaned and allowed his head to fall forward. "I'm sorry but it's probably best you hear it from me. I'm guessing it would have come out sooner rather than later."

Gary knocked JJ's hand away. "No, it wouldn't. It bloody wouldn't. I've been seeing Amber. Me." He thumped his chest. "It was me she came to see in Bristol. I don't know who Steve is, or this mystery man, or whether they're one and same, but we were getting back on track. We were! You must have known." He jabbed a finger at Emma.

"I'm sorry, love, I didn't. She never mentioned it. How long has this been going on? Why wouldn't she say? Are you sure?" Emma lurched back as Gary jumped to his feet, his finger inches away from her face.

"Of course I'm bloody sure. Here look." Pulling his phone from his pocket, he tapped at it and handed it to JJ. "Should that make me sure?"

JJ scrolled through a string of messages exchanged between Gary and Amber, and he nodded.

"It does. Sit down, Gary. It's early days. I'm just poking around at the moment. Clutching at anything that blows my way because I've got no authority to ask outright questions, and people sure as hell have no obligation to answer them. Perhaps Amber meant you, if things worked out. You know what kids are like, they get muddled. Don't read too much into it and don't go putting pressure on Luke. He said he'd never met the man, so all you will do is upset him."

"He's right, Gary. Amber wasn't telling me anything. That's clear now, so why would she say anything important to Luke? She would know he'd ask me. JJ's right, did you hear what he said? No talking to our Luke about it."

Running his fingers through his hair, Gary nodded. "I hear you. Next question."

Before JJ could answer, there was a banging on the door, and Luke's voice reached them as he shouted through the letter box.

"Dad. Nan. Let me in. Can I go to school for sports day? Miss Elliott said it was up to you. Where are you?"

"Oh, that's a positive." JJ got to his feet and followed Emma and Gary into the hall. "I'll leave you now Luke's home, but if I could grab that laptop, I'll pop back in tomorrow and go over a few more things. Is that okay?"

"Of course, JJ, and thanks." Emma opened the front door and Luke flew into the hall.

"Well can I?" Luke demanded.

"Ask your dad. I need to get something for JJ."

By the time Emma returned with the laptop, they had agreed that if Luke wanted to go back to school he could, and that Miss Elliott could always ring to have him collected if it was too much for him.

Handing the bag to JJ, Emma ruffled Luke's hair. "If you're sure. It won't be all mucking about on the field, you know. There will be normal lessons, too."

"That's okay. But I'm fit, aren't I, JJ? We've been training," Luke assured her, and JJ agreed.

"In which case, it's way past your bedtime. Kiss your dad and get up those stairs."

Gary asked JJ to wait as he scooped up his son and kissed him goodnight.

"Get off, Dad, JJ will think I'm a baby."

Gary laughed as Luke shot up the stairs. "You'll always be my baby," he shouted after him before turning back to JJ. He jerked his head and the two men stepped outside. "Password is Babyluke21. Capital B. I doubt she's changed it. I think it's good Luke's going back to school, don't you?"

"I do. But that's not what you wanted to speak to me about. Just say it,"

"Well, it's the funeral. It's two weeks until the end of term. When do you think we should arrange the funeral for? I think it's best that we wait until the holidays, that way Luke will have time to get over it all over again. Oh. Do you think he should come? Oh God, JJ, I don't know what to do for the best."

JJ's face clouded. "Have they released Amber's body? That was quick. This is just what—"

"What do you mean, released it? Why wouldn't they release it?"

"With an unexpected death like this, whatever the cause, there is always a postmortem. That takes a while to get written up, for tests to come back, for reports to be read, and only when everyone is satisfied that any findings have been dealt with, and recorded properly, will the body be released for burial. If everything is straightforward, that's usually two weeks minimum, then you have to book everything, so the answer to the first question is yes, it will be in the holidays. The answer to whether Luke should go is I don't know. That's for you and Emma to decide. Off the cuff, I'd say he's too young, but funerals bring closure, and you can have some sort of memorial down at the church. It might help him. I don't know, Gary, I've not got kids, and I was a teenager before I went to my first funeral. Have a chat with Emma. You don't have to decide now."

"I've not heard anything about the postmortem. How do I find out about that?" Gary began pacing up and down the path. "You're right, JJ, that Evans bloke has his head up his own arse. I'm sorry, but I am going to have to complain about that too."

"You do what you need to, Gary. You don't need to apologise to me. Not on that score."

"Thanks, JJ. You're a genuine friend. Nice to know you're looking after our interests. I'll see you tomorrow." Keen to get his complaint started, Gary headed inside.

Chapter Ten

When JJ got home, he had a quick word with Sharon, who was on her way to bed with a book, before opening Amber's laptop. He had no issues accessing any of the key programmes as Amber had saved all her passwords. He didn't notice the hours flying by, and when Davie appeared a little after midnight he was so startled he knocked his mug from the table.

"Blimey, Davie, are you in stealth mode?" he asked, glad his favourite mug hadn't broken.

"Apparently. Sorry about that. What are you working on? Your exhibition?" Davie filled a glass with water and took a seat at the table. "Forgot to take one up with me. I'm parched."

"I wish, although I've already broken the back of it. This is Amber's laptop. I've been having a poke around."

Davie looked from the laptop to the notebook and the neat lines of information JJ had written and held out his hand. "How long have you been at it? I heard you come back just after eight. Let's have a look."

"Pretty much since then. You won't make sense of that. Headlines. Amber had no financial worries. Nice little sum in her savings account, healthy balance in her current account, and she does her books at the end of each month. All suppliers paid, all income listed. That surprised me. She always seemed a little...I don't know, dippy, in a cuddly artistic sort of way. I didn't realise how much she sold. Not just her paintings, but notebooks, cards, coasters, in fact, anything you can put a print on. Some of it is lovely. Gary should keep it going for Luke."

"Do you think she was putting on an act, then?" Davie asked.

"No...I don't know. Maybe. She certainly appeared to be scatterbrained but wasn't."

"Get to the juicy bit, JJ. I want to go back to bed." Davie held up his glass. "Have you got anything stronger?"

"Yes, coffee. But have instant, the percolator might wake Sharon. And how do you know there's something juicy?"

"Because you've been at it for over three hours, and although there might be a lot to go through, you don't make that many notes for organised, honest and tickety-boo. So, what did you find?"

"I'll tell you what I didn't find. I didn't find any threats, and I found nothing to or from anyone called Steve. We're going to have to go back to your source on that one. Nor did I find anything on her messenger account that would indicate she had fallen out with anyone. On that note, Gary claims they were getting back together. He let me read an exchange of texts. Some were quite racy. She was making him date her again, and it seemed like they were both enjoying it. He's devastated that Luke thought his mum had a boyfriend who she hoped would ask her to marry him."

"We need her phone records. What about dating sites?" Davie asked. "To all intents and purposes she was a single woman."

"Never found any."

"How hard did you look? Did you check her history? I can tell by your face you didn't. Open up her history. I doubt she cleared it or went incognito. You're losing your touch, JJ. Lucky you've got me to push you along."

"We had a team that did this sort of stuff. Right, let's have a look." JJ fell silent as he opened the browsing history and scrolled through the results. "Oh."

"Told you. Get it open." Davie moved around the table to look at the screen.

JJ attempted to navigate the site, and Davie nudged him and took control of the mouse. He gave a throaty laugh.

"Here we go. She's been in touch with six different men. Pick a man, let's see what they've been chatting about. Not that it's too much of a strain on the imagination."

"That's Sean Manton. But it's late. It's half twelve. Let's do it tomorrow. We need sleep, because we've also got to come up with a plan of action." JJ pulled the lid of the laptop down.

Davie tutted. "You're no fun. But yes, I'm knackered, some shuteye will be beneficial. What time am I clocking on in the morning?"

"What time do you get up?"

"Depends on what happens first. My back says no more, and I have to get up and walk off the cramp, or I'm awoken by the wonderful sounds of nature. By which I mean pigeons tapdancing on the roof."

"Sounds bloody awful. Get up when you wake up. Young Luke is going to school tomorrow, so I'll be here when you arise. But I'm not a chef, and I'm not cooking breakfast. You can have cereal or toast." JJ walked to the back door and checked it was locked. Taking Davie's glass, he topped it up and got one for himself. "You can help me move stuff around in there." JJ jerked his finger towards a door in the corner.

"What is it, a cupboard? I don't think we should muck about clearing out cupboards, JJ. I don't mind giving you a hand, but we need to prioritise.

"It's my photography room. Used it as a darkroom before I went digital, still do sometimes. It started life as a dining room but as we eat at the kitchen table or on a tray in front of the telly it wasn't needed. But we're going to have to set up something visual because it seems this case is going to get a little more complicated, and I can't keep shuffling the cards up here." JJ laughed and tapped the side of his head. "I'm getting old."

"Ooh. An incident room. I like the sound of that. See you in the morning, boss. Or is it Guv? Which would you prefer?"

"'Night, Davie. JJ will do just fine."

The next morning, Davie found JJ sitting at the table eating toast.

"Morning. What's new?"

"Not much. I've been up as long as it took me to butter this toast. Tea in the pot if you want some."

"Chuck a couple of slices in the toaster for me. I want a peep in here. I feel quite excited. Rejuvenated. Well, almost. I'd like a peep at the office. It's been a long time since I had one." Davie opened the door and walked into the dining room.

"Carry on."

JJ filled the toaster, and with a half-eaten piece of toast in his hand followed Davie. He watched him nodding as he took in the current setup, which consisted of a small desk, two battered filing cabinets, a trestle table holding a printer, and stacks of photographs it had produced. Many others had been tacked to every wall. On the floor beneath were various boxes of photographic paper, and a stack of empty frames. JJ finished his toast.

"I thought I'd get the stuff I need for the exhibition finished, or as near as damn it, I'll probably change my mind at the last minute. Then we can rearrange it so we can work in there as needed. The thing is, I don't want Sharon bogged down with this stuff. The living room's not suitable, and we can't keep using the kitchen because we'll be in the way. She breaks up from school soon, and she likes to cook. That's why we set it up this way."

"Sounds perfect. I take back my original thoughts on your photography. Some of these are quite good. Not sure about the arty ones. Blurry doesn't do it for me. Oops, toast's ready." Davie went back to the kitchen. "Mind you, you have got three bedrooms and we're only using two of them. I'm surprised you didn't use the box room."

"Oh, are you? The box room is too small for this lot, and for me, and I have four nephews and nieces who stay when their parents want some me time, and Sharon also has family who stay. Apart from anything else that printer is ancient, and as I do most of my printing at night, it would disturb Sharon. But thanks for the suggestion. Eat your breakfast. I'm going for a quick run, then we'll get started." JJ emptied his mug of tea, picked up his phone and camera, and left Davie with a smile on his face.

By midmorning, they had rearranged the sparse furniture, commandeered a chest of drawers from the box room, and borrowed a chair from the kitchen. Davie was now putting JJ's chosen prints into the frames, while JJ agonised over the final three choices.

"When is this exhibition?" Davie asked.

"A couple of weeks. Why?"

"Because, my friend, I am itching to get on with our investigation. If you've got six you like, but can only use three of them, let someone else choose, or put them to one side and look again tomorrow, or the next day, or both. But can we please get on?"

"This is what I do. I'm glad you're keen, but this pays the bills." JJ jabbed his finger at the photographs. "Or bits of the bills, anyway. But yes, stack those in that box and ..." There was a blast of Mozart. "You put those away, I'll get the door, and then we'll get on." JJ was laughing as he wandered off to answer the door.

"Another suggestion is to change that bloody doorbell. It's horrendous!" Davie shouted as he loaded the box with the framed prints. He paused in his task, as he heard JJ invite Gary Wilton in.

"Come on in, Gary. Did Luke get off to school okay? I'm guessing not. You look a bit out of sorts."

"I'm bloody fuming, is what I am. As far as I know, Luke's fine. He was a little nervous, but very excited. I'm here because I'm about to do an email, but thought I'd better speak to you first. You know, make sure I get it right." Gary pulled out a chair and sat at the kitchen table.

"I have no idea what you're on about. I'll put the kettle on. You start at the beginning." JJ filled the kettle and joined Gary at the table.

"Once I'd taken Luke to school, I came back to call the police, you know, to make a complaint like I said I would. I started off softly-softly because there's no point in upsetting people if you've got the wrong end of the stick. My head's been all over the place. So I asked for DS Evans and was put through to his office. I spoke to someone who wasn't actually working on the case and was told he'd call me back. Two hours later, he does. I asked him how the investigation was going, and he said everything was under control. I asked what that meant, and he waffled, told me how long things took, and the more he waffled, the madder I got. Eventually, I interrupted him and asked if I could see the results from the postmortem. Someone had murdered my wife three days before and I wasn't happy that enough was being done to find out who had killed her. I said a lot more, but that's the gist." Gary ran out of steam and then looked shocked as Davie appeared. "Who are you?" he asked, but looked at JJ.

"Davie, meet Gary, Amber's...husband. Gary, this is the friend I mentioned last night."

"Ah yes, nice to meet you." On his feet, Gary shook Davie's hand.

"You two sit back down and carry on. Sounds like you've got something to sort out. I'll make the tea."

"Carry on, Gary. What did he say about the postmortem, and what do you need from me?" JJ asked as Gary sat down.

"He said it would be easier to do face-to-face, which I heard as, I can bamboozle you easier if I'm looking you in the eye. He's coming around at two. So, I've made a list of what I can remember you said, but you wanted to look at Amber's stuff. I didn't know if you wanted to do that first, you know, in case he tells you to back off. Also, should I give him the card?"

Davie placed the pot of tea on the table. "Do you mind if I put my oar in? First, he can't tell anyone to back off anything. That's for you to do. He's had long enough to go through her stuff, and he didn't. Just say it was you. You could have destroyed all sorts of evidence by now. Don't look at me like that, I know you didn't kill her, I'm just saying. Second, investigators investigate. Police ones or private. JJ and me, we're private. The police can't tell us we can't go about our business if we're not breaking the law, especially if they're not treating it like murder. Tell him I'm right, JJ." Davie waited until JJ had confirmed it. "Thank you, and finally, what card?"

"I'll tell you about that later. Is it alright if we pop down now, Gary? We won't take anything, but I might take a few photos if that's okay?"

"Yes, of course. I can run through my list with you, too. Is that what you do now, JJ? Private investigation? Because I'm happy to pay you. Apologies, I didn't realise. I thought you just dabbled with the photography. Oh, will you still be part of the exhibition? Please say yes, I haven't got the willpower to sort someone else out to replace you."

Davie grinned. An offer of payment. This week was getting better and better. Murder victims excepted of course.

"Yes, he's still doing it. But once we've had a look-see, would you mind coming up here and giving him some advice, he's stuck on the last three choices and it's driving him mad." Davie ignored JJ's eyebrows, as he jerked his thumb towards the dining room. "In fact, you could do that now. Won't take long. It's not twelve yet, so we've got a couple of hours."

It took an hour, but satisfied they'd made the right choices, JJ helped Gary carry the crate of soon-to-be exhibits and load them into the back of his car.

"This is great. Emma is picking up Luke, so as soon as Evans has gone, I'll get these down to the gallery. I promised Ellen I'd pop in today. We're never rushed off our feet, but she's held the fort like a trouper. I'll arrange for you to come and get set up nearer the time. Shall we?" He held his hand towards the front door of his cottage.

JJ took his camera from Davie, and they followed Gary into the house. They found nothing in Amber's studio, a wooden cabin at the end of the garden, except that Davie had a newly found appreciation of watercolours.

"I should get up here and sort through some of this stuff. I'm determined that she will have the exhibition she'd been invited to at the castle," Gary told them as they made their way back to the cottage.

"Yes, you should, and find a way of keeping her business running as long as you can. I had a quick look at her computer last night, Amber was running a tidy business. You could set up a trust up in Luke's name," JJ suggested as they followed Gary up the stairs.

"Already been speaking to Emma about it. Just need someone to 'do' it." Gary made speech marks with his fingers. "We'll get there. This is it. Her office." Gary pushed open the door to the box room. "Her bedroom is the one at the front. A few of my bits are back in there now, but they shouldn't get in the way. I'll leave you to it."

"One room at a time, or shall we take one each?" Davie asked as Gary went back downstairs.

JJ pulled him into the main bedroom. "No disrespect, but we've got limited time to search properly. I don't want to risk either of us missing anything. We'll do it together."

"What you mean is you don't think I'm up to it. How little you know of what my previous employment required. I'm used to looking for stuff people don't want found. Still, have it your way. Let's do the bed first. Those divan drawers look inviting."

They found nothing of interest in the bedroom. JJ's camera never got used. And it appeared the office would be much the same. JJ sighed as he picked up a box full of pens, clips, and other essential office equipment.

"Nothing doing here. I suppose that's a good thing, really. I don't like to think that Amber was troubled, but it doesn't help our cause." He slid the box back into its slot and pulled out the wicker basket next to it, the last but one to be searched, and handed it to Davie, who placed it on the desk. "Nearly there. You do that one, I'll do this last one. Then we can get out of here before Evans arrives."

Davie lifted the pack of envelopes from the box and punched the air. "Hello, hello, hello. I think we've found something." He lifted a transparent folder and waved it at JJ. "Looks like Amber was getting hate mail."

"Don't touch it. Put these on." JJ pulled some blue nitrile gloves from the pocket of his shorts and handed two to Davie.

"Where did you get these from?" Davie asked.

"Picked them up while we were in Amber's studio. She had a boxful. I thought they might come in handy. I was right."

Davie slid the contents onto the desk. There were three items. One was an envelope which simply said Amber. One was a sheet of A4 paper folded into quarters, and one was a greetings card, although not one of Amber's.

JJ photographed them as they had landed, before asking Davie to hold open the card. To his eye, the same hand had written the text as the card sent to Gary, but in a felt-tipped pen.

STUPID WOMAN.

YOU CAN'T SAY I DIDN'T WARN YOU, BITCH.

TOO LATE NOW.

JJ photographed it before unfolding the A4 sheet, which was typed out and printed.

Amber,

A quick note to tell you that you're messing about with the wrong man. You need to stop. Now. What might seem like fun to your warped mind is wrecking lives.

Stop or I'll wreck yours. Heed my warning.

A well-wisher.

"That confirms this is related to her romantic activities. There you go, JJ. We have a motive. We just need to find out why and who." Davie grinned as JJ took several more photographs.

"You forgot when. There is nothing to show when either of these were received. They weren't posted. Amber kept hold of them, as she knew someone might need them as evidence. If we knew when, we might narrow it down to which man." Allowing his camera to drop back down to rest against his torso, JJ placed the items back into the wallet. "Come on. Not long until Evans is due. I could do without that aggro."

"Me too. We need to get back to that dating site. That might shed some light on it. What are you going to do with those?" Davie asked, pointing at the wallet.

"Leave them there for Evans. That should make him get his finger out."

JJ led the way downstairs and found Gary staring out into the back garden. He turned to face them.

"Anything?" Gary asked.

"Yes. A couple of letters she'd received. Not nice. I've left them on the desk for Evans. He might want to poke around himself, but there's nothing else to find. Let him do what he needs to," JJ replied.

"Letters? What sort of not nice letters?" Gary walked across the kitchen, and JJ placed a hand on his shoulder, halting him in his tracks.

"Don't touch them. Might be fingerprints. They're evidence now. Look on here."

JJ showed Gary the images of the letters. Gary shook his head, unable to believe what he was seeing.

"That's the same writing as the one I got, isn't it?"

"It looks that way, yes, where is it? You should give that to Evans, too."

"In the drawer. We didn't touch it after yesterday. What do I do if he doesn't take it seriously?"

"He will. But if it puts your mind at rest, ask him what he's going to do to step up the investigation in light of this additional evidence. I'm sure all will be well, but if it's still okay with you, we'll keep looking into it."

"Of course it's okay with me. In fact, I insist, whatever Evans says. She was a good woman, JJ. A bloody good woman, and you have to make sure she gets justice. Promise me. Look, I'll pay you. Don't be embarrassed, I'm far from broke, and...just let me do something."

"I don't want your money, Gary. I'm just doing what's right. If you want me to carry on, then that's what I'll—"

"Hang on a minute, JJ. Think about that. I'm not saying go mad, but while we're doing this, we're not earning elsewhere. Sorry, but it's true. I'm not working. You might be able to say no, but I can't. Gary, can we get back to you on this?" Davie gave what he hoped was a charming smile.

"Davie, will—"

Gary held up a finger and pushed JJ towards the front door. "Your partner sounds smart to me, JJ. Have a chat about it. We'll speak later. I've got some stuff to do before Evans gets here. I can't stand around arguing the toss. Thank you for your help so far. Just keep going. We can dot the i's and cross the t's later."

JJ opened his mouth to protest again, but deciding his words would be better directed at Davie, he nodded and shoved Davie towards the door. Davie winked at Gary as he closed the door behind them.

JJ marched off towards his cottage. Hands in his pockets and shoulders rounded, he left Davie standing there. JJ didn't want to speak because he wasn't sure how he felt. Gary had more than enough money to hire a private detective. But was he that man? If he was, how much should he charge? Should he charge? If the police didn't get their act sorted, he'd investigate whether or not Gary approved. He didn't really need the money. It would make things easier, of course, but he didn't need it, so was it right? Then, of course, there was Davie to consider. He might need the money. Probably did if he was living in his car in his condition. He might have a free roof over his head now, but what about his living expenses?

Food, car, insurance. JJ groaned at that thought. Did Davie even have insurance for the car?

"Don't go groaning, JJ. We got work to do, partner." Davie grinned at him. "We've got six blokes on a dating site to investigate, and a string of women to chat to. It's lunchtime, Evans will be after that laptop, and you're standing in the street groaning. Come on. Let's do this thing...partner."

"You call me that one more time and you'll be sleeping in that car again. Is it taxed and insured? If not, move it. You keep on about how you need money. You don't want to add fines to your list of expenses."

"JJ, you're not a copper any more, and you're not my dad. First, they'd have to find me, then they'd have to hope I was still alive by the time it got to court. Are you going to open this door or not?"

"I'm not dropping this, but you're right, Evans will want the laptop. We'll discuss this later. I won't forget." JJ opened the door and led the way to their newly organised office.

It was a little before two when Davie placed a plate of sandwiches in front of JJ. The printer was churning away on top of the acquired chest of drawers.

"Cheese and pickle as requested. Bloody hell, that printer makes a racket. I can see why you don't work upstairs. Now, before we set to work on that lot, are you sure there's nothing else we can use on that laptop? He could turn up at any minute. Shall I have a look?"

JJ picked up a sandwich and bit into it. "Knock yourself out. But eat, Davie, it's been a long time since breakfast."

Davie nodded, and they ate in silence as Davie searched the files and records held on Amber's laptop. Reasonably satisfied they'd got all they could, he pointed at the pad. "Make a list."

JJ picked up his pen. "Of what? I've printed all we had on the men."

"Printer, external hard drive. You should have one of those for yours anyway. White board, and there was something else. It'll come to me."

The pen in JJ's hand hadn't moved, and he stared at Davie.

"Don't look at me like that. You need a new printer. What if that broke down on the eve of one of your exhibitions? And on that note, your computer is ancient too. How much memory has it got? What if it goes kaput on you? Where's your backup storage? You need both for the PI business and the photography. White board, that's just so you have something visual. Blu-Tacking sheets of A4 all over the walls won't be very efficient. Doesn't that stuff leave greasy marks? And for the photographs, you would be better to use tacks. Write it down, you can always ignore it."

"Or I could just remember the three things my lodger thinks I need." JJ lifted the printing onto the desk. "Shall we get on with it?"

"Partner JJ, partner. Until we talk about the money thing, I'm an equal partner like Gary said. Lodger would imply that a payment is being made. It's not, so I'd refer you back to Gary's offer. If sorted, I might become a lodger, but until then you'll have to make do with having me as a guest. Now that's settled, who's first?"

JJ leaned forward and blu-tacked up the list of the six men Amber had been in contact with. Davie had extracted a little more information, but they had limited IT and hacking skills, so it was lucky that JJ had identified three of them. All but Manton had used pseudonyms, and he was hoping for luck with two of the others.

Flash Harry
Big Ben (Sean Manton)
Hot Wheeler (Mark Baxter)
Lonely Heart
Urban Cowboy
Night Watchman (Brian Gates)

"For the time being, we can discount Flash Harry. From the brief exchange they had, that went nowhere. The chat with Sean Manton, who wasn't scared to show his face, stopped months ago. I'm guessing because they got it together. We need to look into him. We could put Mark Baxter on the back burner, for the time being. Amber worked out who he was and told him to behave. He's not subtle, is he?. Why she was then caught kissing him, who knows? Despite the Zorro mask, I think Amber recognised Brian Gates, alias the Night Watchman as easily as I did. He's old enough to be her grandad, how he thought he would get away giving his age as forty-five, I don't know. He didn't bother her once she'd said she was in a relationship, so he goes down the list too. So, my dear guest, we have to find out who Lonely Heart and Urban Cowboy are before we do anything else. If we can, of course."

"Okay. I suggest we start with Lonely. She liked him, she met him, and judging by the number of messages they exchanged on here, I'd suggest he was married, or at least in a serious relationship, because otherwise why not do it via your phone without having to log in here. Although, that said I suppose—" The sound of Mozart interrupted Davie, as did the sound of the constant knocking on the front door. "War party has arrived. I'll keep out the way but bring him into the kitchen so I can eavesdrop. This will be fun."

Chapter Eleven

Clive Evans pushed past JJ but followed his pointed finger into the kitchen. Evans walked to the open back door and turned to face JJ.

"I understand you are in possession of goods which might be pertinent to an ongoing murder inquiry. I want everything you have. Now," Evans demanded.

"Hallelujah. So, you are treating it as murder now. Is that since you saw the hate mail, or because of the postmortem results?" JJ asked with a beaming smile.

"Wipe the grin off your face, Jenson. Get what I need, and I'll be out of your hair. Don't bugger about."

"I'm not. I'm genuinely pleased. That family needs justice for Amber. Everyone needs justice for Amber. Otherwise, what's the point? Come on, Clive. This isn't a competition."

"No. It's not. If it was, you'd lose. It's not a murder either, but now I've got to waste time going through the motions because your addled brain has told you that you're capable of investigating anything?" Evans held a palm up towards JJ. "Don't say anything, just get the gear. But let me tell you this, if you get in my way, or piss me about, I'll arrest you for obstruction. Understand?"

JJ bristled. Generally, he saw little point in ever looking for trouble, but Evans was always the exception. "You didn't say it."

"Say what?" Evans' foot was now tapping the floor.

"You didn't ask properly. You don't barge into my house and make demands without proper manners. Now, try again." JJ offered a smile.

"Fuck off. Will that do you?"

"Afraid not. Now, moderate your language or I'll have to ask you to leave." JJ's tone remained calm and friendly, but his eyes bore into Evans.

"Ha! What, now you've found Jesus, you don't like the swear words? Listen, JJ, you failed as a police officer, you failed with the church, and you have obviously failed as a photographer. Can't say I'm surprised there. What makes you think you'll succeed as a private investigator? Don't bother to answer that, you're living in cloud cuckoo land, but it's sad that you are taking advantage of a grieving family. Get me the gear, *please*, and I'll leave you to your delusions." Evans put an emphasis on the p, and spittle sprayed from his mouth.

"What do you want?" JJ tried to keep his anger bolted down, and his tone was calm.

"The laptop and anything else you took. Duh!"

"Just the laptop, then. I'll get it."

"That's all you've got? Wilton led me to believe there was more." Frowning, Evans resumed the foot tapping.

"Oh, I have more. I took none of it, though. I investigated a crime and found it."

JJ went into the office area and a grinning Davie handed him the bag. JJ peered inside. Laptop, power cable, mouse. It was all there. Returning to the kitchen, he held it towards Evans.

Evans took the bag. "If I find out you've withheld anything, JJ, there's going to be trouble."

"What you forget, Evans, is that I'm an honest man. I don't lie, I don't cheat, and I don't take backhanders. I'll see you out."

JJ held his hand towards the door as Evans hurried past

"You shouldn't go throwing accusations like that around, not with your history, and not without proof," he snarled, his face an apoplectic red. "Watch your back, JJ."

"I made no accusations, Evans. If you've got a guilty conscience, you can't hold me responsible for that. Give my regards to Tom. Tell him I'll give him a ring later."

"Why? What do you need to speak to him about?" Evans was almost frothing at the mouth.

"'Bye, Evans, have a good day. If you want to know what we've found out, just ask." Now at the front door, JJ swept his hand towards the street.

Evans stormed past. "Like that would ever happen!"

JJ sighed as he returned to Davie. He didn't like Evans, but nor did he like confrontations. Not any more. The only positive thing he could take from it was the boost it gave to his determination to solve the case.

"If you want to know what we've found out? Have you gone mad?" Davie demanded, as JJ entered the room. "We're going to whip his arse and then rub his nose in it."

"Possibly, but the top priority is to find Amber's killer. If we can help the police, then we will. Even if that means helping Evans. Think how smug we'll feel if we can take enough evidence to him to enable an arrest and God willing a conviction."

"I'm not going to argue, JJ. I just want to get on with it. What do...I'll get to finish a sentence in a minute. Bloody bell. If that's Evans again, tell him to sling his hook. I'm putting the kettle on."

Seconds later, Gary hurried into the kitchen. "I'm sorry, JJ. Hello, Davie. I had to come and apologise."

"Why? What have you done? I'll get an extra mug out." Davie lifted another mug from the cupboard.

"I thought he was paying me lip service. I showed him the notes, and he asked me questions he knew I couldn't answer about when they arrived and what have you, but he didn't search the house like you did. Then he said he'd be in touch. I told him I'd have to go back to work, but it might be better if he spoke to the investigator I'd hired, and he could collect Amber's laptop from them. He asked me who, and I said JJ Investigations, and assured him it was all legitimate because I knew you were an ex-copper. I thought he was going to have heart failure. He spluttered a bit, grabbed the folder, which he threw into his car on his way to you, and I've just watched him drive off now. He didn't say a word about the postmortem, or when we're likely to be able to have a funeral. Evans is short-tempered for a police officer. I was shocked, and glad you're working on this. I know you said to leave it, but I'll have to pay you now, or I've lied to the police. Not for me, Davie. I'll leave you to it. I want to get into Bristol and back here as quickly as possible. I want to hear how Luke got on."

"Did you not want to go?" JJ asked.

"Of course, but I wanted as little fuss as possible for Luke. People feel obliged to pay condolences. That would have upset him. One can only hope the other parents will use a little common sense, but I'm sure Sharon and Connie Gerrard will do their best to protect him. Right, I'm off. I'll see myself out."

JJ wagged a finger at Davie, who was rubbing his hands together. "We're not discussing it now. We're going to the pub."

"I like your thinking, JJ. Have you worked up a thirst?" Davie asked.

"Nope, but it's Friday and Sean Manton always goes to the pub on a Friday afternoon when he finishes work. Let's see if he does today."

It was a glorious sunny afternoon, and JJ would have preferred to sit outside, but he knew that to achieve what they wanted, they'd need to stay inside. He waved to Old Sam as he entered.

"Blimey, you're here again! These daytime visits are getting to be a habit. Jemma will be back in a minute. Don't make me get off this stool." Sam looked around. The four men at the nearest table were engrossed in a game of crib, and the others were too far away to hear much, so he asked, "How's it going? Are you getting anywhere?"

"Early days, but yes, it's progressing." JJ walked closer and lowered his voice. "Has Manton been in?"

"Not yet. Any time now if he comes. Do you need to speak to him?" Old Sam asked.

"If I can get him to talk, yes."

Jemma appeared and JJ ordered some drinks.

"You want to sit over by the fireplace. That's his preferred spot. Seen him get people to move just by staring at them." Sam jerked his finger over his shoulder.

JJ thanked him and he and Davie settled themselves to wait. They were rewarded ten minutes later when Sean Manton walked into the bar. He glanced over and tutted as Jemma came to serve him. Davie watched Sam beckon Manton over as Jemma pulled his pint and say something to him. Manton glanced over again, and Davie nodded.

"I think Old Sam's had a word." Davie nudged JJ. "He's coming over. He's a big lad, isn't he? Don't go upsetting him. I couldn't fight my way out of a wet paper bag."

Manton stopped a few feet away. "Old Sam said you were looking for me. What do you want?" Despite his words, his tone suggested just standing there seriously inconvenienced him.

"Yes, have a seat. It won't take long." JJ pushed a stool forward with his foot.

Rolling his eyes, Manton lowered himself onto the stool, took a swig of his pint, and sucked the froth from his lips. "What do you want?"

"I want to talk to you about Amber Wilton." JJ watched Manton's features harden. His eyes seemed to darken despite the forced smirk.

"What about her? I shagged her and moved on."

"I think we both know it was a little more than that, even if you had moved on." JJ mentally crossed his fingers. It was a long shot, but based on Manton's demeanour when he'd come into the pub the other night, JJ guessed he'd been genuinely upset about Amber's death, even if it was him who pushed her off that bridge.

"Who told you that?" Manton asked, not denying it.

"I hear things. People say a lot when they're trying not to gossip. I'm sorry for your loss."

Manton knew JJ was genuine, and he nodded acceptance. "Like I said, I'd already moved on. But she was nice. Why are you asking questions?"

Before JJ opened his mouth, Davie jumped in. "Because her family has employed us to find out who killed her."

"Why? Is that what you are now, a private investigator? I thought you were a vicar or a photographer or something." Manton pointed at the camera hanging against JJ's torso. "What about the police?"

Once more, it was Davie who answered, "The family don't think the police are making enough effort." He paused as Manton snorted agreement. Here was a man who didn't think much of the police. Davie took that idea and ran with it. "Jobsworths. More worried about someone dealing a bit of weed or taking bets in a back room than fighting serious crime. Bastards, the lot of them." Davie tutted and took a sip of his beer. Dabbing his mouth with the back of his hand, he looked Manton in the eye. "Look, Sean, can I call you Sean? We've been given a lot of conflicting information about Amber. For the best part, she comes across as a lovely girl, a wonderful mother, a fabulous artist, and kind. You know, a good neighbour to have. But, and there always is one, some would have us believe she was flighty in the romance department, but having looked at her personal stuff, we don't think that's true. For instance, we know she thought a lot about you." Davie didn't continue, hoping Manton would give his own opinion.

Manton was nodding as Davie spoke. "I had no complaints. We had a good time. She was a good mum. Her boy always came first. I liked that about her, opposite of my mum because she couldn't get rid of us quick enough. As to putting herself about, not that I knew. Bet it was a woman who told you that. Probably jealous. I've never heard that. After her old man left, I didn't hear of her being with anyone but me. That was only a couple of months ago. So, it's true, she was murdered. I hope you catch the bastard." Manton's mouth drooped, and he sighed. "Shame."

"It is a crying shame," JJ agreed. "Tell us about her. What did she talk about? Was she worried about anything? Was anyone giving her a hard time?"

"Not that she told me. We just had a laugh, and the other, of course. Look, I'll be straight with you, we weren't love's young dream, but for a while it felt like it. Neither of us wanted to trot up the aisle. We just wanted a bit of fun. I don't think I can help you, but I'll let you know if I hear anything. Are you going now? Only I sit here."

JJ smiled at the unmasked invitation to move. "We're going to sit outside, but one more question, if I could. Do you know anyone called Steve? Particularly a Steve she may have been involved with after you."

"Nope. I'll ask about." Manton stared into his pint as he considered this, a frown creasing his brow.

JJ nudged Davie and got to his feet. "Give us a shout if you hear anything, even gossip. Some gossip might be relevant. Do you know where I live?"

"Yep, next door to...Yes, I know."

JJ patted him on the shoulder as he and Davie picked up their glasses. "Thank you."

"That's another thing for the list." Davie took a seat at JJ's favoured bench.

"What's that?" JJ asked.

"Business cards. You need to get business cards with a telephone number on. People will pick up the phone, but there are many who wouldn't want to climb that hill on the off chance you were in."

"I suppose you're right."

"Ha!" Davie clapped his hands together. "You agreed with me. Now we're getting somewhere. What next?"

"Next, we pop down to the shop and speak to Will. Seems like he knows who this Steve chap is. But we'll finish these first."

"Sounds like a good plan. Should we grab something for dinner while we're there?" Davie asked.

"No. It's fish and chip Friday. I'm going to introduce you to the best fish and chips you've ever tasted."

"That also sounds like a good plan. But I'm hoping we'll take the contraption you call a car because I've just remembered I need to drop into the surgery and pick up that prescription."

"I'm going to get fat working with you because I tend to run everywhere. School's out, there's Luke and Emma. He looks happy enough. I have to confess I was worried about him. Finish your beer. We've got somewhere to be."

When they arrived at the supermarket, Will Clarke, the manager, was stacking tins on a shelf.

"Hello, JJ. You're the talk of the town again. Shit. Sorry, mate, not engaging brain before opening mouth. Anyway, you are. What are you after?" Will grimaced at Davie, having inadvertently mentioned JJ's past troubles.

"If they're talking about me, everyone else is safe. I wanted to speak to you about Steve. Amber's Steve." JJ decided there was no point in dragging it out.

"You know about that already? I was told you only got hired last night. You don't mess about. I'd love to help you, JJ, really I would, but all I know is the gossip from the customers. I wouldn't be telling you anything I know as a fact." Shelf stacking completed, Will tore up the box which had held the cans.

"Give me the gossip and I'll work out who can give me the facts." JJ leaned against the bread stand to show he wasn't going anywhere.

Will glanced around, and content no one was listening, he stepped closer to JJ and kept his voice low. "I don't know how long Amber had been involved with the doctor, or how serious it was, but rumour has it she was smitten, and getting impatient with the skulking around." Will held up his hands. "That's it. That's all I know."

Davie looked blank, but JJ frowned as the pieces fell into place.

"Okay, do you know what happened between Amber and Sandy Bentley in here?" JJ asked. "I heard Sandy left her shopping without buying anything after their encounter,"

"I couldn't hear what was said, but I'd heard the rumours about Amber and the doc, and I kept an eye on them when they ended up in the same aisle." Will pointed up at the mirror suspended from the ceiling. "They exchanged words, no shouting or anything, then Sandy marched to the counter, slammed her basket down and left. She came back in later but barely said a word. Understandable, I suppose, if she knew, and I'm guessing she knew because I've never seen her like that before. But being the doctor's wife is a bit like being married to a vicar, isn't it? Got to be on your best behaviour all the time."

"And how was Amber once Sandy had stormed off?" Davie joined the conversation, having worked out that Steve and Dr Stephen Bentley were one and the same.

"Okay, I suppose. Not bouncy like she usually was, but polite and bought some of the wife's raffle tickets for her latest charity."

Someone entered the shop and walked straight to the counter. Will glanced over. "That's Keith in for his evening paper. I'd better get on, but I've got no more I can tell you."

"One last thing. When did everyone start calling Dr Bentley Steve? I'd never have guessed that's who they were on about."

Will shrugged. "As far as I know, when Kerry Snell had a barney with Amber at keep fit or whatever it is they do these days. They were in the changing room, and Kerry thought they were alone, so told Amber, in no uncertain terms, that she should drop Steve. An argument ensued, and it was Steve this and Steve the other. One of the other girls was in the toilet and quickly worked out who it was when Kerry told Amber to think of Sandy. And as you know, you can't keep a secret in this place for very long. The school mums were talking about it. Better go, he's looking at me again." Will hurried away to the counter.

"That was useful as we're going to the health centre next. Are you sure we don't need anything?" Davie asked, browsing the shelves as he headed for the exit.

"Go on then, grab some biscuits and a loaf of bread." JJ tutted as Davie handed them to him at the counter.

"Bit short, JJ. The sooner we get paid, the better," Davie told him with a straight face.

At the surgery, they were in luck of sorts. Doctor Bentley was in, but Davie would have an hour wait, minimum, if he wanted to see him. Kerry Snell was working, but not on reception, they could see her coming and going from the main office behind a glass screen.

Davie took a seat in the centre of the waiting room and patted the chair next to him.

"Not sure I want to sit around for over an hour." JJ dropped onto the chair. "This only needs one of us."

"You wait and see. Now the gossips know you have been formally instructed, I bet they'll all be wanting to sit next to you. Although I could go and question him on my own, I think we'd get more out of him if you come in with me. I'll tell him you're my next of kin, which I suppose you are."

"You must have other family. I mean, who are you going to leave your worldly goods to?" JJ asked.

"Haven't got any, nor if I did, have I got anyone to leave them to. I've paid for my funeral, didn't fancy lying in a drawer for weeks on end while they decided what to do with me."

JJ shuddered. "Let's change the subject. But if that's right, that's something else we have to sort out. You need to make a will. My life was simple until you turned up. I like simple."

"No, you don't. It was boring. You can't like boring. Mine was pointless, now it's not. Like I said before, it's a win-win. Dr Singh must have done well yesterday, there's not as many people here today."

Davie wasn't wrong. Over the next fifty minutes, numerous people came to sit next to JJ, and all brought the conversation around to Amber. JJ downplayed his involvement and was relieved when Davie's name flashed up on the screen and a robotic voice asked him to go to room three. He led the way.

Dr Bentley was finishing typing up the notes from the previous patient and didn't look up when the door opened. They looked at the healthy mop of blond hair and his elegant fingers as they tapped out his diagnosis.

"Take a seat, Mr George. I won't be two ticks."

Davie sat in the chair and JJ hovered by the door once he'd closed it. Dr Bentley was shocked when he looked up.

"Hello." He glanced back at his screen. "Mr George, I can see you're living with JJ, but we don't need him to verify that. Are you happy for him to stay?"

"Oh, yes, to get that stuff out of the way, JJ is my next of kin. I've not done any sort of power of attorney, but I'm happy for you to discuss with him anything you might want to discuss with me. Is there something we need to sign for you? There is one crucial exception, that being the DNR. When I'm getting to the end, let me go, and let me go quickly. Don't string it out with drugs, I'm not interested. JJ's an old softy. If it was down to him, he'd drag it out."

Dr Bentley was nodding gently as Davie spoke. When Davie folded his arms, Bentley linked his fingers. "Okay, I understand. I've only skimmed your notes, but looking at you now, we have a while before we need to worry about that, so I'd suggest you should formalise it. Although I know that, and I can even put a note on your file, I'm afraid it won't be good enough if it comes to life or death and someone else is treating you. I'm not sure how complicated your final wishes are regarding bequests etcetera, but I understand these things are quite simple, and not expensive. I'm sure Brenda Saunders could sort you out."

"Who?" Davie asked.

"Solicitor, above the café," JJ told him. Silently relieved and concerned at the same time. Uncharitably, he'd questioned Davie's honesty when stating the extent of his illness. That had been confirmed by the lack of challenge by Bentley.

"Ah, gotcha. Talking of complications, Doc, I'm sure by now you've heard that JJ has been instructed to investigate the death of Amber Wilton." Davie hoped his face looked sympathetic, and taking a leaf out of JJ's book, added, "By the way, condolences."

Bentley's head jerked back. "Condolences? Surely they should be directed to—"

"The man she loved. Yes. That's why I said it. Must have come as a shock, Amber's murder." Davie pressed on, aware of JJ fidgeting behind him.

The colour drained from Bentley's face. He attempted to speak, but his voice was no more than a croak, so he cleared his throat and tried again. "Murdered? Amber? I don't understand. Why are you telling me and not the police?" He looked to JJ for an answer.

"Because Gary Wilton isn't happy that the police are doing enough. We're just asking around, trying to find out what was going on in Amber's life immediately before her death, and, of course, anything we do find will be handed to the police. But it's better that these things are done quickly before too much time has elapsed." JJ walked further into the room and leaned against the examination bench. "We know you were in a relationship with Amber. I'm guessing you met on the dating site, and you are Lonely Heart. We'd like to ask you a few questions, if that's okay?"

"Not here, not now. I've got another half a dozen patients to see. Can I meet up with you later?" Bentley asked. "I'll come to you if you like. Not sure what time. After dinner. So eightish?"

"That would be good. Before we go, just so we can keep up the momentum, do you know if Amber was having trouble with anyone? Threats, nuisance calls, nasty correspondence, anything like that?"

"No. No, I don't, I'm sorry. I'd help if I could. Can I ask how Amber was killed?"

"She was pushed off the bridge. Down by the mill. It was quick, she didn't suffer."

Bentley looked into his lap and remained silent. Davie got to his feet and held his hand out. "We'll see you later, Doc."

"Yes. Yes. Sorry. Nice to meet you, Mr George. Don't forget to see a solicitor."

"Call me Davie. And yes, I will."

Back in the car, Davie suggested they may as well go to the solicitor's to make an appointment. They were in luck. Brenda Saunders was in the reception area: a buxom middle-aged woman, with a white streak of hair, wearing a black skirt suit that had seen better days. She stood clasping several files to her ample bosom, as she listened to why Davie was there and interrupted Fran Jones, the receptionist, who had opened the diary to make an appointment.

"That sounds fairly straightforward. I'll need to ask a few questions, so if you have time, we might as well do it now, and I'll get you something drafted for next week. JJ, you'll need to stay there. You can't be party to this if you're going to have power of attorney."

"Not much to take power of," Davie quipped, as he followed her through to her office.

Knowing Fran from the church choir, JJ tried to make small talk while he waited. "How are you, Fran? How's the kids?"

"Yes, all well, thanks. You? We don't see you at church any more." Fran didn't look up from her typing.

"No, well, that's a long story for another day." JJ wished he'd kept quiet.

"Shame. I thought you were going to be a photographer when you didn't come back. Now I hear you're a private investigator." Resting her fingers on the keyboard, Fran looked up for an answer.

"News travels fast. Just dipping my toe in the water. How did you find out?"

"Popped down to the shop for some biscuits and there were a couple of mums in there. The school gates are a hotbed of tittle-tattle, you know. Can find out anything you want there. Apart from the fact that Amber died, are you enjoying it?" Fran waved a mug at JJ. "Do you want one?"

"Not for me, thanks. And yes, I suppose I am. Would rather it wasn't Amber's death though." JJ grimaced. "It's knocked the Wiltons for six, as you can imagine."

"Yes, it's awful. Absolutely awful. What else would you investigate then? Cheating spouses? I can't think of any other use for a private investigator. Oh, I suppose some sorts of fraud might come up."

"Who knows? Still early days, but I'm guessing it will mainly involve tracking missing people. Have you never had to employ someone to track down a beneficiary or the like?" Instead of replying, Fran looked down at her hands and seemed to be in a world of her own. JJ leaned forward. "Fran, are you okay?"

Fran gave herself a shake. "Yes, sorry, JJ. I'm fine. Just set me thinking, that's all. I'll get back to you."

"On what? I wasn't touting for business, although I'd be happy to help." But would he be? JJ wasn't sure he liked how quickly the idea of him as a private eye was gathering pace.

"On a missing person? I won't say more now, it's not my missing person. Like I said, I'll get back to you." Fran looked at the door to Brenda's office, as Brenda's throaty laugh reached them. "Sounds like they're finishing up. Before they come out, can I ask you something?"

"Of course."

"Was it Gary Wilton who asked you to investigate?"

"It was. Why do you ask?"

"No reason. Um, a little surprised, I suppose. Do you know why he asked you?"

"I know they weren't together, but he wanted to be, and they seemed to be trying to rekindle the relationship. He wants the murderer brought to justice. Not that surprising, is it?" JJ was confused, he thought that would have been obvious.

"I guess not. Look at the time, I'd better get on, otherwise I'll sit here and ask you questions until the cows come home. I'm pleased for you, JJ, good luck with it all. Hopefully see you in church one day soon." Fran looked up and smiled as Davie returned. "All sorted?"

"Bar the shouting and the bill, yes thanks." Davie clamped his hand to his stomach. "Did you hear that? What time does the fish shop open, JJ? I'm starving."

Ten minutes later, they were sitting in the car outside the little chip shop. They had twenty minutes to wait until it opened, but they weren't alone. A queue of half a dozen people had already formed.

JJ called Sharon, and having taken her order looked at Davie. "What do you want? I'll phone it in. Cod or plaice, I'd recommend cod. Large or small, large is the size of a small shark. They do sausages and pies and similar, but it's fish night, so cod or plaice?"

"Small cod and chips. I haven't got the appetite I used to have. Seems I need little and often these days. Why does it have to be fish? Your religion? My nan always had fish on a Friday."

"Mine too, but no, just because it's an end of the week treat."

"So what happened on the religion front? Did you stop believing or have you had a falling out with the bishop?"

"Neither and both. I lost faith in many things, and stopped going because it made me feel like a hypocrite. That and the suffering I saw. I wasn't even working in a war zone. It was awful. Anyway, I tried to get home to see Dad, and never went back. Not to Africa or the church. Now shut up and let me call this in."

Davie nodded, not really caring why JJ had given it all up because it had worked out perfectly for him, instead he watched an old man shuffle into line at the end of the queue. He was, however, interested in why JJ needed to get back to his dad, but that would wait for another day.

A few minutes later, a woman approached the queue and spotted them. She waved before joining the queue.

"Who's that?" Davie asked.

"Teresa Burns, from the café. You've met her, Davie. Not sure how good an investigator you're going to be. What's that smile for?"

"Because you've admitted we're a team. I didn't recognise her. She looks totally different without the overall and she's had her hair done."

"That's because it's bingo night at the church hall. I used to call the numbers, legs eleven, bang on the drum seventy-one, overweight twenty-eight. You'd be impressed, I know the lot. Had a lot of fun making some up."

"A man of hidden talents. We should go. Room full of women looking to hear and share gossip. Might be worth a punt. Here we go. They're open."

"Give it five minutes. Let that lot go in. Charlie is well organised. He knows he has a rush on Friday at teatime, it won't take long. As for bingo, not tonight, Dr Bentley is coming round, although you could go if you like."

"Forget about bingo, I'd rather hear what the doctor has to say for himself."

Chapter Twelve

SHARON SHOOK HER FIST at JJ. "How did you forget to mention he was coming? I'll have to get dressed now because I can hardly entertain the doctor dressed like this." Despite the warm summer evening, Sharon was wearing a teddy bear dressing gown over her nightie.

"I meant to, then we had the pickled onion saga and it escaped my mind. Davie," he shouted up the stairs, "remind me tomorrow that we need to buy pickled onions." JJ rolled his eyes, then winked at Sharon. "You could always go to bed with a good book. It's Friday. No work to do for next week with the holidays fast approaching. Or you could binge watch the soaps. You could have a field day."

"Yes, like that's going to happen. I'm still in shock. I want the nitty-gritty and from the horse's mouth. Not from someone in the staff room or even you. Amber and Dr Stephen Bentley. Wow. How did it even get started?"

JJ hadn't told her about the dating site yet, and he pondered if he should. Davie removed the choice as he came back downstairs.

"What are we talking about, the doc's affair? Online, Sharon. That seems to be where she hooked up with all of them. Are we going to sit in the garden? It's a lovely evening."

Sharon gave a squeak. "A dating site! JJ, why didn't you tell me that at the beginning? I am certainly not skulking up to the bedroom now. And, yes, Davie, let's sit in the garden. You two move the table further up, so we can keep an eye out for prying neighbours. I'll grab a T-shirt and some shorts. We have no wine in. Should we have something? We need to offer him a drink."

"Sharon, he's coming here to be questioned, not entertained. You can offer him a cup of tea," JJ replied. "Come on, Davie. We should do as instructed while she takes the time to calm down."

As they moved the furniture further up the garden, Davie asked, "Can I be nosey? Why don't you have alcohol in the house? Is it allowed? What I'm trying to say—"

"...Is, which one of you has a problem? The answer is me. I never know when to stop. When I drink I get nightmares. Wake the entire street up type of nightmares, and the hangover lasts about two days. Sharon has never been a big drinker, so we've stopped, well as near as damn it. She lost a few pounds, I lost a lot of headaches. Yes, I have a pint of Guinness occasionally, but I can keep that to one. I'm not an alcoholic. I don't think so anyway. More of a teenager who can't handle booze but doesn't realise that until it's too late."

"What sort of nightmares?" Davie asked.

"Do you ever have a normal conversation? You know, looks like rain, or the price of...Oh no, what's she got there?"

JJ pointed down the garden, and Davie turned to look. Sharon was carrying a stacked tray and had a tablecloth over her arm.

"We didn't have a tablecloth when we ate out here. How come he gets special treatment? Here, let me take that."

JJ took the tray, and watched with a small smile as Sharon shook out the cloth, allowing it to settle across the table. She then set a jug of iced water and glasses on it, and lit two fat candles in glass jars. Once finished, she turned to JJ.

"Say nothing or else you're sleeping on the couch. You go in and wait for him to get here, and I'll get settled with Davie."

"Why do I have to wait inside? He's not due for ten minutes and that's if he's on time." JJ was already walking towards the back door.

"Because it means I've already joined you. I won't have to ask if he minds if I do." Sharon turned to Davie as JJ entered the house. "He can be so dense for an intelligent man. Who's Daniel Boyd?"

Davie's mouth fell open, and he held out his hands. "Really? You don't know?".

"I wouldn't ask if I did. I can see that's shocked you. Who is he?" Sharon wound her finger in circles to make him hurry.

"It was huge. Catastrophic for JJ. Sharon, I know we're out in the sticks, but have you heard of Google? Why are you asking now?" Davie asked. "It was years ago."

"Davie, come on, they'll be coming out here any minute. I only knew the name Daniel. I didn't have the Boyd bit until you mentioned it. And I haven't had the time. Quick, who is he?"

"Have you asked JJ?"

"Okay, please yourself. I'll speak to JJ."

Davie shook his head and rapped on the table. "No, don't do that. It would probably upset him. Daniel Boyd was a six-year-old murder victim. Nasty case, and...and here they are. Don't ask him. Google it. I'll answer what I can once you've done that. Now smile. You've been waiting for this."

"Ah, he looks so nervous. He's usually so outgoing. Jeans too. Never seen him in jeans before," Sharon whispered and raised her hand in greeting as she got to her feet. "Hello, Dr Bentley. There's water here, but would you prefer tea or coffee? Haven't got anything stronger, I'm afraid."

"Hello. Water's fine, I'm driving." Bentley looked at JJ. "Are we sitting out here?"

"We were planning to but we can go in if you prefer?"

"No. I've been cooped up inside all day. This is perfect. Shall I?" Bentley pointed to an empty chair and sat down when JJ nodded. "What do you need to know?"

"Well, I know how you met, or probably more accurately, how you got together. That was what, three months ago? It wasn't clear from the exchange when you actually started seeing each other."

"You've read the messages? Gosh. That's embarrassing. But you'll know that as soon as I realised it was Amber, she was very open about herself, I confessed I was married but not who I was, and...well, you read that, I'm sure. Amber said it was fine. We had done nothing wrong. Then I bumped into her in the street. We were alone, and I had to tell her who I was. I wasn't comfortable with the dishonesty."

Bentley pushed his hair back. "Sounds odd, I know. I was being dishonest to my wife by omission. But damn it, I was lonely. Amber was a breath of fresh air. My wife and I...look, this is very uncomfortable and embarrassing. We'd been seeing each other for about a month when Sandy, my wife, realised something was going on. I'm a terrible liar, so I confessed all, and we were working through whether Sandy wanted our marriage to continue when Amber died. Such a bloody waste. She was so...so vibrant. How's Luke doing? I usually call in on the family when a sudden death occurs, but given the circumstances, well, you know."

"He's getting there. He came to school today. Sports day, so it was manic, but it meant the other kids were too invested in that to worry about Luke. He won his egg and spoon, and the skipping dash, so he was happy. Great way for him to get back into it. JJ can be quite clever on the quiet," Sharon answered. "I think with the love of his dad and Emma, and the support of the school, he'll get there."

"Were you still seeing her?" Davie asked as soon as Sharon uttered her last word. "You know, when you were working things out with the wife?"

Bentley lowered his head and mumbled, "Yes."

"Did Amber know that Sandy had found out? That you were working on your marriage?" JJ asked.

"Of course." Bentley sounded irritated.

"No, not of course." Davie ignored the sharp look from JJ. "Until you told her you were married, she didn't know. Your profile, which is still live by the way, didn't say 'married but my wife doesn't understand me'. Your wife didn't know you frequented dating sites until she found out. You didn't tell her. So there's no 'of course' that Amber knew you were trying to sort things out with your wife. If that's what she thought was happening."

"What's your point?" Bentley had resumed his slightly superior air, the one necessary when he needed to convince a patient that a change of lifestyle was needed.

"My point is someone killed Amber. You don't do that without a motive. When Amber climbed up on that bridge, she couldn't have known that her companion harboured ill intent. So, if she knew your wife was aware of your relationship, would she have done that? Where was your wife on Tuesday evening? If she was out, could she have been down by the bridge?" Davie raised his eyebrows to emphasise the question. "You see?"

"Of course she didn't kill Amber. She was angry with me, not Amber."

"She knew Amber. And that Amber should know you were off limits. Yes, it was your fault, but she might have thought Amber should also have known better. So, are you sure about that?" Davie asked.

"Of c...As far as I can be, yes. Sandy went to the Bums and Tums exercise class. She wasn't walking in the woods."

"So did Amber," JJ said quietly. "Yet, she still went to the woods. What time did Sandy get home?"

"I don't know. I had a call-out. The Jacksons' baby. I had to send her to the hospital, so I waited for the ambulance with Mrs Jackson. By the time I got home, Sandy was asleep in bed,"

"What time was that?" JJ asked.

"I don't know. After ten, I suppose. Look, I didn't kill her either, if that's where this is going." Bentley rapped the table with his knuckles.

"Did Sandy tell you about the meeting in the supermarket with Amber?" JJ asked.

"What meeting? Why would they meet there?" Bentley's eyes moved from side to side as he considered this. Sandy hadn't told him that.

"Sorry, I phrased that wrong. They bumped into each other. It wasn't arranged. There was an exchange, and Sandy stormed off without buying anything. Left her full basket at the checkout."

Bentley's relief was obvious. The frown disappeared, his shoulders relaxed, and he blew out a breath. "Well, there you go. It wasn't a meeting, or anything near. It would have been embarrassing for both of them. I'm sure Sandy wanted to avoid a scene. She doesn't like confrontation. And frankly, nor do I. I'm finding this all rather uncomfortable."

"I'm sure you do. But it can't be avoided, and I'm sure you want to catch Amber's killer. Only a few more questions." JJ patted the doctor's shoulder. "Nearly done."

"You're right, I do. But I'm not sure how I can."

"Did you have feelings for Amber? Were you close, or was it just a sex thing?" Davie asked bluntly, and Sharon picked up her water to hide her smirk. She liked the doctor, but he was a cheating bastard, so a bit of discomfort would do him good.

"Yes, we were close, I had thought...that is we, oh God! Yes, I thought we had something, but Sandy didn't take it well. I thought she'd be grateful to have an escape route she could blame on me. She'd walked out before, you know. But I was wrong, and I couldn't walk out with her in that state, could I?"

"Well, that depends," Davie answered. "Did you finish it with Amber? Or were you more careful not to get caught?"

"It was finished. Done. She was thinking of getting back with her husband, Gary." Bentley was looking at his lap again. JJ knew he wasn't telling the truth, not the whole truth anyway, just his version of it.

"Who finished it? You, Amber or Sandy?" JJ asked.

"Does it matter?" Bentley turned to face him. "Over is over."

"Not always, Doctor. No, it's not. Might have been over for Sandy, but not Amber. Or over for Amber, but not you? Tell me, did you ever discuss marriage with Amber?" JJ watched the colour hit the doctor's cheeks.

"You clearly know I did. That was before. Look, I'm going to go now. Sandy is waiting for me. I've told you everything I know, which is nothing about Amber's death." Bentley got to his feet.

JJ held up his hand. "Two more questions and I'll see you out."

"Make them quick ones." Bentley stepped away from the table and stood with his hands on the back of the chair he had occupied.

"Did Amber tell you she was getting hate mail?" JJ asked.

"Hate mail? No, she didn't. What sort of hate mail?"

"The 'you're messing with the wrong man, so watch your back' sort of hate mail. We don't know, of course, but our best guess is that you were the cause."

Bentley didn't reply, but his shoulders had drooped, and he looked forlorn as he shook his head.

"Last question, for now. How did Sandy find out about your affair? It wasn't a secret in the village when we started investigating. Did they find out before or after Sandy?" JJ stood to join the doctor.

"I told her. Whatever you may think of me, I didn't like the deceit. I didn't enjoy sneaking around although I'd be a liar if I didn't admit that it was exciting, but it's not real life. I wanted a real life. Like I said, I knew my wife would be angry, but I thought once she'd calmed down she'd be glad to be free of me. Sandy is not content. I don't know why, I've tried to find out, but it's almost as though she enjoys being miserable. Now I've said too much. Thank you for the water, Miss Elliott." Bentley gave Davie a curt nod and headed for the door.

Sharon watched them leave as she nudged Davie. "Considering your condition, and the fact he's going to be your doctor, you were very...not sure what the word is. Confrontational. You were very confrontational. You purposely made him feel uncomfortable."

"What's the worst he can do? Kill me? I'm not worried about that. Let's just say when it's time to move on, strap a pair on and do it. But don't cheat on your other half. Not when they're busting their balls trying to keep you in handbags and shoes. It's not the end result, it's how you get there. Enough said?"

Sharon nodded and patted his knee. "So, what's next?"

"In my book, we need to speak to Sandy next. If she did it, she'll lie. If she didn't, it might be obvious. We also need to speak to whoever the doc said he was waiting with for the ambulance. Find out what time he left for home. I've not ruled him out. Then we'll need to go back to the gossips."

JJ appeared in the doorway, and after a brief pause, hurried towards them. He was wearing blue gloves and waving a white envelope at them.

"That doesn't look good. Have you had post?" Davie asked.

"Yep. But I haven't opened it yet. I had to get the gloves and a letter opener. I told you they'd come in handy. And before you say it, yes, I'll add gloves to the list, maybe. I'm glad you put the clean tablecloth on now, Sharon." JJ smiled and hoped he sounded light-hearted. He felt anything but and was already questioning the wisdom of opening it in front of Sharon, but they'd promised no secrets, so he placed the envelope on the table.

Only one word was on the envelope. Printed in blue ink.

JENSON.

JJ pulled the letter opener from his back pocket and sliced it open. He tutted. It was one of Amber's cards again, this time depicting snowdrops.

"From the same pack I expect," he muttered as he opened the card.

BACK OFF.

IT WILL DO NO GOOD AND COULD HURT THOSE CLOSE TO YOU.

HOW IS MISS ELLIOTT?

"Shit. This is a threat. I'm going to have to call Evans and report it. I was hoping to call in a favour from Denise, but mentioning Sharon is off limits. Damn it. That reminds me, I must phone her about the postmortem report. It's nearly nine. Too late, do you think?"

Sharon shook her head. "Do it. This is clearly connected to Amber's murder, and now they've made me doubly mad. Do Denise first and leave Evans until tomorrow. I don't want to have to put up with him tonight."

JJ inclined his head. "You're not worried about this?"

"Nope. I don't plan on being anywhere that there's not many people around, and I hear tell you were a good copper, so I have every faith that you'll catch this bastard soon."

"That sounds like you think it's a man. I reckon it's a woman." Davie got to his feet. "Ring the pathologist, JJ. Let's see if that's going to help us. I'll make some tea, too late for coffee for me. Anyone else?" Davie wandered back to the house to make drinks, while JJ sat next to Sharon and called Denise Thompson.

Denise Thompson was happy to speak to JJ, and he explained what he was doing for Gary Wilton and why. Denise gave a guarded response.

"You know if this is a crime, I can't speak to you officially. You'll have to wait until the inquest for my evidence, but I can tell you that your photographs were as you thought by the look of it. Possibly. The police might think differently."

"Someone hit her thigh, causing her to fall?"

"Yes. If there's an inquest, I'll be telling the coroner that I wouldn't have considered it to be bruising from an assault had I not had the privilege of seeing the photographs. I would have suggested death by misadventure, but the age and position of the bruise, when taken into consideration with your photographs, suggest foul play, and not any other scenario."

"Have you told Evans this?" JJ asked.

"Of course. Preliminaries on Wednesday, full report with the nitty-gritty on Thursday."

"If I attended such an inquest who would give evidence that I might be interested in, evidence which might tell me why Evans didn't open a murder enquiry?" JJ asked.

"Good question, JJ. You've not lost it, old boy. Glad you're sort of back in the saddle. Other than you, me and the police, I would have thought the only other witness likely to be called would be a doctor."

JJ's eyes shot to the chair where Dr Bentley had been sitting. "I've just been with Amber's doctor. Called you as soon as he left. What evidence would he be giving?"

"JJ, you know I can't tell you that. Are you allowed to search Amber's house? If so, I'd suggest the bedside drawer or medicine cabinet. Oh, another call coming in. I must take it. Good luck, JJ." Denise ended the call before JJ could respond in kind.

"What's the doctor done now?" Davie asked as he returned with the drinks.

"I don't know. Was he her doctor? I assumed so, but perhaps she saw Dr Singh. Either way, they might be required to give evidence that it wasn't necessarily a murder. Denise said to check places where someone would keep medicine."

"Oh, my bet is antidepressants. If Amber was on the happy pills, it suggests depression. Most suicide victims are depressed." Davie shrugged. "That gives Evans a reason to think it wasn't murder."

"Except, of course, the hate mail. First to Amber, then Gary, and now to me. Only one way to find out if she was. I shouldn't be long." JJ checked the time as he hurried away. If he could see a light, he'd knock. If not, he'd leave it until the morning.

Davie smiled at Sharon. "He's got the bit between his teeth. Do you mind?" He held up a packet of cigarettes, took one out, and lit it on a candle.

"Yes. They'll kill you." Sharon raised her eyebrows. "But as you're not worried about that, they'll speed it up. Make your breathing more difficult sooner. I'm sure there's a list of negative things they're doing to your body."

Davie blew smoke into the air. "Yep. It's huge. But I've cut back, although more because of the cost than the effect, and I've only got one left now until my money comes in. I'll probably go over to roll-ups and smoke even less because of the hassle, but for now, I'm savouring this." He took a long drag, which caused a coughing fit. Sharon patted his back and held out a glass of water, which he pushed away when the fit had passed.

"If that's savouring it, I'd hate to see you when you were forcing yourself. Put it out, Davie. Have you tried vaping? I hear that it's recommended to help you give up."

"I'm not inhaling hundreds of chemicals that I've never heard of, not in my condition." Davie was shaking his head, a look of horror on his face. Sharon opened her mouth to counter this, but Davie dropped the cigarette onto the grass and held up his hand as he ground it out with his foot. "Say nothing. I'll make sure you're not around when I smoke this one." He tapped the pocket holding the packet. "Didn't think JJ would live with such a killjoy."

Sharon laughed. "But a healthy killjoy, Davie. A healthy one. Now we're alone, let's go back to Daniel Boyd."

"No. Google it, read the newspaper reports about it. You won't have questions then. But if you do, I'll answer them. I don't want to go there tonight."

"That bad?"

"Worse."

Sharon could feel the presence of her phone in her back pocket, and was itching to do the search, but given Davie's reluctance she would wait until he'd gone to bed. She looked up as JJ spoke.

"What is? What's worse than bumping into Connie,? I'm still chewing a wasp, Gerrard, when you're least expecting it!"

"Giving up smoking," Sharon replied quickly. "Where did you see Connie?"

"She was leaving the Wiltons' cottage. Looked like someone had smacked her arse as usual. I expect she was checking up on whether we'd dropped the tin of goodies in. Gary welcomed me like a long-lost brother. I think I rescued him by speeding up her departure. But the answer was yes, Amber was taking antidepressants. Not for long. She had started taking them when they split up. Gary threw them out when he moved back in, so they weren't hanging around, and didn't know which doctor had prescribed them. I explained why I was asking, and he said the bottle had been almost full, and that if Amber wanted to kill herself, why not sit down and take them all, why go to the bridge with someone and hope it was enough, and I said we were with him on that."

"We need to speak to that woman in the surgery. The one Amber gave two fingers to. Her and the doctor's wife. Might be worth another word with the doctor too, although I don't think he likes us much." Davie raised his arms above his head and yawned. "I'm off to bed, if there's nothing else."

They agreed they'd done as much as they could, and Davie left JJ and Sharon sitting in the semi-darkness of the flickering candles.

"Well, that was a close shave. His memory is not what it was." JJ picked up his mug of tea and drank it down in one.

"That must have been freezing. You're disgusting. And what was a close shave, not having to get into conversation with Connie?" Sharon's nose wrinkled.

"No, but yes, now you come to mention it. But Davie forgetting to pressurise me into making this investigation into more than it is."

"You're not interested?"

"Not sure. Part of me is, but then part of me isn't. That's not a way to start a new venture, is it? He wants me to buy a new printer, and an external hard drive, probably wants a flashy laptop too. I don't know, Sharon, I really don't. What do you think?"

"I think you should do what you feel is for the best because I don't mind one way or the other. You never know, I might be able to help, although that's probably going to put you off." She took hold of his hand. "I want you fulfilled and happy, whatever that takes, and I want you to go to bed at night and sleep soundly because you're content, or perhaps even knackered. I don't want you worried about anything, especially anything that gives you nightmares and has you weeping like a child but unable to share. You know I'll back you whatever.

There's no time limit, is there? Although I suppose there is for Davie, but you can't decide something like this based on someone who may not be around for long."

"I know, but perhaps it will give him something he needs. It might just be me, but I think he was like a different man today. Still got winded easily, but a bit of colour in his cheeks, a spring in his step. Not a hint of the sneaky, miserable little whatsit stalking the Wiltons I first spoke to. Perhaps he wants to do something good before he goes."

Sharon shifted in her seat. "Let me get this straight. He's not an old buddy you owe a favour to, he's a sneaky, miserable little whatsit, and you invited him to live in our home. Is that right?"

"Not quite, and yes, I think I owe him. He used to be good you know, still a pain in the arse as far as the police were concerned, but if it wasn't for him...Let's just leave it at I owe him, but is starting up as a private investigator too big a price? I know you don't know, and nor do I, and like you say, I don't need to decide immediately. I'll humour him while I get my head around it. Let's take a few days to sleep on it."

"That sounds like a plan. Let's sleep on it now. Come on." Blowing out the candles, Sharon got to her feet. "We can clear this lot up tomorrow."

"I'll do it. You go on. If I go to sleep now, I'll be awake at four." JJ took her hand and pulled her in close. His kiss was deep and heartfelt. "You're a wonderful woman. Do you know that?"

Sharon pecked the end of his nose. "I do, yes. Don't be too long."

Chapter Thirteen

SHARON PUT HER PHONE on the table. "Dr Bentley is covering surgery this morning, but only until twelve-thirty. If you want to speak to him, that would be a good time to do so. You never know your luck, Kerry Snell might be working too."

JJ checked the time. "I also want to speak to Sandy Bentley, and if he's working this morning, she might be more inclined to speak while he's out. Are you coming?" JJ called to Davie, who was in the room now referred to as the office.

Davie appeared in the kitchen. "I am. Like I said, I reckon it was a woman, and it might be her. I want to look her in the eye. We can hang around at the surgery after."

"A plan in the making. But before you go swanning off, you have a choice, shopping or bed changing. Neither will do themselves, and I'm not doing both."

"Nor would we expect you to, but I always forget something, so I'll take the—"

"Shopping. You bump into people shopping. My chest won't cope with changing beds. Have you tried stuffing a duvet back into a cover? It's hard work. What do you need, Sharon? I have an excellent memory."

"I have a list. Here you go. Where there's a question mark, it means whatever you fancy or whatever is on offer. Child's play."

They made it as far as the door, before Sharon yelled, "Bags!"

JJ went to the cupboard under the stairs and wrestled some shopping bags out from behind the vacuum.

The Bentleys lived in a substantial home on the outskirts of the village, formed post-war when two cottages were knocked into one, and it looked picture-perfect with a climbing yellow rose around the door, and a white picket fence protecting it from the road. To the right-hand side, an area of garden had been cleared to create a driveway. A small red Fiat sat there, but there was no sign of the doctor's Volvo.

"It looks perfect, doesn't it?" Davie observed as JJ pulled in next to the Fiat. "If only houses could speak, I'm sure that one has a few tales to tell. Especially at the moment. Oh, we've been noticed."

Although the cottage had a crazy-paved path running up the centre of the garden to the front door, a second door at the side gave access to the drive. The door had opened, and Sandy Bentley stood looking at them. JJ raised a hand in greeting.

Sandy was a plain-looking woman, tall and slim, she wore a white shirt neatly tucked into a blue skirt. Her shoes were flat, black ballet pumps.

"Well, she's the polar opposite of Amber. Looks like she's been crying. This might not take long," Davie commented as he climbed out of the car. JJ ignored him and gave another wave as he approached her.

"Good morning, Mrs Bentley. Might we have a word?"

"Nothing good about it. I thought you might turn up. Come on in, but if it saves you the bother I didn't kill Amber Wilton." Despite her words, Sandy Bentley turned her back on the men and went into the kitchen. They followed her. "Ask away. I've got things to do. You're not the police, so I might choose not to answer. That said, I've done nothing wrong, so I've nothing to hide, other than from the gossips, of course, so gloat away."

"We're not here to gloat. Far from it. Would you mind?" Davie pulled out a chair at the small, round kitchen table, and sat down. "We know you're the wronged party," he continued. "And we don't think you killed Amber. But Gary Wilton has employed us to do a job and we need to do it properly, and that means eliminating suspects, of which, for obvious reasons, you are one. Ask JJ. He used to be a police officer, but I expect you know that."

JJ was still getting used to Davie's bull at a gate way of addressing things, and sighing, he joined Davie at the table. "He's right. Both you and Dr Bentley will be suspects. We aren't here to make your life more difficult, more to get a full picture of what was going on in Amber's life, so that when we give our findings to the police, they won't waste time bothering the wrong people. I thought your husband would have explained that." JJ's brow furrowed. "You know we spoke to Doctor Bentley, don't you? That is why you were expecting us?"

"I do. Why did Mr Wilton employ you? Why aren't the police knocking at my door?" Sandy Bentley didn't join them at the table. Instead, she leaned against the sink, her arms folded across her chest.

"They thought it was more likely to have been an accident than murder. I have photographic evidence that suggests otherwise," JJ explained. "Gary wants justice to be done, and I'm sure the police will step up their game now that threatening letters have been discovered, but speed is of the essence in these matters, as I'm sure you'll appreciate."

Sandy nodded acceptance, but didn't speak, so JJ carried on.

"So the first question we need you to answer is where you went after the Bums and Tums exercise class? Your husband couldn't answer that, as he'd been called out."

"I went to see Mrs Wilcox. Stayed until just before nine. Then I came home. Stephen wasn't here, so I showered and went to bed. I'm sure you'll want to check that. She lives in Rhododendron Cottage, on the bend."

"You didn't go for drinks with the girls first?" JJ asked. "I understand there was a birthday."

"Don't be ridiculous. It was bad enough that the woman was there. She hadn't been for weeks, but then she probably had been meeting someone else's husband instead. I certainly wasn't going to socialise with her."

Davie nodded. "And I don't blame you. I've been on the wrong end of a cheating spouse. It's nauseating what you have to put up with. I don't think people realise. What time did the doctor get in?"

"I don't know. You'd have to ask him."

"Will do. What was the row in the supermarket about? A couple of weeks ago, you stormed off, leaving your shopping behind."

"God, I hate this village. They make up what they don't know. There was no row. No shouting, no pushing, no shoving, no embarrassment, except, of course, there was. Someone was watching and judging. Who was it?"

"Honestly, we don't know. Someone's cleaner was told about it and shared it on. You know how gossip works. I don't get village life either. I'd rather be in a town. So, no words were exchanged? You just shot off to avoid the embarrassment, did you?" Davie asked.

"Ran away with my tail between my legs, you mean? No, I did not. But nor was I going to stand there and have a whispered conversation about my husband." Sandy Bentley's fists had clenched, and she stamped her foot. "If you have lived through this, you'll understand why I didn't think the local hippy chick knew more about my husband than I did." She trained her eyes on Davie, who agreed.

"What did she say? You didn't understand his needs, you didn't appreciate the stress he was under?" Davie asked.

"Something like that. I won't discuss it. Of course, I'm sorry she was killed. Actually, that's not true. I'm glad she's gone. I'd have preferred she or we simply moved away, but that's not what happened. So yes, my life is easier now she's gone, but I didn't kill her."

"Would you have moved if the doctor had wanted to? Or did you suggest it?" JJ asked.

"Yes, and yes. Like a shot, but this is where Stephen's work is. He's looking for another position, probably a little harder now he knows everyone is talking about him. My husband has many qualities but being brave isn't one of them," Sandy replied.

"Are you content that their relationship was over?" JJ watched her closely. He hoped to see any sign that she was lying.

"As much as one can be, yes. I mean I didn't know it had started because I trusted him completely. I won't be so stupid in the future." Sandy stepped away from the sink. "Look, is there anything else that you can ask that will convince you of my innocence and not give the impression you're simply collecting gossip?"

JJ got to his feet. "We're not collecting gossip, and we'll leave now. But for what it's worth, if you're going to build a healthy relationship, you'll need to trust him again. Otherwise, life will be miserable for both of you."

"Are you an expert on relationships too? I've got to like him again first before I can trust him. Goodbye. Be careful reversing out, it's difficult to see oncoming traffic."

"How long do you give them?" JJ looked at Davie as he started the engine.

"About two years. They're both too stupid to sort it out before then. It's only eleven. Let's get the shopping done out of the way. I'll push the trolley you can zig-zag about."

JJ rolled his eyes, and a few minutes later parked as close as he could get to the large supermarket on the outskirts of town. He passed Davie a pound coin. "You'll need that for the trolley."

Trolley collected, Davie unfolded the list. "There's a lot of veg on here. Which way is that?"

"That way I think. I don't come here often. Oh, look. That answers one of our questions." JJ jerked this thumb towards the first aisle where Kerry Snell was reading the label on a jar. They watched her shake her head as she replaced it before walking further down the aisle.

"Home baking. We've got eggs and sugar on this list. Let's go." Davie set off to follow Kerry Snell. "With any luck, we'll have a trolley clash. There are the eggs. One dozen, free range." He flipped the shopping list to the left and kept moving. "Quickly, we don't want to lose her." His eyes scanned the shelves, and a bag of flour was in the trolly by the time JJ had caught up with him.

"Loaf of bread and some biscuits," Davie told him. "Make it two packets. You two get through a lot of bread and biscuits. I'll be in international foods."

Davie steered his trolley around an elderly lady, leaving JJ to collect the items. Biscuits chosen, JJ picked up a large sliced wholemeal and set off to find Davie. He wasn't in international foods, so JJ walked the central aisle, looking left and right until he found Davie in sauces and pickles, talking to Kerry Snell while waving a bottle of ketchup at her.

"... because I just haven't got the strength these days. Whoever invented the squeezy bottle deserves a medal. JJ, grab a jar of pickled onions. Those pies look good. Have you had them before?" Davie pointed at the pack of pies sitting in the child's seat on Kerry's trolley.

"They are. Fresh and as close to homemade as you'll get without doing it yourself. They get them from the farm shop. But if you're buying meat, go there. It's more expensive, but their meat is beautiful."

"Thanks, Kerry, I'll make it the next stop, well, after we've spoken to the doc again, anyway. I'm doing Sunday lunch. My mouth's watering at the thought of a nice leg of roast lamb."

"Hello, JJ. Dr Bentley, again? I didn't realise you'd spoken to him. I hope everything is alright. It is, isn't it?"

"Hello, Kerry. We got the short straw, or I should say Davie chose it. I'd have rather changed the beds. As for Dr Bentley, I hope you're not fishing. Difficult to say anything without knowing what you already know. We're investigating a murder, not after gossip."

"I heard Gary Wilton had called you in. But surely you don't think it's Steve, do you?"

"What do you know about Steve and Amber? If I know that, I might tell you more. It would be wrong to gossip about either of them."

"I blame myself." Kerry stepped closer and lowered her voice, "Do you know I met the current hubby via a dating website? So, when anyone is bemoaning being single, or lonely, I tell them to get online. That was fine for Amber, although some of her choices were a little unwise in my opinion, but not for Steve. He was married, for goodness' sake. I don't hold with that. I know Sandy is a challenge at home, but that's no excuse. Like I told him, if he wasn't happy with her, he should have told her, not gone pretending he was something he's not online. Silly man."

"You spoke to him about it? Are you close? Mind you, with trouble at home, and you being his senior member of staff, I'm sure he valued your opinion," Davie said.

"You'd have thought so, wouldn't you? Neither of them wanted my opinion. I told them it would lead to trouble and tears, but they both told me to keep my nose out. Well, not in those words, but I got the message."

"It must have been awful for you, having to keep their secret when you didn't approve."

"Is that what the argument was about?" JJ asked.

"Which one? There were many." Kerry raised her eyebrows.

"Amber gave you the V sign in the street. The lady who saw, said she was shocked as you'd seemed such close friends." Davie tutted. "You were right, Kerry. Nothing but trouble and tears."

Kerry was frowning, trying to recall the incident. "Was this recently?"

"In the last couple of weeks, we were told," JJ replied.

"Ah, that would have been about Gary. I don't know how much Gary has told you, but as he's paying you to look into his business, I doubt it will matter. Gary wanted Amber to take him back. She'd had her fun with the dating site, and I think she was going to. Rightly so, in my opinion. Then Steve tells her it's him she's talking to online, and they start an affair. Two weeks it took her to tell me, so I gave them both my opinion and backed off. Then when it all hit the fan, and Steve called it off, she was distraught. She really did like him and believed him when he said they had a future together. But once that wasn't on the cards, she told me, on the day you're talking about, that she was going to take Gary back. She was going to date him for a couple of weeks and then let him come home."

"I'm not sure he knew that. He hoped it was what would happen, but he didn't know that was the plan."

"She wouldn't have told him. It was a test to see how serious he was, or if he, too, was after the easy option."

"So what happened, between you two, I mean?" JJ asked.

"I told her she was being selfish. That she should only take Gary back if she was sure she was over Steve, and that if she wasn't, she was messing him about. She reminded me he'd done a lot of messing about himself, and he was big enough and ugly enough to fight his own battles. Which, when you get down to brass tacks, is true. But Amber didn't like what she saw as my interference and demonstrated that, which is what your informant saw. Only lasted a couple of hours. I went round to see her that night. Not that I apologised. I was right. But you don't let too much water flow under the bridge, do you?"

"No, very wise. I'm glad you made up before she was killed. I didn't know Gary had messed about."

"Only the once, and it lasted all of two minutes, but it's enough to cause ructions, isn't it? I thought he'd meet someone else, and Amber would regret not sorting out their marital problems. When she started seeing Steve, I told her as much. But she said as far as she knew Gary was seeing someone, and that was fine, as he was a free agent too. My retort was unlike Stephen Bentley, and she laughed and said not for long. People are unnecessarily stupid sometimes, don't you think?"

"I do. Since our last chat, Gary has asked me to investigate who killed Amber. Can you think of anyone who might have held a grudge against Amber, or would have wanted her out of the way?" JJ asked.

"Oh no. Not Steve and I'm sure not Sandy. Steve would never hurt a fly, and I got the impression he was fond of Amber. Sandy never, look at the attention the affair has brought. Sandy doesn't like undue attention."

Kerry was waving her finger, and for a moment JJ thought she was going to bring the conversation to an end, so he jumped in, taking a leaf from Davie's book, and agreed with her.

"Exactly what I thought. Can you talk me through what happened on the night she died? I understand you went to Bums and Tums with her, and then on to the Three Bells for a drink."

"I can, but not now, I'm afraid. Got an appointment at twelve-thirty, and I've not finished shopping yet. Would you like me to pop up and see you later? I know where you live."

"Yes, of course. What sort of time? I'll make sure I'm back."

They agreed on four o'clock and went their separate ways. As Davie pushed the trolley into the next aisle, he summed up his thoughts.

"She's very protective of the doc, but I agree with her. He's a bit wet. I doubt he's got it in him. Good that she's coming to see us, though. Also, was Gary Wilton the cause of their breakup, and did you know he was playing the field too? You didn't mention it. Toilet rolls, jumbo pack." Davie jerked his thumb at the display and consulted the list again.

"But you wouldn't necessarily need to have anything *'in'* you, would you?" JJ placed the pack in the trolley. "I doubt it was premeditated. If you were planning on killing someone, pushing them off that bridge wouldn't be near the top of the list. She might have landed on her arse, not her head. We could be looking at manslaughter. And that being the case, getting irritated and lashing out is possible, even for the weakest of men."

"Yet you've been calling it murder since you clicked that thing." Davie looked at the camera hanging from JJ's neck. "You can get little ones, you know. Ones you can slide into your pocket."

"I do know. Got two. I like this one. What's next?"

They finished the shopping, and with twenty minutes to spare headed for the surgery. The doctor was with his final patient, and they took a seat in the empty waiting room. Bentley looked irritated to see them as he showed the patient out.

"So, give me a ring next week, Mr Jones. Let me know how you're getting on." Turning to JJ, he added, "I've said all I can. There's nothing to add."

"Oh, but there is. It won't take long. And better us than the police." Davie stood up and walked to the doctor. He glanced at the receptionist. "But not out here, aye?"

The receptionist raised her eyebrows as they followed Bentley through to his consulting room. He turned to face them, not offering a seat.

"What?"

"Were you prescribing Amber Wilton antidepressants? Don't come the patient confidentiality thing, she won't sue, and her husband wants us to get to the bottom of it. This might be the reason for her death, as far as the police are concerned, so it's important." JJ perched on the edge of the examination table.

"I'm not following." Bentley pushed his hair from his forehead. "What do you mean, the reason?"

"Nor are you answering the question, doc. Did you prescribe them or not? How depressed was she, how many was she taking? You must know the drill."

"Yes, I did. She was finding it hard to focus and keep on top of things when she split up from her husband. It was a mild tranquilliser, a low dose, which she found helpful."

"So she wasn't depressed enough to kill herself?" Davie asked bluntly.

"No!" Bentley was shocked at the suggestion. "Who is saying that? Amber wasn't depressed. She was a live wire, possibly on the autistic spectrum. She took them to keep calm. To help her remain focused. Look, ask Dr Singh, he took over prescribing once...once it became necessary. I don't even think she took them daily. I can check her records if you like."

JJ asked him to do that. The doctor hadn't meant there and then, but JJ didn't want to chase him. Who knew when Evans would appear asking the same questions? Bentley sat at his desk and called up Amber's record. He pointed at the screen.

"There, her last prescription was for sixty pills, issued three months ago. I don't know when she collected them, of course. The pharmacist will have to confirm that. But the prescription is one a day. She'd not requested a further supply, which indicates she wasn't reliant on them." Bentley tapped a button, and the screen went blank. "Was there anything else?"

"No. Thank you for your time. We'll leave you to it." JJ walked to the door, which had remained open, and pushed Davie forward. "If you think of anything which may help, please call. Oh, and you have been stupid, that goes without saying, but for what it's worth I hope you sort things out with your wife."

Bentley nodded, and JJ pulled the door closed.

"That's another thing we need to think about adding to the list." Davie said as they made their way back to the car.

"What's that?"

"Business cards."

"Already on there." JJ slammed the door.

"Just checking." Davie grinned and fastened his seatbelt.

Back at the cottage, JJ opened the boot of the car and handed Davie his keys. "You open up. I'll carry this lot in. You can manage these." He passed Davie the pack of toilet rolls.

Davie left the gate open, and placing the pack on the doorstep, attempted to open the door. "It won't open," he told JJ, who was heading towards him with a bag in each hand.

"Why not? Try again."

Davie turned the key again and shook his head.

"Two secs," Sharon called from inside, and the two men listened to the bolt sliding back. "We've had visitors." Sharon pointed at her car. It listed to one side as the tyres were flat. "There was a card under the windscreen. I'm sorry but I was so mad I've touched it."

"And it worried you enough to bolt the door in the middle of the day?" JJ stepped into the house, and leaving the bags in the hall, said, "Show me."

Sharon had laid the card out on the table. The envelope had been torn open roughly and the last two letters of her name separated.

"Whoever this is, JJ, knows us well enough to know my name."

"That's not necessarily true," Davie said. "People would volunteer that information without being asked. People round here couldn't keep a secret if they tried, and there'd be no reason to think your name was a secret. What did it say?"

"Not much." Sharon opened the card.

STOP HIM BEFORE I DO!

"I've put it off long enough, I'm calling Evans. Sharon, love, I'm not saying this to make you feel better, but these things are almost always a bluff. Whoever it is, they fear being caught. They think this might help because it's personal. But what if I was still a copper? I couldn't stop investigating, so they'd say something like, I'll do it again. And even with that threat, we'd have to keep on looking. I don't think either of us is in danger, but if you want me to stop, I'll stop. If you want me to bolt the doors, I will. I'm just telling you it's probably nothing to worry about."

"If that's the case, then why are you calling Evans?" Sharon's hands were on her hips.

"Because it means he has to do something. We need him to do something. Fingerprint these cards for one thing. Amber's killer needs to be caught. It really is that simple."

"Right, but I want to be there when you hand them over," Sharon replied.

"Okay, but why?"

"Because if I don't think he's taking this seriously, you will not be giving anything to him."

"Well, I'm glad that's settled. Shall I get the rest of the shopping in? Because we've got work to do, JJ, Evans will never convince her." Whistling, Davie headed back to the car.

Chapter Fourteen

Evans watched Rachel Sampson slide the cards into the evidence bag.

"We'll get them off to lab for printing, but I doubt we'll get anything."

JJ could see he wanted to say more. "Thank you, and you'll let me know the results as soon as?"

"Yep."

"How's your investigation going?" JJ asked.

"Slowly."

"Why's that? Amber's nearest and dearest have been very talkative with us. All are very keen to get her killer caught. What did you think of Mrs Bentley?"

"Mrs...JJ, you know I can't share the detail of an ongoing investigation with you. I'm sure you'll know as soon as we know. We'll be off. Have a good afternoon. We'll see ourselves out."

Evans hadn't reached the door before Davie said loud enough for him to hear. "He didn't know who she was. He was going to say Mrs Who. What a waste of space he is. No wonder Gary Wilton employed you to see that justice was done."

Evans' step didn't falter, but he slammed the door behind him.

"That wasn't necessary," JJ said. "We need them to help."

"JJ, do you know you're too nice for your own good sometimes? He's never going to help you. Davie is right. And perhaps a few home truths might help shove him in the right direction. Don't give up on this, JJ. But humour me, and let's bolt the doors at night."

"If you're sure, then there's no time like the present. Davie, who else do we need to speak to?"

Davie walked into their office and looked at the sheet pinned to the wall. "Sara Dent, Jo Harris, Kerry Snell, and anyone else who saw her that night. It's a shame the Three Bells doesn't have cameras."

"No time to do any of that before Kerry comes, but once she's been, we're off to the builder's merchants. I want a camera on that front door and on the Wiltons'." JJ looked into the hall as the doorbell sang out. "Perhaps she's early. That would be a stroke of luck."

Sharon went to answer the door and JJ and Davie exchanged glances when they heard Gary's voice. He stepped into the kitchen.

"I saw him leave. Did he tell you, JJ?" Gary asked.

"He said very little. What in particular?" JJ pulled out a chair and invite Gary to sit.

"They are officially treating it as a murder investigation, and I can arrange for Amber to be collected by the undertakers. Do I need to do that immediately?"

"Good news. It doesn't need to be today. I'm sure Monday will be soon enough."

"Which reminds me, JJ," said Sharon. "I spoke to Lynn while you were out. I was explaining what you were doing, and why, and she recommended Jackson and Son in the precinct. That's who arranged your dad's funeral. They were very good. So that's someone you can think about, Gary." Sharon patted his arm. "Tea?"

"No, I don't think I could drink another cup. I'll call in on Monday. So, how's everything else going?"

JJ took the seat opposite, and gave Gary an abridged version of Amber's involvements, ending with what Kerry Snell had told them.

"So, she'd decided that if dating you worked out, she wanted you back." JJ returned Gary's smile. "But up to that point, she might have stepped on a few toes. While we're putting cards on the table, we're told that when Amber was warned that by messing about with the doctor she might lose you, she implied that not only were you not innocent in that department, having stepped out on her while you were together, but also she thought you were seeing someone recently, despite saying you wanted to come back to her. You don't have to tell us, but it might shed light on other matters arising."

Sharon could see Gary was embarrassed and busied herself loading the dishwasher. Davie wasn't so sensitive and leaned forward, crossing his arms on the table.

"I was a fool. It was something and nothing and already over when Amber found out. She tried to work through it, but it was hard for her, so I offered to move out and give her some space. I suppose she needed to sow some oats before she knew whether she wanted me back or not. Who knows? The lady in question thought that meant I was on the market, but we didn't see each other again. Not romantically. I took her to dinner and explained." Gary flipped his hand. "Amber knew nothing about it. How could she? Nothing to do with this, I'm sure." Rubbing the palms of his hands into his jeans, Gary got to his feet. "I'd better get back. We promised Luke we'd take him into Bristol for some new trainers. Apparently, Velcro is for babies. Anything to keep him occupied."

With a sudden movement, Gary pulled something from his back pocket and handed it to Davie.

"There you go. I don't know how much it will be but let me know when you want more." Gary turned and almost ran down the hall. "I'll let myself out."

Davie opened the envelope and counted the money. "One thousand smackeroos. We need to discuss our daily rate, JJ."

"We also need to discuss if there *is* a daily rate." JJ watched Davie divide the money. He ignored the five hundred pounds Davie pushed across the table.

"Fifty-fifty. I reckon that's fair. I've done most of the legwork so far, but you supplied the office." Davie counted off another two hundred pounds from his wad. "And you'll need some housekeeping." He handed Sharon two hundred pounds. "Not sure how much that will cover, but I want to pay my way. Especially now I'm earning my living. Shall we go to the Italian tonight? To cement all these new relationships? Don't worry, we can go Dutch. I've got money. That bloody bell. When we go to get the cameras, which I think is a good idea, we're buying a new one."

"You won't," Sharon told him when JJ went to answer the door. "His dad loved it. He won't change it. Please don't try to make him."

"Enough said. Hello, Kerry, come and take a pew. You've been to the hair salon, it looks nice. I like the colour."

"There's a breakdown truck outside. I'm guessing it's for you, Sharon." Kerry jerked her thumb outside. "JJ's sorting him out. Trouble?"

"Pranksters," Davie answered. "Here comes JJ, sit down, let's get started."

Kerry took a seat, a pot of tea was made, and JJ asked her to run through the hours before Amber's death, giving as much detail as she could remember.

"Everything, Kerry. You might think it inconsequential, but it could help point us in the right direction."

Kerry sipped her tea and cast her mind back to that fateful Tuesday, and placing her mug back on the table, started where she thought it had begun.

"Oh, hi, Amber, what can we do for you?" Jackie, the receptionist at the surgery, smiled as she spoke, but gasped as Kerry Snell rushed over and put the call on hold.

"Sorry, Jackie, I need to speak to her. I'll pick it up over there." Kerry pointed to the desk in the corner of the admin room. Snatching up the phone, she waited for Jackie to transfer the call. "Amber, it's Kerry. What do you need?"

"You, actually. It's Bums and Tums tonight, so I had two questions. Are you going? Is Sandy Bentley still going? And do you think I should go?"

"That's three questions, but yes, she has been going. Yes, I will be and you can't hide forever, but only come if it's over. I mean that, Amber. You can't socialise, or I suppose more accurately, exercise with the woman if it's not finished."

"Jesus, Kerry, I've told you it's over. I'm dating Gary." Amber giggled. "Sounds weird saying that. Right, I'll come to you before. See you at half six."

As always, Amber was running late, and it was six forty-five when Kerry opened her front door, and immediately turned her to face the other direction.

"I don't think you've been on time for anything in your life. Get a move on. Glenda said she's starting at seven sharp because she's fed up with hanging around for stragglers. Did you bring a change of clothes?" Kerry eyed Amber's kit bag. "A proper change, I mean. It's Amy's birthday. We're going to the Three Bells for a drink with her."

"Not specifically, no. But what I have will do for the Three Bells. How are things at work? Slow down a bit. I've only got short legs." Amber hurried to catch up with Kerry.

"I won't be late. If you're really asking is Steve moping about because he no longer has you chasing after him, the answer is no, not that I've noticed. Other than that, same as usual. The supplies for the clinic were not only late, loads of stuff was missing. The printer had a jam none of us could reach, so we're waiting for an engineer. Oh, you've stopped listening. How's Gary?"

"He's okay. Very keen, more so than before we got married. He's coming round on Friday to help me choose which paintings to use for the exhibition. Did I tell you I was invited to the castle exhibition? Yes? So bloody excited. My other stuff is selling well too. I've just had to put an order in to the printer. My winter flora cards are selling like hot cakes."

"That's because they're lovely. Sounds to me like all is well with the world for you. Don't mess it up, love."

"Agreed. Been a bumpy, although in some ways entertaining year, but the stars have aligned, and everything is falling into place. I promise to be good." Amber licked her finger and crossed her heart.

"Don't make promises you can't keep. And stars aligning? I'm a Capricorn. You get out what you put in for the best part. Get a grip." Kerry pushed open the double doors leading to the entrance to the school. She gave a wave to a cleaner as the muffled sound of an amplified voice reached them. "Bugger, they've started. We'll have to dump our bags in the corner."

"Ladies." Connie Gerrard appeared at the door of her office.

"Evening, Miss Gerrard. Can't stop, we're late. My fault," Amber called.

Bags dumped, they made their way to the back of the class. Amber made a point of not looking at anyone, but Kerry waved to Sandy Bentley, who gave a curt nod, before she began jogging on the spot.

At the end of the class, they lay on padded mats to wind down. Amber rolled over to look at Kerry as the sound of crashing waves filled the gym, and the instructor used a soothing voice to tell them how to breathe.

"Blimey, I'm out of shape. That was hard. The exercise was bad enough without her glancing over every five minutes."

"Shut up, I'm relaxing. Anyway, she wasn't, and even if she was, suck it up. You're a big girl."

Amber clasped a breast in each hand and grinned. "I am, and I shall, oh wise one."

In the changing room, everyone going to the pub freshened up, mainly with wet wipes and copious amounts of deodorant because of the lack of shower facilities. Amber and Kerry found themselves alone.

"I'm glad Sandy Bentley isn't going to the pub. I might have given it a miss. Her eyes follow me." Amber pulled a colourful stripy top over her head.

"They don't, and even if they did, can you blame her? She's checking out who caused her husband to fall off the straight and narrow. I still can't believe Steve did that. Anyway, that's the past. Let's get to the pub. I've burned off enough calories to deserve a drink or two."

The two women left the changing room and headed for the exit. Kerry stopped halfway there.

"I left my ring on the sink. He'd never forgive me. I'll be two seconds."

Connie Gerrard was standing by the door, keys in hand.

"Be quick, I'm locking up, the caretaker is visiting his mum in hospital."

Kerry ran back into the changing room, almost colliding with Jo Harris.

"Oh, I thought we were the last. Miss Gerrard is locking up. I'd better hurry or I'll get a detention," Kerry joked as she collected her ring.

They found Amber standing outside with Connie.

"Are you coming to the pub with us, Miss Gerrard?" Jo Harris asked.

"Afraid not, Mrs Harris. Got some errands to run. No peace for the wicked." Connie smiled as she pushed the door shut and inserted the key. Pulling her phone from her pocket, she set the alarm. "Technology. Don't you just love it. I used to have to push buttons, close doors and run for it."

The four women walked as far as the carpark together, where Connie left them and headed for the solitary car. She waved her keys at them.

"See you later. Have fun."

The three women chorused "'Bye, Miss Gerrard", as though they were pupils.

The Three Bells was lively, and once the birthday party had imbibed their first drink, a little rowdy. Old Sam grumbled he couldn't hear the television, but other than that, everyone enjoyed themselves.

One of the school mums, Shelly, waved goodbye to Jo and moved around the table to sit with Amber and Kerry.

"Alright girls? Wish her birthday had been on a Friday. I'm going to have to go in a minute, too."

Amber checked the time. "Me too. Did your mum like her painting?"

"Ah, she loved it, Amber. Said it was the best birthday present she'd had. She also told me I was conceived near that bench. They had a shotgun wedding, but it's their fortieth anniversary soon, so all's well etcetera. I told her that was too much information. She should keep her love life a secret. Talking of which, how are you doing in that department?"

"I'm not listening to this. Far too sordid for my ears." Standing up, and collecting her glass, Kerry gave Amber a warning glance before asking, "Who wants another drink?"

Taking their orders, Kerry went to the bar. When she returned with the drinks, Amber gulped hers down. "That's it. I've got to go. See you soon, ladies."

Sara Dent wandered over. "Are you leaving too, Amber? Blimey, you lot have got no staying power. It's not even nine yet."

"Things to do, people to see. Don't forget to check my site if you're looking for a present for your parents. I've got some new stuff on there. Or come to the castle. I'm exhibiting, don't you know? 'Bye, ladies."

"And with that, she was gone. I wish I'd asked her if she did have someone to see, but it's just what you say, isn't it?"

"It is. Yes." Sharon made a sad face. "No one could have known, Kerry."

"Did you notice anyone else leave after?" Davie asked.

"No, but I wasn't looking. I drank my drink and walked back down to the village with Jo about twenty minutes later. We left Sara there with a couple of other stragglers. Even the birthday girl had gone."

"So you left about twenty past nine. Did you see who else was still in the pub?" JJ asked. "Whoever was there couldn't have killed her. Not enough time to get ahead of me."

"I wasn't taking any notice, not really, but I know Jemma and Sara were there, and Harry Brown was sitting at the bar with Sam. There were two young lads on the slot machine. Oh, and you were sitting outside, JJ. And there was a couple out there as well, don't know who they were." Kerry fiddled with her cup before shaking her head. "I can't remember anyone else. Jemma came outside for a ciggy and we left. It was cold. I remember that. It had been so hot all day, but the wind had picked up, must have been a northerly. I've not been much help, have I?"

"Yes. We now have a few we can eliminate. You've confirmed that Amber was trouble-free when she left the pub. And maybe, somewhere in what you have told us is a clue to what happened that night, we simply don't know it yet."

"I hope so. I really do. Must dash now, though. Hubby is taking me out tonight, not that I feel like going, but life goes on."

JJ showed her out, and when he returned, Sharon and Davie were deep in conversation.

"What are you two whispering about? Are you okay, Sharon? You look pale."

"No makeup. We're not whispering. I was just asking if you'd confirmed Sandy Bentley's alibi. She knew where Amber was going. She could easily have hung around out of sight. Might not even have been hiding. After all, you said it might have been a spur-of-the-moment thing. Perhaps she wanted to talk to her, not kill her, and that pushing her was a reaction to something Amber said. That or she did intend to kill her, but Amber climbing up on the parapet made it easier. What's next?"

"I think Sharon is hooked, JJ. She'll be wanting a cut of the profit next." Davie opened the tin of biscuits and lifted one out. "Next on the agenda is the builder's merchants for the cameras. Are we going out for a meal? It is Saturday, after all. And, if we are, have we got time to check out the Bentleys' alibis? His needs checking too."

"I think we should go out. It's not five o'clock yet. JJ go and shower and then go to get what you want. While you're gone, Davie and I will get ready, you come back and pick us up, then you can do your alibi checking, and we'll go for a meal. It's a while since we've been out. I'll book a table."

"What about getting the cameras up?" JJ was already walking towards the stairs. "I suppose tomorrow will be soon enough."

JJ knew Sharon was avoiding being left in the house on her own. The cameras needed to go up immediately, but if keeping busy made her feel better, then that's what they would do, he hoped they wouldn't miss anything by waiting until the next morning.

Sharon waited until she could hear water running before returning to the conversation interrupted by JJ.

"And JJ found him. Dear God, Davie, no wonder he has nightmares. That poor man. Add to that what he saw in Africa, and I'm surprised he can still function. The report I read said that the suspect, Jenkins, walked away free because of a police error. Please tell me that wasn't JJ's fault."

"Are you kidding? No. JJ didn't cut corners. He gave the copper who cocked up a slap, and then he just sort of collapsed. The other coppers who were in the pub took the other bloke home. Imagine how he felt. JJ ordered another drink. Both of them left the force because of it. But JJ...Oh, he's out. Let's leave it at he almost drank himself to death, and having sat through the court case, I joined him. But I got us home, and I stayed with him until he could manage himself. It wasn't pretty."

Sharon glanced at the ceiling as JJ moved about.

"Things are making sense now. He doesn't talk about anything much before his dad's funeral. That's how I met him. Not at the funeral, in the graveyard the next day." Sharon fell silent for a while. "I never knew."

"He's coming. Don't go all soppy on him or he'll know something's up and blame me."

Chapter Fifteen

JJ LEFT THE NEWLY purchased cameras on the table, and double checked that all the windows and doors were locked. Dressed in a striped, short-sleeved shirt and jeans, which had frayed a little at the bottom of one leg, he looked the other two up and down.

"You two look very smart, I must say. You're not up to something, are you? No surprise party or the like. I don't like surprises."

Davie slapped his shoulder. "Some of us have higher standards, old boy. Can we get going now you've checked Fort Knox? I'm starving and there are alibis to confirm."

"Says the man who was sleeping in a car. Come on."

Five minutes later, they pulled up outside the Jacksons' house. A row of cards had been arranged on the front windowsill.

"She had another boy. That's four now. Jake is in my class, so if you don't mind, I'm going to stay in the car and not get dragged into it. Mr Jackson is home. That's his car in front."

Davie also opted to stay in the car, and they watched JJ knock on the door. A small boy opened it and disappeared, to be replaced by Mr Jackson. The two men had a brief conversation before JJ was invited inside.

"Oh boy. This might take a while. What time did you book the table for?" Davie opened the glove compartment and rummaged around. "Nothing edible in this car. Not even a packet of mints."

"Eight. And JJ doesn't snack. Not even a bag of popcorn to watch a film. He might have a starter, but he won't have a pudding." Sharon stretched her hand forward and handed Davie a small bar of chocolate. "Emergency supplies."

"Ta. Why's that then? Is he watching his figure? He's in good shape for a bloke of his age, so it's working."

"No. He's weird. He has no interest in food at all. It's simply something he has to do to stay alive. Fuel. He's not fussy about carbs, or sugar, although given a choice he'll lean towards healthy eating, but he has breakfast, lunch, although he sometimes forgets that, and dinner." Sharon tapped Davie's shoulder. "That didn't take long."

JJ climbed into the car. "Not conclusive. Neither of them took that much notice of the time. They called the doctor out before eight, they know that because *Eastenders* hadn't finished, he arrived about fifteen minutes later. He examined her, and they were discussing the options when her water broke. She insisted hubby clear it up. Then they had to wait for her sister to arrive to look after the other kids. By this time she was in full labour and Bentley insisted she wait for an ambulance, and he stayed to wait with them just in case. They didn't keep track of the time. Their best guess was it was somewhere between nine and ten. The baby was born at ten forty-five. The only way to clarify that is to check with the ambulance service. I'll have to get Evans onto it, I suppose. If it's not him, I feel sorry for the doctor. Gossip about his whereabouts being questioned will fly around."

"Don't feel sorry for him. Remember why he's a suspect. Let's go and find out if Sandy is in the clear. Davie is hungry."

As they approached Rhododendron Cottage, the door opened, and Rachel Sampson stepped onto the doorstep. JJ bumped the car up onto the grass verge behind the other car parked there, guessing it was Rachel's. As she approached, he got out of the car.

"Evening, Rach. Evans not with you?"

"No, thank goodness. Bear with a sore head. To be fair, we are up against it at the moment. Still, every cloud, I'm on time and a half for this shift. You've certainly been busy, JJ. Dare I ask how it's going? Oh, hello." Rachel smiled at Davie as he got out of the car, narrowly missing her with the door.

Davie held out his hand. "Davie, nice to meet you. I'm JJ's partner."

"Oh, so you're to blame, too. Just passing?" Rachel raised her eyebrows as a smile played around her lips.

JJ laughed. "No. Here to confirm Sandy Bentley's alibi for the night Amber was killed."

"Then you won't get it here. I never told you this, but it will save disturbing Mrs Wilcox again. Mrs Bentley arrived a little after *Eastenders* finished and left before nine because Mrs W was in bed by nine. She watches her detective series in bed. She can't say exactly what time. It could have been five minutes before, could have been half eight. They had a chat and a cup of tea. Mrs Bentley sorted out an issue with the energy company, and then she left. Mrs W washed up the cups, put the dog out for a pee, then they went to bed." Rachel shrugged. "Not conclusive."

"Same as her husband's then. How did you find out about the affair?"

"Come on, JJ. Evans would have me for sharing that. We have Amber's phone, remember?"

"Of course. I'm rusty, forgive me. Would that be texts to the doctor or to Sandy Bentley?" JJ leaned against the wing of his car. "We've seen the exchanges on the dating website, so I'm guessing the latter."

"And you'd probably be right. I think I've said enough, although you might want to tell me about the doctor not being in the clear. You're one step ahead of me."

JJ told her what he had found out from the Jacksons. "So, you'll need to check what time the ambulance arrived. That will give you a good idea."

"Will do. Thanks, JJ. Anything else I should know? I could do with earning a few brownie points."

"Let me have your phone number. I'll text you if I think there's anything you should know." JJ tapped her number into his phone and messaged her. "There, if I can ever be of any help, just shout."

"Will do. Better get going, I'll be in touch." With a wave of her phone, Rachel left the two men.

"Do you reckon she'll let us know about the ambulance timings?" Davie asked as they got back into the car.

"Yep. That was the message I sent." JJ tapped the clock on the dashboard. "We're going to be early."

"Good, then we can order promptly. Did I mention I was hungry? Drive on." Davie settled back into his seat. "We need another angle. We've reached a dead end for the time being. I'll put my journalist's cap back on."

"I take it you mean work out which bit of dirt you'd start digging up next?" Sharon called from the back seat. "I'm not sure there can be much more."

"I do. And there will be. There's always more dirt to dig."

"Well, I for one, hope not. That little family has enough on their plate." JJ said as he pulled away. All three looked at the Bentleys' cottage as they drove past. Dr Bentley's car wasn't there.

Ten minutes later, they found out where Dr Bentley was. Sharon spotted him as they walked to the entrance of the restaurant.

"Look who's here. I hope they don't put us close by."

Davie stopped walking, and Sharon bumped into him. "Of course you do. Blimey, JJ, she's got a lot to learn. How can we hear what they're talking about at the other end of the restaurant? Wrong, Sharon, love, we want the table next door."

"No, you want that. I'd be happy to be as far away as possible. Let's see where fate places us, shall we?"

JJ winked at her as he held open the door. Davie scanned the restaurant while they waited to be seated. It had a retro feel to it that was comforting. Red and white checked tablecloths, strings of chianti bottles suspended from the beamed ceiling, and plastic ivy draped around the bar area. It was full apart from two tables, one of which they'd reserved.

He nudged JJ. "Is this the only joint in town? Even I know half the clientele."

"One of two, the other is a bit more upmarket on the outskirts. View over the river. This one is always popular on Fridays and Saturdays. The other one is more so on a Sunday when you fancy a posh roast."

JJ fell silent as the waiter appeared and Sharon apologised for being early. Her concerns were swept away, and three huge menus collected from the dresser. They weren't seated next to the Bentleys, but Davie gave a wave to Teresa Burns at the next table. She was sitting with Fran, the receptionist at the solicitor's, who smiled acknowledgement.

Their orders taken, Davie looked around and counted the number of people he had met since arriving in the village.

"Seven people. In a little Italian. That would never happen in Bristol. Wish it did, because it would make my job a lot easier."

"Stop being so obvious," Sharon hissed. "Not everyone enjoys being ogled, you know."

"They're all fine. They've all waved. The pizzas look good, but they're massive. Glad I went for pasta." He gave Sharon a wink. "What are you having for pud, JJ?"

"I doubt I'll have one. Like you say, the pizza is more than enough. Why do you ask?"

"Just wondering if you're watching your figure. You don't eat much," Davie replied.

"No, my figure watches itself. I eat if I'm hungry. More people should try it. Saves a fortune."

"Ah, you're mean. I knew there was a reason. Oh, hello, Teresa."

Teresa patted the back of the empty chair next to Davie. "Do you mind? It won't take a minute."

"Carry on. What can I do for you?" Davie asked.

"Well, it was both of you, really. Our Fran said you were starting up an investigation business, and I might have a job for you. If you think it's worth it."

"It's always worth it to us, Teresa. It's whether it's worth it to you. What did you have in mind?"

Sharon grinned at JJ, who had yet to say a word.

"Not here. It wouldn't be appropriate. Come round and see me. Tomorrow if you like, I'm in all day. I don't open on a Sunday. See you then. I'd better get back to Fran. She doesn't get out often, not with the kids." Teresa was back on her feet. "Shall we say afternoon, got church and Sunday lunch to get out of the way first?" She looked at JJ. "Unless you're coming to church, then I could see you between the two."

"I'll see you at about half three," JJ replied. "Your pudding has arrived. Looks nice, I might try one."

As she left, Davie rubbed his hands together. "Sounds promising. I wonder what she wants us to do?"

"Missing person." JJ moved his napkin from his lap as the waiter appeared with his pizza.

"How do you know that? Don't tell me on top of all your other skills, you're psychic." Davie waved his hands from side to side.

"Nope. Fran mentioned something while you were with the solicitor. I didn't think it would come to anything."

"But you didn't say no." Davie winked at Sharon. "Off and running. This looks fabulous," he told the waiter as his food was placed in front of him.

"Good. Shut up and eat it."

Meal eaten, Sharon went to the toilet, leaving Davie trying to convince JJ that he should try a pudding, and that in moderation, eating for pleasure was allowed too.

"But I'm not hungry, and you didn't finish your pasta, and yet you're now going to eat more," JJ countered.

"I didn't eat it all, nice as it was because I'd seen the dessert menu. I knew I'd want one, so I left enough room. You see. Eating for pleasure. Best of both worlds." Davie flipped his hand. "I can see that I'm not going to convince you. But be warned, I'm not sharing."

"Nor would I expect you to. I've seen awful things, Davie. Kids queueing to get a drink from a standpipe, hoping to stave off their hunger while they await aid. Racing for dropped scraps or hanging around bins with the feral dogs. It teaches you priorities. I can't do it, but I don't begrudge you, or anyone else come to that. I only apply it to me. So let it go."

"So your abstinence is from guilt. I can understand that to a point, especially if you were somewhere where leaving a little for others would be the right thing to do. But here? No. Can't see what difference it makes. I'm having the blueberry cheesecake, but I'll wait for Sharon to get back in case she wants one. I take it she eats for pleasure?"

JJ laughed. "Like a professional. She'll want one. And the thing about location, Davie, is it's always with me. Here." JJ tapped the side of his head.

"Then perhaps—"

"Sharon's coming back, and she looks angry. Are you okay?"

"Fine." Sharon plonked herself down and rapped the table. "Sandy Bentley has lost the plot. She just had a pop at me in the ladies."

JJ glanced up as Sandy Bentley left the toilet, and seeing JJ watching her, lowered her head. She walked to her table, said something to her husband, and walked out. Flustered, Dr Bentley called for the bill and hovered by his table as it was prepared. Once paid, he hurried after his wife.

"What did she say?" Davie turned back, having watched the departure over his shoulder. "But before you tell us, what are you having for dessert? Let's get our orders in." He beckoned the waiter, and with the order placed, returned his attention to Sharon. "You were saying?"

"I was washing my hands when she came out of the cubicle. I knew she'd assume I knew about the affair, so I didn't avoid eye contact, but I wanted to let her know I wasn't judging or gossiping, so all I said was, 'It's a lovely evening again. The food is good here, isn't it?' And she rounded on me. Wagged her bloody finger in my face, and told me...in a nutshell, I was a judgemental bitch, who had no reason to feel superior. She used a lot more words than that while working herself into a frenzy. Completely lost it. So, I told her I had no idea what had just happened, but she might want to lay off the wine." Sharon grinned. "I thought she was going to choke."

JJ shook his head and took hold of her hand. "I'm sorry, Sharon. What I do shouldn't affect you like this. Are you sure you want me to carry on?"

Sharon snatched her hand away. "What! Of course! JJ, I'm not made of porcelain. I have a backbone. It was only a sad, cheesed off woman sounding off. Davie tell him."

"Agreed. JJ, you have developed some very odd outlooks on life. It's concerning. But what's that saying? The lady doth protest too much, or something like that? Could be her guilty conscience taking hold. You'd know all about that," Davie replied.

"Who does? Me or JJ?"

"Him, of course. Hopefully, I'll get him back on the straight and narrow again."

"Oi. I'm happy as I am, thank you. Now, while you two stuff your faces and discuss my shortcomings, I'm going to get some shots of the viaduct. It's quite stunning with the sun setting behind it."

As JJ went to open the door of his car to collect his camera, he stepped back and peered at it. Someone had scratched it from front to back. The scratch was new, and as it was on the side next to the pavement, it was deliberate. He glanced across the road at the buildings opposite and smiled. He'd deal with it in a moment. First, he was going to do what he liked best. Lifting his camera from the footwell, he headed for the bend in the road, and the view of the viaduct. Davie and Sharon found him there some thirty minutes later.

"Now I can see why you wanted to come. That is quite pretty," Davie said.

"Not pretty, spectacular." JJ walked further round the bend and took more shots of the valley below. "That should do it. One more little job, and we'll head home."

"Job?" Sharon queried.

"Yep, someone has keyed the car. There's a doorbell cam on the house next to the restaurant. They might have caught something."

"How did you even notice?" Davie asked, nudging JJ with his shoulder. "Just kidding, but I'm guessing you won't be going for a respray. Not with the state it's in."

"Probably not. But as it's probably related to the case, I want to know who."

Reaching the house opposite his parked car, JJ knocked on the door. A middle-aged man holding a slice of pizza answered.

"What can I do for you?" he asked, taking a bite and looking confused.

"My car's been vandalised, any chance your door cam is working? And if it is, can I have a look?"

Jo Harris appeared behind the man and pushed him out of the way.

"I thought it was you. How can we help you?" she asked.

JJ explained again, and she invited them in.

"Ignore them. Saturday night treat." Two children looked up, the eldest did a double take.

"Hello, Miss, why are you here?" the larger child asked.

"JJ's car's been damaged. Eat your pizza, please, you're in bed as soon as that finishes. You're way past bedtime already." Jo winked at Sharon and said quietly, "They think I don't know that they purposely choose the longest films to watch. I don't mind, no school tomorrow and I get a chance of a lie in. In here." She showed them into the little dining room, in the corner was a table, on top of which sat a laptop. "Dave, you'll need to log them in. I've never used it."

Dave, minus his pizza, flipped open the lid of the laptop, and leaning forward so they couldn't see the password, he opened the app for the door camera. "There you go. Click on the date, and then go to the time you want." Pulling over a chair, he handed JJ the mouse. "I'll leave you to it, or the kids will polish off my pizza."

Jo didn't leave and stood watching the screen over JJ's shoulder. When the vandal appeared, she grabbed his shoulder.

"Oh boy. That's the doctor's wife. Why the hell would she do that? Play it again, she did do it, didn't she?"

JJ went back a few minutes and hit the play button. He now had three bodies leaning over him.

"It looks like it. Is there a way of sending me this? I'm not familiar with the system, although I've just bought a door cam, so I'll have to learn."

Davie tapped his shoulder. "Get out of the way, I'll do it. Look and learn."

After a couple of false starts, he used Jo's email to send the attachment. JJ checked his phone, opened the attachment and nodded.

"That's it. Thank you...um, sorry I didn't catch your name."

"This is Jo, and don't worry, she won't tell a soul, will you? Jo doesn't gossip. That's Sara." Davie stood and returned Jo's smile. "Thanks, Jo. I'll catch you in the café, I'm sure."

Back in the car, they all spoke at once, and Sharon took control of the conversation.

"So was it Sandy sending the notes and damaging our cars? You wouldn't have thought it, would you? And if it was, then it stands to reason she killed Amber. Oh, my God. What do we do now? Call the police?"

"When we get home, yes, but let's go and confront her first. I might put that to her," JJ replied.

"Oh, he's gone official. Can't remember how many times a copper has said to me, 'I put it to you'. Come on then, JJ. Start the car, or we'll never get home."

When they arrived at the Bentleys', only the doctor's car was on the drive.

"You two stay here. Looks like we won't be confronting her tonight." JJ pulled into the vacant space, and leaving the others in the car, knocked on the side door.

"You!" Doctor Bentley looked JJ up and down, as if seeing him for the first time. "What do you want?"

"I was after Mrs Bentley. I'd like a word if possible."

"Good luck tracking her down. She's gone again. I don't know where she went last time. I really don't need this. You got what you wanted. Goodbye."

JJ began to protest that wasn't what he wanted, but the door was closed, and he heard the key turn in the lock. He returned to his car. "He said—"

"We heard. I kept the window open. Where does she go, I wonder?" Davie asked.

"No idea. Let's go home." JJ started the engine.

Chapter Sixteen

JJ COULD HEAR DAVIE was on the move, and unable to get back to sleep, went to join him. He crept out of the bedroom. Sharon deserved a lie in. The night before they'd spent an hour talking in circles, although they had agreed that calling the police was best left for another day. JJ hadn't slept well, despite not having nightmares and now felt completely drained. He needed coffee.

"Bloody hell, you look rough. It's supposed to be me that looks like that. Tea?" Davie held up the pot.

"No thanks, coffee. The stronger, the better. I barely slept last night. I heard you had no such problems. You snore like a pig." JJ scooped some coffee into the cafetiere.

"I've never had any trouble. I put it down to a clear conscience." Davie replied and spun around when JJ barked out a laugh. "What?"

"It's not a clear conscience you have, it's the total lack of one."

"Not true. So, what's on the agenda for today? Shall I put some toast on?" Davie was already loading the toaster.

"Cameras first. You also have to give me a crash course in how they work so I don't have to read the manual. But we'll set it up on Sharon's phone, as she'll get more comfort from it. Then I'll call Rach about Sandy Bentley keying the car, and we'll take it from there."

Breakfast over, they set about setting up the camera on JJ's front door.

"You should get a dash cam too. They're not expensive," Davie commented as JJ screwed the fitting to the door frame.

"When did I win the lottery? You're very keen on spending my money." JJ clipped the last piece in place. "Now what?"

"Now you position it at the angle that suits you. Open the app on Sharon's phone."

Ten minutes later, they were done. JJ had a clear view from his doorstep to the street beyond.

"Nine o'clock. I don't reckon that's too early to speak to Gary. Come on." JJ collected the other camera and his door keys.

"Were your ears burning?" Gary asked as he opened the door.

"Why, who's been talking about me? Was it you?" JJ asked Luke as he appeared by his father's side. "If you want to go running, I'm up for it. Davie made me eat a whole pizza last night, and I didn't run at all yesterday, and that's not good enough."

"No, it was Dad. I'll come running though, and you can tell me about church." Luke stepped out onto the step. "What's that?" He pointed at the box containing the camera.

"It's a camera. I'll tell you about it in a minute. What's this about church?" JJ asked.

"Come on in, and I'll explain. Go straight through to the garden. We had breakfast outside today. Luke, if you're going running with JJ, go and clean your teeth. You can show him what we bought then."

Remembering his new lace up trainers, Luke needed no encouragement, and scooted off. While they were alone, Gary explained to JJ that Luke was still concerned that he wouldn't find his mother in heaven. The latest argument being he didn't know God and felt he should if everything was to work out.

"I've never been a churchgoer, JJ. I don't believe. Not that I'd ever tell him that. He needs to find his own way, but how can he do that if he's not taught about it? I know they skim it at school with assemblies and what have you, but that's not enough to satisfy him. So, I thought, who better to ask than you." Gary grimaced. "Sorry, I know you already run with him, but you're far more qualified than I am. Would you take him to church? I'll come too if you like. I've no problem with that, but I'd feel better if someone who believed was there."

JJ rubbed his hand along his stubble. This was the last thing he'd expected or wanted. But his own issues shouldn't impact on Luke. Luke was after peace of mind, and at his age, the church might help.

"I'll tell you what. I don't think he should jump straight in with a full church service, but Sunday school would be an excellent place for him to start. We'll swing by the church on our run, and I'll see what time it starts."

"Perfect. Now tell me what the camera is for?"

"Yes. I probably should have mentioned it before I got it, but it was a spur-of-the-moment thing."

JJ explained why he had the camera, and about its value in catching Sandy Bentley vandalising his car.

"The doctor's wife. She's only one peg lower than the vicar's wife. Why? And more importantly, do you think she might have killed Amber? Bloody hell, JJ, is there no one you can trust?"

"I've certainly rattled her cage. As for Amber, I don't know, but I'm going to hand the recording over to the police as soon as I get a minute. I...hello, Zed. What's that on your feet? You've got lace ups!"

"Velcro is for babies. I'm not a baby. Are you ready?" Luke asked.

"I am. Can I leave you two to set up the camera? Davie's better at it than me, anyway. Not sure how long we'll be because we'll pop into the church on the way. Is that okay with you, Zed?" When Luke nodded, JJ got to his feet. "Come on then. Let's go. Jog down to the signpost and run to the church or the other way round? And we'll have to warm up first."

"It's sunny. I'm not cold."

With a wave to the others, JJ led Luke away, explaining the science of warming up before physical exercise.

After a little stretching and a few jumping jacks in the front garden, they sprinted to the signpost, then jogged further down the hill to the church. Leading Luke through the churchyard, JJ headed for the church hall where the Sunday school was held. The doors were locked.

"That's a nuisance. Come on, we'll have to go back to the noticeboard."

Luke pointed at a nearby headstone. It had fresh flowers, and the surrounding grass was neatly trimmed. "Will my mum have one of those?"

"I'm not sure. You'll have to ask your dad, but she'll have something somewhere where you can go to leave flowers or have a chat, I'm sure."

"A chat! Can she talk to me?" Luke had stopped walking.

"No. But she'll listen. You can tell her what you're up to, what's on your mind, stuff like that. And you can tell her your secrets and any worries. Just like you would if she was still here. It'll make you feel much better."

Luke didn't look convinced, and the crease in his brow showed he was considering this. Eventually he asked, "Why is that one nicer than the others?"

"Different. Not nicer, and because someone has come to visit and tidied it up. They all get tidied, but not as often as they should." They had reached the noticeboard and JJ scanned the information pinned behind the glass door.

"Well, my mum's will always be nice. Who's that man waving at you? He came to school at Easter. I don't think Miss Gerrard likes him. She kept doing that thing with her eyes. He couldn't see her, but we could. Zac laughed and got told off." Luke smiled at the memory.

JJ had noticed Andrew Parsons, the vicar, approaching, and he ignored him for the moment, instead he turned to Luke. "What, like this?" JJ made a meal of exaggerating an eye-roll and grinned as Luke laughed confirmation. "She does that to me a lot, too. I don't think Miss Gerrard likes many people. Here's the man we need to speak to." JJ held out his hand. "Hello, Andy, this is Luke Wilton. His friends call him Zed. Luke, this is the vicar, Mr Parsons. Luke thinks he might need to learn a little more about God. So we're here to find out about Sunday school."

"No, not school. I want to go to church. I can't go to heaven if I don't go to church, can I?" Luke looked from one man to the other.

Andrew Parsons smiled and patted Luke's shoulder. "Everyone can go to heaven, Luke. Or may I call you Zed? I think going to church just helps you find your way a little easier, and Sunday school is not like proper school. No tough headteachers like Miss Gerrard here. I think you'll like it. You're a bit early, though. It doesn't start until ten thirty."

"We're just out for a run. Your dad can bring you back later, Zed. We'll finish our run, then you can go home and change first. We'd better get going."

"If I didn't know better, JJ, I'd say you were avoiding me. Will you be coming back with Zed? I can call you Zed, can't I?" When Luke nodded, he smiled. "In which case you can call me Andy. We don't need titles here. Will I see you later, JJ?"

"Not unless you're coming to lunch. We need to get on, or Zed will be late for his first time."

The vicar held JJ's gaze. "Will you come and see me on another day? I'd like to try to help."

"I might."

JJ led Luke around the other side of the church and, cutting across a well-worn path, took him into a tunnel formed by trees and bushes. It was too long to see the end, and shafts of sunlight managed to pierce their way through the foliage and glinted against the smooth rocks laid down many years before. JJ lifted his camera and took several photographs.

"Have you been in here before?"

Luke shook his head. "No, it looks spooky. Where does it go?"

"Spooky? I think it looks like the beginning of an adventure. When I was a boy, I used to make up different stories about what I would find at the end. In winter it looks spooky. Especially with the cobwebs trying to get you. But not today."

"It does to me. Where does it go?" Luke asked again.

"Shall we find out? Be careful, the ground can get slippery. We should be alright today, though, it's not rained recently."

With no further warning, JJ took off at a jog with Luke chasing after him. Luke was disappointed that the end of the tunnel led only to a field. It was pretty enough, with clumps of wildflowers straining to reach the sun through the long grass, trees that looked climbable, and a small murky-looking pond, but it wasn't exciting. JJ took a diagonal route across the field, slowing his pace for Luke.

"Where do you think this comes out?" JJ asked as they entered the trees at the far side of the field.

Luke shrugged as he looked up the path that ran through the trees. "I don't know."

"What if I tell you there's a coke and a packet of those bacon things at the end?" JJ asked.

"Is this the hill above the pub? How?" Luke looked back the way they had come and couldn't find the answer, but he was smiling.

"Because our village is wonderful. You think you're in the middle of it, and in the blink of an eye you're in the middle of nothing. Ready? Go!"

JJ took off again, and only slowed as they approached the steps which led out of the woods and to the pub. Luke pushed past him, and by the time he found Old Sam sitting on the steps of the pub reading the paper, his face glistened.

"Zed! You look like JJ has been putting you through your paces," Sam said as he folded the paper.

"I won. But he's a cheat. He didn't say it properly again. Did you know there's a tunnel behind the church?" Luke looked down at the church and then back to the steps as JJ emerged. He still couldn't work out where they'd been.

"I know you're not open yet but I promised him a coke and a packet of bacon bites. Only a small one though, he's got places to be."

"I expect we can manage that." Sam accepted JJ's offer of help and got to his feet. "Come on, young 'un. Or I'll be dobbed in to the police for breaking the licence."

"Who would do that? And what's a licence?"

Sam explained the UK licencing laws as best he could while filling a glass with coke. JJ had water.

"I can't charge you, you see?" Sam finished. "I reckon that's why JJ comes so early. Where are you going, anyway?"

"Sunday school, which isn't a proper school, and Miss Gerrard won't be there. I'm going to learn how to find heaven."

"Sounds like a good plan. Did JJ tell you to go?" Sam glanced at JJ from the corner of his eye. JJ ignored him.

"No. I decided. He just showed me where it was, and we met Andy. He's a vicar, but I'm allowed to call him Andy. Can I take these with me? I don't want to be late." Luke picked up his snack.

Sam told him he could, and they headed for home. The camera was set up, and Emma, who had arrived to make the lunch, was standing on the path waving at it. Seeing his grandmother in the garden, Luke took off at speed. JJ slowed to a walk and watched the reunion. By the time he'd reached them, Luke had told his grandmother about his adventure with JJ, and that he needed to change and get ready. Their conversation was now about what to wear to Sunday school. As she escorted Luke into the house to change, Davie came out. He told her the camera was perfect and went to meet JJ.

"All sorted, JJ. How did you get on at the church?"

"Okay. He's going to Sunday school. Where's Gary?"

"That's why I've come away. He's on the phone, and in the nicest possible way is telling whoever it is to go forth. I wasn't sure if he was being polite because I was there, or if he simply can't do nasty. Either way, I was seconds from snatching the phone off him and hanging up. It is possible to be too nice. Glad Emma turned up, or we'd still be sorting it out. Oh, and yes, she asked if we thought she should have a door cam for her house too, and I told her if she got one we'd fit it."

"Understandable. Until we find out who killed Amber and why, it's reasonable for the family to think they might be next? I need to run through everything again. You can read the paper or something."

"Which one? I'm choosy."

JJ shut himself in the office and ignored the chatter from Sharon and Davie as they prepared lunch. He reappeared when Sharon announced lunch was ready.

"Did it help?" Davie asked as JJ sat at the table.

"What?" JJ asked before turning to Sharon. "Looks lovely as always."

"What? You being on your own. Have you come up with a new angle or something we might have missed?" Davie speared a potato with his fork.

"Oh, I see. No. Nothing. Got a couple of new prints sorted for the exhibition, though. Now stop talking shop, we need to show due appreciation to this meal. Once we're done, we need to discuss this afternoon's meeting. I know Teresa

Burns is financially comfortable, but depending on what she wants, I wouldn't like to charge. I know we have to, I'm just saying."

"Well, if you—"

"Davie, not now. After lunch. What are you doing this afternoon, Sharon? I'm guessing there's not much schoolwork to prepare."

"None. Film and a bag of jellybeans. *Four Weddings and a Funeral* is on. I don't mind you talking shop, you know."

"Again? How many times can you watch the same film?" JJ shook his head at Davie. "Be grateful we have a reason to escape. Unless, of course, you like Hugh look-at my-cheeky-smile Grant."

"More of an action movie fan, although haven't watched one for years. Sharon said we could carry on, so what do you think we should charge?"

JJ put his knife and fork down. "I'm going to get indigestion, but my thoughts are to find out what other people are charging, and then charge what we think our clients can afford. You don't need the money, you've got food on the table and a roof over your head, and we have two and a bit incomes already. Will that do you?"

"What they can afford, who ever got rich doing that?" Davie asked, his horror at the suggestion not hidden.

"We're not doing it to get rich. Well, I'm not. I'm doing it to help. If you have different motivations, perhaps we should reconsider."

"Don't go all churchy on me. Or threaten me. All I'm saying is that people expect to pay the going rate. We need to have one. It's me going to have indigestion at this rate."

"Which is why I said to leave it." JJ tutted and picked up his cutlery.

"He considers everything, every possibility. Always," Sharon told Davie. "He's not the strong silent type, he's the, I'm going to mean every word I say, type. And as much as it pains me to say it, he's rarely wrong. I don't think he is on this either. If someone can afford to pay the going rate, take it. If they can't, so what? As long as it covers your expenses, of course. I don't think you should be out of pocket. And after all, Davie, what else have you got to do? Hang around the homes of grieving families, and sleep in your car? Tell me he's wrong."

"I don't think I like you two any more. How are we going to buy the gear we need if we don't make a profit? Tell me that as you pass the mustard." Davie held out his hand.

JJ didn't have to answer, Sharon did that for him. "Because those you do charge the going rate will all be profit, or most of it, anyway. There you go. Don't use that mucky knife and contaminate it. That's a hanging offence in this house."

"I won't argue. No point when you're talking to people who are clearly a few shillings short of a pound. And I have never knowingly contaminated a jar before." Davie snatched the jar.

"Oh, so it was JJ that left toast crumbs in the marmalade, was it?" Sharon asked.

"I couldn't possibly say. Why are you grinning?" Davie asked JJ.

"Red-handed, mate. I don't have marmalade. Do everyone a favour, shut up and eat."

Lunch over, they took a pot of tea to the garden. JJ explained he'd already done his own research and would like Davie to hear him out before he put forward any arguments.

"So, to summarise, I'll speak to the bank about a business account next week. I've already applied for a licence, which should be a formality given my background, although I am rusty. I'm going to have to brush up my legal knowledge on data protection and the like, and I won't be charging over eighty pounds an hour, and that's for both of us. Any more would be greedy. And, and this is the most important thing, I have the final yea or nay on the jobs we accept. We won't advertise. We'll simply see what happens. Is that agreed?"

Davie lifted a nonchalant shoulder. "Sure." Inside, he was doing a jig. A business account and a licence application told him JJ was taking it seriously. He'd be signing out as an upstanding pillar of the community, or close enough, anyway. "When we see Teresa, I'll let you do all the talking."

"I can't see that happening for a minute. But thanks for the thought." JJ laughed.

"Notebooks. Or better still a recorder. Or are we going to use our phones? I favour the latter, but some people get really jumpy about that."

"Jeepers, Davie. Every time we clear one hurdle...I've got a couple of notebooks. This is only Teresa. It should be sufficient."

JJ uttered the words with confidence. If he'd had even an inkling of what the case would involve, he might not have been so flippant.

At three fifteen, armed with the notebooks, JJ drove the short distance to Teresa's home. A detached post-war semi at the end of the row of shops on Main Road. JJ would have preferred to walk but knew the hill on the way back might be too much for Davie. Perhaps he'd suggest that Davie considered a mobility scooter, but that was a conversation for another day.

The front door opened as they walked up the path.

"I saw your car go past. Are you going somewhere?" Teresa asked as she ushered them into the living room.

"Not that I know. Why do you ask?" JJ sat in the armchair next to the window.

"I'm minutes away from you. You could have walked. I'd have thought you'd be big on saving the planet. Do me a favour, open that window. I don't use this room often. Could do with some air in here."

JJ got back up, choosing not to answer, and with the window ajar, sat back down and flipped open his notebook, waving his finger at her as she opened her mouth to speak.

"No tea, coffee or anything else yet. Let's cut to the chase. Why are we here?"

Teresa settled herself on the sofa next to Davie.

"I want you to find my brother, although I think I should say I want you to find out who killed my brother. I'm convinced he's dead, but as there's no body, whoever did it hid it well." Teresa delivered this without a hint of emotion, and although Davie hid his smile, JJ looked shocked. "I can see I've shocked you. Understandable, I suppose. Two murders in one week. I've done my best to find something for you to go on, but what with the café, and keeping on top of this place, I've not got much. Come on, I'll show you."

"Hang on a minute, Teresa. Let's back up a little. What do you mean you've tried to get me something? We haven't even got this business going yet. So you've not had long to try? And, if as you suggest your brother has been murdered, why aren't you talking to the police?" JJ asked, ignoring the eye-roll from Davie.

"Oh I have. And it wasn't for you, not in the beginning. I was just going to hire someone. Brenda did what she could with her contact, but like she said, he's more of a notice server than an investigator. But he got some bits and pieces. I shelved it for a while with all the Covid nonsense, and meant to get back to it, but it's a minefield. Fran tried to help, but even she got overwhelmed trying to work out who would be our best bet. It's not the money, there's plenty of that, but you need to spend it wisely when it's other people's, don't you think? Shall I show you now?" For the first time, Teresa seemed hesitant.

"No. Stay where you are, start at the very beginning, and get to the bit where I'm sitting here refusing a cup of tea."

Teresa pointed to the mantel. "That's Ted. Edward officially. The one on the end. It's a bit creased. He's my older brother by ten years. It's his seventieth birthday on the first of August. I was a happy accident, my mother used to tell me. Anyway, he left home when I was ten. Over the next ten to fifteen years, he turned up occasionally. Sometimes that was a good thing, mostly not. He usually came home when he had some kind of trouble. My dad used to get so mad. But Mother was a soft touch. We were never wealthy, think all Dad's money went into this house, but we were comfortable, so she always found what he needed. I didn't care. I thought the sun shone out of his rear end. He was such a funny man. To the best of my knowledge, he's been married twice. Both ended in divorce, and he's lived with I don't know how many. The last we heard was about three years before Mother died. He was in Liverpool working on the docks, or boats, or something. Settled with a nice woman, although I've forgotten her name. And they seemed settled. We had an address then, or so we thought. So I suppose I don't even know if that was true."

"Which bit?" Davie asked.

"The address. Mother told him he'd missed enough birthday cards, and he scribbled it in her address book. Anyway, then Mother died. That was a bloody shock, I can tell you." Teresa patted her chest.

"Unexpected?" Davie asked.

"Oh no. She'd been ill for over a year. It was the will." Teresa looked JJ in the eye. "Can I trust you?" She jerked her head towards Davie.

JJ smiled. "Of course."

"She left nearly a million. All came from Dad and his trading stuff. But I had no idea, and I'm guessing she didn't when he popped off, either. She never said a word, though. But with our Kathy gone, she left it to all three of us. Me, Fran and Ted. I also got the house, and Fran got some jewellery. She put a little aside in her will. Is that what they call it?"

"Do you mean a caveat?" JJ asked.

"That's it. It said if Ted couldn't be traced, the money was to come to me. What would I do with another three hundred and twenty thousand? I couldn't spend what I've got if I live to be one hundred. So, I wanted him found. Still do, especially now I've worked out he's probably dead."

"Yes, but why do you think that?" JJ asked. "It seems to me like Ted has led quite a life. Sometimes people make sure they can't be found easily."

"We wrote to the address we had. Me and Fran even caught the train up to Liverpool to knock on the door. Brenda organised adverts in all the major newspapers, especially the sporting ones. He liked a flutter, and Fran got it posted all over Facebook and what have you. We didn't hide the fact that there was a significant inheritance. Then we offered a reward for information. But I've got all we found out there." Teresa flipped her hand towards the door. "Yes, we went to the police but because of his past lifestyle, having no fixed abode, and there being no body, the best they could do was put him on the missing persons register, and there he stays. I want you to find out what happened to him, JJ. I need to know. Will you do it? I'll pay whatever it takes."

JJ refused to look at Davie, knowing he'd be grinning. Instead, he nodded at Teresa, but held up a finger.

"I will, Teresa, yes. But I want whoever killed Amber Wilton found first. We all knew Amber. We know absolutely she met an untimely and unlawful end. That's my priority. So much so, I'm not even going to look at whatever you've got until that happens, or until I throw in the towel. Might be a few weeks. Is that okay?"

Teresa was beaming. "Of course, JJ. It's been years, so a few more weeks won't hurt. Months even. Thank you. Now, can I get you that cup of tea?"

Knowing they'd only get drawn into more detail about Ted Burns, JJ refused.

"No, thank you. I promised Sharon I'd do some jobs for her. I'll keep in touch. Do you mind if I take a snap of your photo of Ted?"

"You can take that one. I'll have it back when you're done, though. He was a handsome man, you wouldn't think it looking at that. But he was. Shall I dig some older ones out for you?"

"That would be wonderful." Collecting the photo from the mantel, JJ looked at Davie, who hadn't moved. "Come on, Davie. Time to go."

Davie got up. "I was going to stay for a cup of tea. Sorry, Teresa, he's a man on a mission now. And he's never thrown the towel in before, so he won't with Amber, and he won't with Ted. I'll pop into the café tomorrow and buy a cuppa."

Walking back to the car, JJ turned to Davie. "Go on. Get it off your chest."

"Nothing on my chest. Don't know why you're in such a hurry. Thought you didn't like Hugh Grant. I wanted to see what they'd turned up. I like poking around, you know that."

"One case at a time, Davie. One at a time." JJ sighed. "If you want to start poking about, get on the internet and see what you can find. He will have been christened in the church, the Burns always went to church, so you can start there."

"But she could have told us all the basic stuff."

"Then wait. I thought you wanted something to poke around in." Smiling, JJ got into the car. "I've just remembered I need to phone Rach Sampson, too. Can't keep putting it off."

When Rachel Sampson arrived, she wasn't in uniform. JJ showed her through to the kitchen.

"You're not in uniform, I'm sorry Rach, I thought you were working. Tomorrow would have done."

"I am. But I've been seconded to CID. I put in for it a while ago, so fingers crossed this could be permanent. I only heard yesterday while I was out. So, here I am, acting DC Sampson at your service. What have you got for me?"

"I'm not sure if you'll want it. Although it could be connected to Amber Wilton's death, it could also be I just stepped on too many toes. Here, have a look."

Rachel watched the video. "Naughty Mrs Bentley. Send that to me, please. I'll go and have a word. If I arrest her for criminal damage, she might say more when interviewed at the station, especially as her alibi didn't stack up. Do you think she's the murderer?"

JJ took back his phone and answered as he forwarded the recording. "No idea. She's top of the list at the moment, but if it was, I don't think it was premeditated. Having spoken to her, I can't believe their meeting was, either. I reckon Sandy Bentley would have gone out of her way to avoid Amber. But that's my opinion. Oh, and you won't find her at home. She's left the doctor again. She keyed my car, went home, and left. He claims not to know where."

"I'll have a word, anyway. She's certainly drawing a lot of attention to herself for someone who likes to keep her head down. What else have you got?"

"Not a lot. Davie is convinced it's a woman, and I tend to agree. Unless there's a bloke on the scene we've yet to come across. What about you lot? Anything you'd like to share?"

"Not that I know. I'm only just officially involved, but I'll know more tomorrow morning after the briefing. I heard they think nothing on the laptop will help, though."

"Well, give me a ring if I can be of assistance. Contrary to what Evans thinks, I'm not working against you." JJ smiled.

"I know. Same here, although if I do inadvertently let anything slip, you never heard it from me." Rachel stood up. "I'd better get round to the Bentleys'."

"There is one favour you could do for me." JJ told her as they walked to her car.

"What's that?"

"I've been asked to look for a missing person. He was a bit of a wanderer, so I doubt much was done about it. But it will be interesting to know what the police know. No rush. When you have time."

Rachel pulled her notebook out. "What's his name?"

"Edward Burns, goes by the name of Ted. Date of birth, first of August 1954. Was living in Liverpool. That's all I've got." JJ opened the door of Rachel's car for her. "Like I said, no rush. I want Amber's case closed first. Unlike you lot, I can queue my cases."

"I'll have a look as soon as I can. Won't be today. See you soon, JJ."

Davie was standing on the doorstep when JJ returned.

"I thought you weren't going to do anything about Ted?" He smirked.

"I haven't yet. That doesn't mean I can't have people beavering about in the background. She's a good girl." JJ jerked his head towards Rachel's departing car. "If she can keep Evans at arm's length, she'll do well."

"Useful contact. You must have others you can call on too, that might be of help further down the road."

"I wouldn't ask. Not unless help was offered. I wouldn't want to put anyone in an awkward position. Anyway, that was years ago. I expect my mates have retired now."

"Never say never, JJ. What's next on our agenda? We're running out of leads."

"We are. Now we're going to speak to all the women who were with Amber in the pub on Tuesday. We've got a few accounts, but we need to speak to them all. One of them may have something they don't know they have. But that's tomorrow. It's Sunday evening. Let's leave them to enjoy what's left of the weekend."

JJ had only just closed the front door when Gary knocked on the glass panel. JJ pulled it open.

"Sorry, JJ, I couldn't find my shoes quickly enough. Any news?"

"Not yet, I'm afraid. Come in."

"No, I won't stop. Luke's on his own and I only wanted to ask if you'd come to the gallery tomorrow. We can look at the venue and sketch out a plan for your exhibits. I've got a sculptor exhibiting too, and I'm going to give Amber's work some space. I got Emma to choose which ones."

"Lovely gesture. What time?"

"Ten? Luke's decided he is going into school. By the way, he loved Sunday school. But I need to be free by one, as I'm meeting the undertaker then."

"That's good on all counts. I'll meet you there." JJ closed the door.

"It's like Piccadilly Circus here this afternoon. Everything okay?" Sharon called from the sitting room. "You'll be pleased to hear my film has finished."

"All good," JJ replied.

"Well, if you're swanning off to Bristol, you'd better give me some idea of where to find these women. I don't want to be sitting in here on my own," Davie said. "Let's do it now, before you get carried away with your arty stuff."

Chapter Seventeen

THE NEXT MORNING, JJ was up early and joined Sharon for breakfast while Davie slept in.

"Morning. You're up early," Sharon greeted him.

"I've decided to leave Davie to it this morning. I'm going to go down to the floating harbour and have a wander around before I meet Gary. Should get some nice shots at this time of the morning."

"What time are you going? You could give me a lift down to school. I want to take those boxes in, and your car will do it in one shift."

"I was going to leave now, but it's a bit early for you, isn't it? It's only half-seven."

"Nope, all I need is my bag and my shoes. I can break the back of it and get away earlier this afternoon. You grab the boxes from the shed. I'll get myself sorted and help you load them."

JJ left a note for Davie, and with the boxes loaded drove to the school. Sharon had already warned John Baker, the caretaker, and the gates stood open. She tapped out a message to Connie Gerrard and slipped her phone into her bag.

"That's Connie told so she won't panic if I mess up the alarm. Park as close to the door as you are able."

Sharon disarmed the alarm on the first attempt, and JJ helped her lug the empty boxes into the reception area, and then on to her classroom.

"Remind me why you need these?" he asked as one slipped from the stack and bounced back down the stairs.

"Because I'm teaching in a different room next year. So I have two jobs to do. Box up the stuff I want to come with me, and box up the rest and label what's in them so Kate can decide if she wants to keep any of it. Supplies are valuable commodities, and their disposal is not to be taken lightly."

Job completed, JJ headed back to his car. The caretaker appeared with a strimmer balanced on his shoulder.

"All sorted?" he called to JJ.

"Yes, she's in there loading up boxes as we speak. Are you gardening today?"

"Nope. Done. Her highness wanted some weeds along the back of the gym sorted. I forgot last week, so thought I'd give her one less thing to complain about. I'm off for my breakfast." With a cheery wave, he followed JJ's car up the drive and to the caretaker's bungalow, which sat to the right of the school gates.

JJ was surprised when he sailed through to Bristol city centre but was soon irritated because he'd forgotten about the clean air zone, and his visit would now attract an additional charge on top of the car parking. He grumbled to himself as he drove into the multi-storey carpark in Millenium Square.

"I'd have caught the bus if it could have got me here by eight. With two changes, do they wonder why people are up in arms? Mind you, probably why I haven't been sitting in a traffic jam, and Sharon keeps telling me it's time to...what the..." JJ screeched to a halt, narrowly missing a stooped figure dragging a kit bag behind him. He lowered the window and called to him, "Are you okay, mate? Sorry about that."

"No harm done. Slow down. What's your rush? We'll all be dead come the end." The man walked back. "Although I'd be better if I could buy a hot cup of coffee."

"Let me park, and I'll treat you." JJ parked, picked up his camera and backpack, and went down in the lift to the ground floor with the man. "What's your name? I'm JJ. Did you sleep here last night?"

"Kevin, and yes. It's too bloody hot. I can't strip off. I've got nowhere to put it. You get a bit of a breeze on the top floor. I shouldn't complain because when it's freezing, I'll have something to moan about, and moan I will. What's your business, then?"

"Well, that's a long story. But at this precise moment, I'm a photographer." JJ patted his camera. "Hoping to get some interesting shots, then I've got to see a man about an exhibition."

"Ooh. Posh. You don't look loaded, you drive a crap car and those jeans have seen better days. What do you take pictures of?"

JJ laughed. "Fashion advice? Give me a break, but point taken. Not posh, not famous, not rich. Better off than you, I agree."

"Do you want to photograph me? I know some great locations around here, and all I'll charge is the cost of a breakfast. Greasy spoon, too. Not one that puts the beans in a little pot. Never understood that."

JJ didn't have any better ideas, and he liked Kevin, so he agreed.

"You're on. Where shall we start, as long as I can get to Queens Road by ten?"

"Depends what you're after. Do you want depressing and moody? You know, like will the downtrodden homeless bloke chuck himself in the river? Or ironic, look at that nice shiny, bright thing, what's he doing there? Or I suppose real life, I could take you round the places the likes of me have to hang out. I'd rather one of the first two options, I can do real life on my own."

"You choose. I'll be guided by you. What's your story, Kevin? If you don't mind me asking, you can tell me to mind my own, but you're well-spoken, clearly educated. How did you end up here?"

"No offence, JJ, but if you've got to be up on the Queens Road by ten, we haven't got time. Let's say wine, women and song and leave it at that. If we meet again, I might depress you with my tale of woe, but I fancy having a good day."

"As you like."

JJ followed Kevin around, taking both candid and posed shots, and by the time Kevin clambered into the fountain at the Victoria Rooms, JJ was excited. He knew he'd captured some great shots and couldn't wait to get home to study them.

"This is great stuff, Kevin. I'd like to get some nighttime shots too, if that's okay with you."

"Are you serious?" Kevin stepped out of the fountain and shook one leg after the other. "My feet feel better for that."

"I am. Walk back this way with me. I'll give you my…have you got a phone?"

"Oh yes, I keep next to my laptop and my iPad. Apologies. That was sarcastic. Yes, I have a phone, no I can't use it. Better things to spend my money on than for something I have no use of. Also a bitch to find somewhere to charge it."

They had reached the shopfront of Gary's unassuming facia. JJ smiled.

"Point taken. Come in here with me a minute."

Kevin looked in at the sophisticated interior, and the face of the woman hovering just inside of the door with a feather duster in her hand. "Somehow, I don't think I'll be welcome. Been nice meeting you, JJ. Now, if we could settle up. A full English is a tenner."

"You're my guest. It'll be fine."

It turned out it would have been fine if Kevin wasn't dripping water over the recently cleaned floor. JJ stood him on the doormat and brought a chair from behind the small counter. Kevin took his boots off, rolled up his trousers, and grinned at Ellen, who watched his every move with suspicion. Gary appeared behind them.

"JJ, sorry I'm late. Time ran away with me. I…is this gentleman with you?" Gary stepped over the boots and looked Kevin up and down.

"Yes, Gary, meet Kevin. Kevin is modelling for me. Can I borrow a pen?"

"Of course. Modelling? Interesting. Do you need paper too?"

Gary walked to the counter and returned with a notepad. JJ wrote his number down and handed it to Kevin. He pulled fifty pounds from his wallet.

"Breakfast for a couple of days, and a tenner goes on your phone. Put my number in it, and call me to arrange a night shoot, or if you ever need help. Promise me."

Kevin took the money and slipped it with JJ's number into his pocket before answering. "Will do. But how do I charge it?"

"Ah. Have you got a charger?" JJ asked.

"Yep. I'm not totally daft."

"Let's have it. You can charge it here while I'm looking at the venue with Gary. Do you know how long it takes?"

"A couple of hours from memory. Are you sure?" Kevin looked from Gary to JJ and back again.

Gary held his hand out. "Yes. Let me have it. We need to make a move. I've got to get back to Frampton."

Needing no further encouragement, Kevin dropped onto one knee and rummaged in the side pocket of his kitbag and located first the phone, and then the charger. He handed them to Gary, who did the honours.

"Where is this place?" JJ asked.

"The old bank building up by the BBC. The top floors are being converted into flats, I think, they've not started yet, but the basement is still a vault. It's a great backdrop, I've already done most of the organising with Ellen." Gary smiled at Ellen, who was still keeping her distance.

"That's only up the road. Kevin can come with us. Do you fancy that, or is your full English beckoning?" JJ asked as Gary's eyebrows rose.

"I'll tag along. Breakfast can wait. Long time since I've seen any sort of exhibition. Monet in Paris was the last one. That was a few years back." Kevin sat on the chair next to his boots and pulled them on. He put his socks in the pocket which had held his phone. "Ready when you are. Thanks for the chair, Ellen, think it should be fine. No contamination that some of that won't shift." He pointed to the antibacterial hand gel on the counter.

As they reached the bank building, Gary's phone rang. He frowned and rejected the call. Minutes later, it rang again.

"Damn it. Two minutes, gents." He walked away as he took the call. "I'm very busy, I have...what? Yes. Oh. Right. Hang on." He walked back towards JJ, the phone held out. "It's Connie Gerrard for you. Yours isn't on, apparently."

"Connie Gerrard, why?" Realising it must be about Sharon, JJ snatched the phone. "Is Sharon okay? What? Where? I'll be there as soon as I can. I'm five minutes away."

Hanging up, he drew in a deep breath, as Gary asked him what was wrong.

"Sharon was attacked at school this morning. They've been trying to get hold of me but my bloody phone ..." he pulled his phone out of his pocket and cursed. "Is dead. Someone saw Davie, who told them I was with you. I have to go. She's in the BRI. Here." He handed his backpack to Kevin. "If you've done Monet, you can do Jenson. Gary, he's homeless, not dim. I'm happy with what he says ..." JJ ran into the street and hailed a taxi. As it made a U-turn, he turned back to the two men. "I'll get my phone charged somehow. Gary, sort Kevin out for me. Kevin, call me later. Or tomorrow, I've got a phone charging problem now." JJ got in the taxi and barked his destination.

When JJ got to the Bristol Royal Infirmary, he sprinted to the reception desk and stood in the queue, his foot tapping out his irritation. As he reached it, he heard Connie Gerrard call to him.

"JJ, this way, she's this way."

JJ ran over to her and tried to remain calm. Connie was clearly upset, her usually immaculate makeup ruined by the tramlines from her tears. Her eyes were red, and she drew in a juddering breath.

"She's still in A and E. I thought you'd come here. She's conscious, and they're waiting for the results of the scan, but said they're moving her to a ward as soon as they've got them. This way."

JJ had a thousand questions, but his need to make sure Sharon was well took precedence. He trotted towards the accident and emergency department. Connie's heels clipped along behind him. Once there, she introduced him to the nurse, who took them through to the curtained bays.

"One at a time, I'm afraid. Why don't you get some coffee while Mr Jenson speaks to Sharon? You look like you could do with it. Go to the café on the first floor. It's cheaper than the chains."

Connie nodded and, with a brief wave to JJ, turned back the way they had come.

"Knock, knock, are you decent?"

JJ's breath caught in his throat as he caught sight of Sharon. Her right eye was swollen, and a lot of bruising was developing. A large white dressing was stuck with tape to her right temple. Blood from her wound hadn't been thoroughly cleaned from her cheek and neck, and the shoulder of her pale blue hospital gown was now tinged pink. She smiled at him.

"That bad? You look like you might faint. Come and sit down. I feel fine now."

JJ perched on the side of the bed and took her hand. “Do you feel like telling me what happened?”

“I don’t know, not exactly. One minute I was packing boxes, the next thing I know someone whacked me on the side of the head. I was stunned, turned quickly to see who it was, and the next thing I know, Connie has hold of my hand and is screeching into her phone. Cue police and ambulance, and here I am. Mild concussion, a black eye, and five stitches which sting like hell every time I move my head. The police officer thinks I probably passed out when I turned, hence the black eye as my head collided with the corner of a desk. I’ve had a scan. I’m waiting for a visit from the doctor with the results. The nurse tells me they’ll keep me in, but if it’s only concussion, I want to come home. If they ask, tell them you’ll babysit me. Promise?”

“I’ll promise nothing until I hear the results. I’d rather you were here so they can monitor you. But if it’s safe for you to come home, of course, that’s where I want you.” JJ lifted her hand and kissed it. “What did the police say about who might have done it?”

“I don’t think they have a clue. They established that I knew nothing, had a word with Connie, who insisted on coming with me, and I’ve heard not a dicky bird since.” Sharon grinned. “Do you want to hear something funny?”

“If it is funny, yes. Your humour evades me sometimes,” JJ replied with a wink.

“I come round, and I’m lying there wondering what the hell has happened and I can hear Connie shouting, and I think I’m having a nightmare. So I decide I need to wake up. I mean, who wants to be dreaming of Connie shouting when you’ve got the real thing the next morning? So I open my eyes and I try to sit up.” Sharon giggled, amused at what’s coming next. “Connie then screeches into the phone. ‘She’s alive, she’s alive. Get here fast. She’s alive.’ Then she hangs up and kisses my hand, telling me she thought I was dead. And I told her to get a grip and help me up. She tried, bless her, but my legs wouldn’t work, so I lay on the floor with Connie’s jacket for a pillow. She’s been so good, JJ, if a little...you know, Connie like. You’re in her bad books, though. She couldn’t get hold of you and had to send someone to the house, then to find Davie who wasn’t there. I’m guessing they found him in the end. I forgot you were with Gary, or I could have told her. What was it, flat battery or on silent?"

JJ grimaced. "Flat. Still is. Have you got your charger with you?"

"That's the other thing. We don't know where my bag is. The police asked if anything was stolen, and I couldn't remember carrying it in. I had my phone to do the alarm, and the boxes, but I don't know if I had my bag. If I didn't, it was stolen. Do you remember?"

JJ shook his head. "I remember you saying you needed to get it. I don't remember if you did. You got your shoes, though." He pointed at the clear plastic bag holding her clothes. "Robbery in a school at that time of the morning doesn't seem likely. I'll phone Davie and ask...ah. I don't suppose you have your phone with you, do you?"

"Nope, as far as I know, it's still in the stockroom on the shelf. I just hope the kids like Adele." Sharon smiled. "My bag was just full of junk. You know all the stuff you wonder why I need to carry around with me. And my purse, of course. Probably should cancel my cards. Can you do that once we know? Oh, hello. This is my partner, JJ."

A young woman in a white coat pulled back the curtain. She smiled at JJ as he got off the bed.

"The good news is that there doesn't seem to be any serious damage up there. The bad news is you're staying for at least one night. There's swelling on your brain that needs to go down. We'll get you on a drip, and then scan you again in the morning."

"But—"

"No, buts. If that swelling gets worse, rather than better, this is where you need to be." She picked up Sharon's wrist and took her pulse. "Bit fast, but nothing to worry about. Must be the excitement. The porter will be here soon. We're a bit short of beds, so for the time being you'll go on general admissions, but there's a chance you'll be transferred to the HITU at Southmead Hospital. We'll have to see how it goes. On the bright side, you're not considered to be serious enough to kick someone out. I'll leave you now but you'll be on my rounds this afternoon.

Oh, here's the porter." The doctor stepped to one side and pulled the curtain back.

A nurse came in first. She looked at JJ. "The transfer and settling on the ward might take an hour or more. Now might be a good time to drink the coffee your friend is nursing, and perhaps go and get an overnight bag for Sharon." She looked at the doctor. "She is staying, isn't she?"

"Yes. I'll see you later, Sharon." The doctor left them, and the nurse allowed JJ a minute to say goodbye before pointing him in the direction of Connie.

JJ walked slowly to the waiting area. Now he knew Sharon was okay, his brain was in overdrive. Was this a random attack, or the warning made good? If the latter were they following Sharon or him? Were there any cameras at the school? Had it been a chance encounter? He spotted the mascara-streaked face of Connie sitting at the end of a row of orange chairs. She attempted a smile and held a cup up. He took the seat next to her.

"I hear you've been quite the heroine today. Thank you for looking after her. They're going to keep her in overnight as there is swelling on her brain. Nothing to worry about, just one of those things they need to monitor. It's going to take a good hour to get her settled. Why I don't I get you home? I've got to get her toothbrush and stuff. Oh. Did you drive or come in the ambulance?"

"I drove. Oh, JJ, I thought she was bloody dead. I knew she'd come in early, and I went to ask her about Friday, and there she was. There was no one to help me. Kath was in the staff room, but I couldn't leave her, could I? I thought she was dead for a minute. She wasn't responding. There was the blood, and I couldn't find a pulse. I'm so relieved. But she's in excellent hands, so we can stop worrying, can't we? I'd better get back to school."

"You don't need to get back to school. They'll cope, and certainly not before you've gone home and repaired the damage. You'll scare the kids to death looking like that. You might need to freshen your lippy up as well," JJ joked, then becoming serious, he asked, "Are you sure you're okay to drive?"

"I'll be fine, JJ. Don't fuss. Where did you park? I abandoned mine on double yellows and I've probably been clamped, knowing my luck."

"I was just up the road, jumped in a taxi to get here, it was quicker. My car is in Millenium Square."

"Come on then. I'll give you a lift to your car." Connie handed JJ his coffee. "It's cold, but it's coffee."

They both got up and headed to the exit.

"Thanks again, Connie. I know we don't see eye to eye on much, but I clearly underestimated how good a friend you are to Sharon. Thanks for this, too. I don't mind cold coffee."

"It was awful, JJ, awful. I thought she was dead, then I was so happy when she woke up, then she bloody collapsed."

Connie put her hand over her face to hide her tears, but the jerky movement of her shoulders gave it away. JJ put his arm around her.

"But she's on the mend, thanks to you. Imagine if you hadn't gone to find her. It could have been a lot worse." JJ stopped walking and looked at her car. He managed a laugh. "When you said you abandoned it, I didn't think you meant in the middle of the road. I can't believe it hasn't been towed away. Have you ever parked in a straight line?"

"No. Not really. Do you want a lift or not?" Connie gave a watery smile. "If you do, get in and shut up. I hate driving in town, too many cars. I need to concentrate."

JJ did as instructed, the only noise escaping his lips were grunts and gasps as he clung to the door handle and braced himself on the dashboard. He was glad it was a short journey to his car, and relieved when his feet were both firmly on the ground.

"Thanks, Connie. I'll call you later and let you know how she's getting on."

With a nod and a wave, Connie pulled away, narrowly missing a cyclist and causing the driver behind to brake violently and slam her hand on the horn. As he walked to his own car, JJ wondered how she'd ever passed a test. Once at his car, JJ checked it for Sharon's bag. It wasn't there.

Davie marched down the garden path, hands on his hips as JJ got out of the car.

"Have you heard of the bloody telephone? What's going on? How's Sharon? All I got was a garbled half story from the secretary at school. Theories are ten-a-penny, mind you, but I'd like it from the horse's mouth."

"Hallelujah. You do want the truth. Put the kettle on, and I'll tell you. I just need to get an overnight bag together for Sharon."

"Hilarious. I almost laughed. Is she alright?" Davie asked, following JJ into the house.

"She's fine. I wouldn't be this calm otherwise."

"Good. Then you'd better see this." Davie pointed to the kitchen. "Another one. And yes, I was careful not to touch it. I've ordered some gloves on your Amazon account."

Walking into the kitchen, JJ looked at the card. It was a lined index card. Printed across the middle in blue biro were three words:

I WARNED YOU

"Same handwriting. Bastard. I can't see that this is a woman, Davie. Have you called it in?" JJ asked.

"Who to? Evans? Not a chance. You've got Rachel's number, let me have it now, then I'll be able to use it in the future."

"Two seconds. My phone's dead. I need to charge it." JJ pulled his phone from his pocket and put it on charge in the office. Returning to Davie, he asked, "Do you know what time this was delivered? As far as I can make out, the attack happened between seven forty-five when I left her at the school, and eight thirty, because school hadn't started yet. Connie mentioned that there were only three of them on the premises. Her, Kath and Sharon, so it may have been earlier."

"I don't know what time. I got up about nine, and it was on the mat. So whoever did whatever they did, and you will tell me what they did, came here straight after, by the sound of it."

They both looked to the dining room, where JJ's phone rang out with a series of alarms.

"That's all the messages coming through. That will tell you. I called you as soon as I noticed it. Before I made breakfast, so near as damn it, anyway."

They went to the dining room and JJ called his answer service.

"You have seven new messages. Message one, left at nine-o-one."

They listened to all seven messages. Three from Davie, four from Connie, both sounding increasingly more annoyed the more messages they left.

"So, what happened to Sharon? How bad is it?" Davie asked.

JJ told Davie what he knew, and what was happening next.

"So I need to get a bag together and get back down there."

"You'll also need a book or magazine, some grapes because they're compulsory, a supply of chocolate and a bottle of squash or Lucozade."

"The bloody camera. Did you check the camera?"

Davie slapped his head. "Never thought of that." Sarcasm dripped from every word. "No, because we set it up on Sharon's phone. And that was because, and I quote, you're useless with that type of thing. Have you got it?"

"No, but I know where it is. Or was. I'll pop into the school on the way. And for the record, I don't think that's what I said. Do me a favour and make a sandwich while I'm getting her stuff together. I've got another detour now. Shop and school, I—"

Davie winced as the Mozart bell did its thing.

"I'm buying you a new doorbell. You can keep that one for sentiments' sake, but we'll have one that doesn't sound like that. You do the bag, I'll get the door."

It was Gary. He looked over Davie's shoulder. "Is JJ about? I need to find out how Sharon is, and update him on the exhibition."

"Come on in. He's just packing a bag for her." Davie swung his arm into the hall.

"I can't stop. I've got the undertakers. Emma is waiting for me, and...ah, JJ. How's Sharon?"

JJ had heard the conversation, and leaving the overnight bag with only Sharon's book and a pair of knickers in it, he hurried down the stairs.

"She looks like she's done a couple of rounds with Joe Calzaghe, but she's fine. Shaken, but fine. What's this about the exhibition? I'm also pushed for time. I have to get back to Sharon at the hospital."

"You were right, your friend Kevin was useful. Too useful in some ways, but I haven't got time to explain now. You haven't got a camp bed, have you?"

"A what? No, we haven't. Got an air bed somewhere. Sharon's sister left it here last Christmas. Can I ask why?"

"JJ, I really have to go, if you could leave it somewhere accessible and message me. I've given Kevin the night watchman's job. Not really needed, but a friend of yours in need and all that. Anyway, he needs setting up. I've left him organising the exhibits. I was hoping you could go and sort him out, but I can see you're pushed."

JJ flapped his hand. "I'll sort it. Not sure when, but I'll do it. No need to go back. Do you have a key?"

"Left it with Kevin. Thanks, JJ. See you later."

JJ closed the door behind him, and his head fell on his chest.

"Who's Kevin?" Davie asked.

"I'll tell you on the way. Make the sandwiches, and make two extra, wrap them up and grab a packet of those biscuits you two like. Get some fruit too."

"Am I going somewhere?"

"Yes, I'll explain on the way. I must pack that bag."

Davie was still smiling as he watched JJ sprint into the school. Kevin was homeless, a tramp, a hobo. Call it what you will, but he wasn't a night watchman, and he wasn't a friend of JJ's, however nice he was. Hopefully, he wouldn't have flogged all the exhibits by the time they got back. JJ was frowning as he returned to the car.

"Not there. Not in the stockroom, not in Connie's office. I'll give Connie a ring, but if she doesn't know, whoever hit Sharon must have stolen it. The police will have to try to track it. Bugger. I didn't call Rach."

Davie rapped on the dashboard. "Slow down. Slow bloody down. You're not acting like a cop...an investigator. You're acting like a deranged husband who doesn't know his arse from his elbow. Call Connie now, before you leave this carpark, then depending on what she says, you can call Rachel."

JJ nodded. His phone was plugged into the cigarette lighter, and he moved the wire around the gear stick and called Connie, putting it on loudspeaker. As it started to ring, Connie's car appeared, and she came to a halt in front of them. Tossing the phone to Davie. JJ told him to call Rachel, as they needed to tell her about the card. He had a brief conversation with Connie, who then reversed in a zigzag movement to allow them to leave.

"He's here now, Rach. I've only got as far as the card," Davie told JJ, who started the engine.

"I'm going to drive and shout, Rach. Let me know if you can't hear me. So, you know about Sharon being attacked and the card confirming it was because I ignored the threat. We're on our way into town to see her now. I fitted a door cam yesterday, and the who it was will be on her phone. But she doesn't have it. She doesn't have her bag either, but I forgot to check that at home. But she knows her phone was on the shelf in the stockroom. It isn't now, and Connie Gerrard, the headteacher, who found Sharon, didn't see it. She said she didn't look, so it could be there, but Sharon was quite adamant that it was blaring out Adele when she was attacked. Any chance you could put a trace on it, and what's the news on the attack?"

"Hi, JJ. Sorry to hear about Sharon. I know nothing about it. Might not even be logged as connected yet. Would the attending officer have known? I'm guessing they didn't. Send me her number and I'll get on to it. Let me know your movements. The guv is bound to want to speak to you."

JJ pulled up outside the supermarket. "Two seconds. Davie, grab whatever you think Sharon might need. Don't overthink it. Rach, tell Tom I'll call him later, and that it's not good enough. A murder, an attack, and other than you, no one seems to be doing a bloody thing about it. Any news on Sandy Bentley?"

"At her cousin's in Somerset. DS Evans is on his way there."

"I won't hold my breath. Keep me posted, Rach. Don't make me have to chase."

"I won't. Give my best to Sharon."

JJ considered what had happened over the last twenty-four hours. He wondered when Sandy Bentley went to her cousin's. Even if she had gone the night before, it wouldn't take long to get back to Frampton. But it would've had to have been early. She wouldn't have known Sharon was in the school alone, unless she'd followed them. He hadn't noticed anyone about, but then he wasn't looking. Davie interrupted his train of thought as he arrived back with a bulging carrier.

"Will says hello and good luck catching the bastard."

JJ glanced at the bag as he drove off. "What have you bought? She's only there for one night, if that."

"Thought I'd better get some stuff for your mate, too." Davie laughed. "Only you could get a bloke you don't know a job doing something he's not qualified for, and leave him in charge of valuable exhibits. It is possible to be too kind, you know."

"One, I didn't give him the job. Two, we don't know that he's not qualified, he's well-spoken and not stupid, and three, I don't doubt his honesty. Oh, and four, he's seen a Monet exhibition in Paris." JJ laughed. "As my sister would say, so there! Now pull yourself together and call the hospital. That place is a warren and the queue to find anything out too long. See if we can find out what ward she's on. Tell them you're me, or they won't tell you."

As they entered Bristol, Davie hung up. "The short version is, they've had several emergencies in, following a double-decker overturning near Temple Meads, resulting in Sharon still being in A and E, but she's sleeping. Her bed was allocated to someone in a more serious condition. Because of the chaos there at the moment, the nurse suggested giving it another hour before you turn up, because apart from anything else, you'll wake her up."

"All that rushing about for nothing. Better head over and see what Kevin's up to. I haven't even seen inside the place yet."

Chapter Eighteen

JJ PARKED HIS CAR in front of the elegant Victorian building, and they got out of the car. Davie looked up at the façade. The windows had been boarded up, and a sign announcing it was under development had been fixed above the sturdy door.

"I remember when this was a bank. In fact, I remember when there were lots of banks on Whiteladies Road. None here now. Big Brother is winning. How many people do you reckon will realise you're here? It's not very welcoming."

"More conspiracy theories? Gary knows what he's doing. I'm sure anyone interested will find it. It's the side entrance." JJ led the way around the side of the building. "This is as far as I got."

The metal gates protecting the door were open, but the door was shut. A key was required to open it. JJ stepped forward and gave it a couple of thumps.

"Have you got your fingers crossed?" Davie asked with a grin.

"Not quite."

They waited a few moments and JJ tried again. "I have now. What was Gary thinking?"

"Burying his wife, I reckon. You won't be very popular, he needs this going tits up like a hole in the head. I'll have a wander around the...Oh, I take it back." Davie watched the door open and quickly assessed the man, who smiled at JJ.

A little shorter than JJ, Kevin was somewhere between forty and fifty. He carried little weight, but certainly more than Davie. His muddy-coloured hair was too long, his face weathered but kind. He had what appeared to be workman's boots on his feet, into which he had tucked his tracksuit bottoms. Despite the weather, he was wearing an oversized sweatshirt, beneath which he wore a polo-necked top. Kevin swung his hand into the building.

"Come on in, you're letting the heat escape. We're through here." He held out his hand to Davie. "Kevin. Nice to meet you. Are you the sculptor?"

"Davie, and no. Wouldn't know one end of a chisel from the other. Private investigator." Davie shot a glance at JJ, who didn't flinch. "And longtime friend of JJ. I hear you've got yourself a new job."

"Blowtorch, not a chisel. This way."

Kevin let the way through several corridors and finally pushed open the door, which led to what had been the main banking hall. It had been stripped of most of the fixtures and fittings from its life as a bank, and what remained was a spectacular space. High ceilings, ornate mouldings, two chandeliers, several marble pillars, and a magnificent cast iron fireplace. In the centre of the room was a stack of crates and boxes, leaning against which were several wooden easels.

JJ sniffed in the faint aroma of disinfectant as he looked around. "Great place, clean too, but I can't see how this is going to be ready in two weeks. I just can't see it. Lighting isn't good either."

"I'm sorting that out." Kevin pointed at the chandeliers. "I'll get them working properly, and then I'll sort some uplighting or spotlights to suit the display. Gary said he's got boxes of stuff from previous jobs in the cellar of his gallery. I'd have gone and had a look, but I don't think Ellen likes me. She's scary."

"You?" Davie asked not hiding his disbelief.

"Yes, me. I had a life once, you know. Electrician by trade. But there's no point in me doing anything until I know what and where."

Davie shook his head. "If you're an electrician, how come you're sleeping rough? You should be raking it in. All tradesmen are these days."

"Yes, so I hear. The thing is, when the mighty fall, they fall hard. Get broken." Kevin's eyes bored into Davie as he weighed the man up. "You've probably led an enchanted life. Didn't stop you from getting ill, though, did it? Shit happens. Sometimes there's too much of it. Are we going to try to sort this out, or do you want to carry on making yourself feel better at my expense? I'm happy either way, but then, I'm not paying the wages. Are you?"

"Nope. And fair point, well made. I'm a wanker. Agreed and seconded by him." Davie jerked his head towards JJ. "He collects broken people. He's an expert, being one himself. What's first?"

"I've cleaned everything. It wasn't too bad. So we need to organise the displays. I've had a look through that lot, and I have some ideas, but thought I'd better wait. There are some display tables coming for some sculptures, and the big one won't arrive until later in the week. Gary said he thinks it needs centre stage." Kevin held his hand towards the stack of boxes. "Probably best where they are. Great work, by the way, looking forward to seeing the results of my shoot," he told JJ.

"Me too. Might be a while getting to it. There's a lot going on at the moment."

"Yes, sorry. How is your wife? I'm guessing not too bad, given you're here."

"She's been better but should make a full recovery. Look, I've got an hour, maybe more. Why don't you show me what you're thinking? Davie can get the supplies from the car, and we'll make a start and see how far we get."

"Supplies? Does that include the full English? I've not eaten yet. Thought I'd better crack on."

"No but judging by the bag he came out of the shop with, you'll be fine, and he made sandwiches." JJ grinned as he pulled a couple of frames from one of his boxes. "I'm going to prop these up along the main wall. Once they are all out, it will give us a better idea of what to do with them."

Kevin helped JJ unpack his framed photographs, talking JJ through his thoughts on the display as they lined them up.

"Have you done this sort of thing before?" JJ asked. "You're surprisingly knowledgeable for an electrician."

"That's because I worked events for years. I've been all over the world. Car shows, caravan shows, cooking shows, museums, I've done most things that needed a light shone on them, and copious amounts of power. Even did a stint at the BBC on set lighting for a while."

"I'm beginning to think me nearly running you over was a good thing," JJ replied.

"Like fate? Not sure I believe in that, or destiny.."

"Nor me. I believe fate is in our own hands once we've wrestled it away from the people who want to control us. You'll get back on your feet, if you want to. Do you? I've met a few people who were glad to be where they found themselves. I'm not judging, it's—"

"What about God? Does he have a say?" Davie appeared in the doorway. "It's like a rabbit warren out there. I got lost twice. I found the kitchen, though. Shall I put the kettle on, or get the bed and stuff?"

"Yes. Go on then. Let's have a quick lunch and crack on. I'll call the hospital while we're not working."

Davie turned back the way he had come. "They said at least an hour. You've got a while."

As Kevin showed JJ the way to the kitchen, he asked, "Is he religious, your friend? He doesn't seem the type, and what bed?"

JJ laughed. "No, he's not. Not at all. We understand you're the new night watchman, together with site electrician, and artistic director. We thought you'd need something to sleep on."

"He might not be religious, but it seems the Gods are smiling on me today. They had a nice little setup for the staff here. There's even a shower. I don't suppose you brought a towel, did you? Can't remember the last time I had a shower. There's some washing up liquid I could use."

"It didn't occur to me. I understand lots of workplaces put showers in for staff who cycle to work, or something like that. I'll bring one in tomorrow."

"You're well set up here, mate," Davie told Kevin as he entered the kitchen. "Even got a washing machine and dishwasher. I doubt the latter will be needed, but the washing machine will come in handy. I had to do mine at JJ's." He looked Kevin up and down. "Tea or coffee? I bought some teabags, but there are some coffee tabs in here. Haven't found any sugar though."

"I'll take it as it comes. Thanks. What do you mean you had to do your washing at JJ's? Were you on the street, too?"

"I certainly was not. I've got a car, I'll have you know. Sit down, you're making the place look untidy."

There was little conversation as the men ate. Finishing first, JJ wandered off to call the hospital. He was smiling when he returned.

"She's on a ward. I'm going down there now. I'll come back later to get that sorted. Sorry. You can sort your sleeping arrangements out."

"I'd better get his gear out of the car then."

"I'll leave the car. It's as quick to walk as it is trying to find a parking place. It's only along Park Row. I'll grab my camera and her things first."

"Rather you than me. But I could say that with most things where you're concerned. What do you want me to do? It's a long way to walk home."

"Anything you like. My phone's charged now. I'll keep in touch."

While they finished lunch, Davie gave Kevin an abridged version of both his own and JJ's lives.

"But JJ's sensitive, so everything affects him more than me. I just get on with it. He looks for the meaning in everything. Sometimes there is no meaning. It just is, and there is bugger all you can do about it. Not God, not fate, just have to accept and move on. Shall we get your gear in first, then you can boss me around while I still have some energy?"

Kevin nodded. "Yep. Nice having a sensible conversation with someone. I've had more today than in the last month. Here, let me put that rubbish in the bag."

Kevin leaned across to collect the wrapping from the sandwiches. Davie pulled his head back and wafted his hand under his nose.

"Kev, mate. Get your gear in that machine, you stink."

"I know. What can you do in this weather? I've got nothing clean to change into." Kevin's nose wrinkled as he sniffed his armpit.

"I think Saint JJ stuck some stuff in a bag for you. Don't know what it'll be like because he looks worse than you most of the time, but it will be clean and odour free. Here's a plan. We'll unload the car, you shower and dress in whatever you can find, then we'll crack on. With no windows to open, it's not optional."

"I haven't got a towel. I'll have to drip-dry," Kevin said as they went out to the car.

"Then drip-dry you shall. Right, you take those two, they're heavy and I'll do this one." Davie flipped his finger back and forth along the heavily laden bin bags in the boot of JJ's car.

"Blimey, it's like Christmas." Kevin pulled out two of the bags and headed back into the building.

When JJ arrived at the correct ward, he reported to the reception desk.

"Ah, Sharon currently has a visitor. I'll see how long they'll be." The nurse smiled as she got to her feet.

"Who?" JJ asked. "No one knows she's here."

"You can ask Sharon that. I won't be two minutes."

JJ pointed at the sign on the wall behind the nurse. "It says there that two visitors are allowed at any one time. How many are in there?"

"Mr Jenson, wait here, please." The nurse wandered down the corridor, and intrigued, JJ followed her.

She held up a finger as she knocked and entered the room. "Stay there."

When the door closed, JJ stepped forward and looked through the slats on the door. Sharon's visitor was Rachel Sampson. The nurse reappeared.

"In you go. I had to check."

"Understood. Thanks." JJ walked into the room, placed the bags he was carrying on the end of the bed, and kissed Sharon's forehead. "How are you feeling?"

"Like I've been hit by a bus. They won't let me have more painkillers yet, and the doctor wants another scan to be on the safe side." Sharon pointed at the chair. "Sit down. We're almost done."

"With what?" JJ asked. "What's the latest, Rach?"

"Not much, I'm afraid," Rachel replied. "Wherever Sharon's phone is, it's not working. If this was opportunistic, the sim card has been removed. If it's more sinister, the sim card's never going to be found. The officers who attended, searched the entire school, including outbuildings, to make sure whoever it was had scarpered. I doubt they checked the bins, but who would dump it that close to the scene? They spoke to the few people who were around, including the caretaker and a teacher. They didn't see anyone. The guv has sent them out to speak to people in the houses that back onto the school, as that's considered to be the most likely point of entry and exit onto school land. That or the lane which Sharon tells me leads up from Main Road. Sharon can't remember any more than she's already told us. Not surprising, the blow from behind knocked her out cold. Haven't heard from Clive Evans yet."

"Why? What's he up to?" Sharon asked.

"He's gone to speak to Sandy Bentley," JJ told her.

"She wouldn't have done this, surely?" Sharon winced as she shook her head. "I shouldn't have done that."

"Before she keyed my car, I would have agreed, but now I'm not so sure. If I'm honest, I was hoping it was some lowlife being opportunistic, but that's not the case. Not unless our card writer heard about your attack minutes later. Which, I suppose, is a possibility with everyone arriving as the ambulance left. Playground gossip spreads quickly, as we know." JJ turned to Rachel. "Anything else on the Amber front, Rach?"

"Nothing of any use. A few more eliminations, but no nearer finding anyone with a motive. Nor anyone without a solid alibi, anyway. Only Sandy Bentley. The times of the ambulance despatch and arrival have been confirmed. Steve Bentley is in the clear." Rachel got to her feet. "What time will you be home? The sooner we get that card processed the better. It sounds like it wasn't planned, or they would have used one of Amber's again. Possibly. Hopefully. Anyway, what time?"

"I'll be here until they chuck me out. What time's that?"

"Seven. And you're not staying here all that time, I'm supposed to be resting. I'm not putting up with you for hours." Sharon smiled. "I'm perfectly safe here. I'd rather you found out who did this to me. Oh, I just thought, you're supposed to be sorting out the exhibition with Gary. Go and do that and pop back in. Or perhaps you should get Rachel the card first? What do you think?"

"I think you're worrying about the wrong stuff. The exhibition is in the hands of Davie and Kevin, and Rachel will get the card. You just worry about getting better."

"Davie? What does he know about exhibitions? And who's Kevin?"

"That's a long story, but he's a homeless guy I met this morning when I nearly ran him over, and—"

"No. Absolutely not. Stop right there. We do not have the room for another lodger. Well, we do, but we're not having one. Get me a nurse, I'm coming home now before I end up running some kind of hostel. It's not that I don't want to help, but—"

"Calm down. Look, you've made the machine beep now. He's got somewhere to stay. He's working for Gary, not me." JJ crossed his fingers. It was near enough the truth.

"On that note, I'll make a move. JJ just text me what time is good to come. But sooner would be better than later." Rachel got to her feet. "Sharon, take care. I'll keep you posted on any developments, although JJ is likely to know before me."

"JJ go now. There might be fingerprints on it. Go with Rachel, then check on Davie and your latest friend in need, and then come back. I promise I'll sleep the whole time you've gone. Although, if that's my book in that bag, I'll have that just in case. I hope you brought me some grapes."

Fingers still crossed, JJ passed her the bag. He had no idea what Davie had purchased. Sharon peered inside.

"Oh, you've done well. Now kiss me and go. Rachel, escort this man off the premises."

JJ told Rachel she could ignore Sharon, and he'd call her, but Sharon was adamant.

"I've got a headache, and I'm knackered. I've been pulled, pushed and poked, not to mention whacked over the head. Now, I'd like to relax with my book, my chocolates and my Lucozade, please. Come back at teatime."

"If you're sure." JJ kissed her and left with Rachel.

As they approached the lift, Rachel's phone rang, and JJ kept a respectful distance while she took her call. He knew it was Evans by the greeting, and he hoped he was the bearer of some good news. He raised his eyebrows in anticipation as Rachel hung up and shook her head.

"Nothing yet. There's no one there. The neighbour says they left in the car at about ten this morning, the sarge is going to grab something to eat and wait another couple of hours. He's not happy because he's left her two messages, so she knows he's there. So we still don't know where she was this morning. Sorry, JJ. Where have you parked?"

"On Whiteladies Road. Do you want to give me a lift to my car?"

"I can take you home if you like. I've got to go there and back, anyway."

When they arrived at JJ's home, Gary was parking his car. Round-shouldered, he didn't notice their presence as he headed for his door.

"He's been to the undertaker," JJ said quietly. "Let's leave him to it. I'll pop in on him later."

Rachel secured the card in an evidence bag and looked around. "Anything else you need to do before we head back?"

"Nope. Oh yes. Let me have a scout around for Sharon's bag. You do down here, I'll check upstairs. You can't miss it. It's a huge brown leather thing, you could fit a small child in it. Weighs a tonne."

He took the stairs two at a time, went into the bedroom, and looked around. He checked under the bed for good measure, and there it was. Leaving it tucked under Sharon's side of the bed, he went back to Rachel.

"It's under the bed. So only her phone was taken. Goes to show that whatever's in it, she doesn't need."

"That saves you the bother of cancelling all her cards. If there's nothing else, I need to get back. If...sorry, JJ I'd better take this." Rachel listened to the caller for a few minutes. "I'm up the road now. I'll go down. Yep, tell him I'm on the way. 'Bye." She looked at JJ. "They found her phone. In the bin by the school gate. We can pick it up on the way."

John Baker was sitting on the wall drinking water from a bottle as they pulled up. He jumped down and went to join them.

"That was quick. Wished I'd checked this earlier, I'd have saved myself hours. I checked along the back lane first," he said to Rachel as she got out of the car.

"I've been looking for clues. Her highness isn't on form today, so I thought I'd make myself useful as I didn't have her foot up my backside. Hot out here today, though. It's still in there. I didn't want to touch it, so I've been sitting here making sure no one else did. How's Miss Elliott?"

"She's okay. Battered, bruised, but over the worst." JJ walked over to the bin and peered inside. There wasn't much in there. A few wrappers, two disposable coffee cups, one shoe, and a very sorry-looking phone.

Rachel handed him an evidence bag and pulled on some gloves. "Hold that open." Leaning into the bin, she retrieved the phone. The back was hanging off, the screen destroyed, and after inspecting it more closely, she shook her head. "Sim's gone. Can you empty that out? It's a long shot, but they might have dumped it in there too."

There was no sim card. Adding the bag to the box in the boot of her car, Rachel thanked Baker, and headed to Bristol with JJ.

"I'll get our tech guys on it. But chances are remote. Such a shame it was on Sharon's phone and not yours."

"It could have been on both. That's the annoying thing. But I said I'd never use it. Bloody stupid. I got it for just this reason."

JJ fell silent as he considered his shortcomings.

As they drove up Park Street, Rachel nudged him. "No point in brooding. Keep your fingers crossed, you never know your luck. Those techy guys can work miracles. Hospital or Whiteladies?"

"Whiteladies. If Davie wants to go home, I'll have to get a move on if I'm going to get a decent amount of time with Sharon."

As he walked past his car, JJ checked the boot. All the bags had gone, and he was keen to see how the two men had done. He hoped he wasn't expected to hang around. The door to the side of the building stood ajar. He could hear a churning noise in the background, and hoping he'd chosen the right direction headed for what would be the gallery.

When he pushed open the door, the sound of Spandau Ballet cutting a long story short blared from Davie's phone. Davie stood with his back to JJ, arms akimbo and foot tapping, and his head angled as he studied the photograph he'd hung. JJ looked around the room. His eyes widened as Kevin, wearing only boxer shorts, and with his hair flattened to his head, raised a hand in greeting.

"Great timing. Do me a favour and lift this onto this pedestal with me."

Turning his hand, he crooked his finger. JJ walked forward and Davie turned and waved his arm around the room.

"Some of this stuff is good. You should try selling it." Davie pointed to the one he'd just put up. "My favourite."

"I do. I don't carry this for the good of my health, you know." JJ tapped the camera hanging against him. Turning in a slow circle, he nodded his head. His grin got wider as he completed his inspection. "I like it. Well done, boys. Great start." He looked down at Kevin's bare feet. A bronze sculpture of a couple nose to nose lay on its side. In front of Kevin was an upturned crate. "Is that the pedestal?"

"Yep. Thought I'd improvise until Gary tells us differently, but this piece goes well with your shots of couples at night." Kevin tapped the photograph on the wall to his left. "Could have been modelled on this."

Agreeing, JJ stooped and took hold of the couple's feet, while Kevin took their heads. He grunted as they shifted it into position. The crate became the couple's seat, their legs dangling over the side.

JJ shrugged. "If I were Gary, I wouldn't even bother to change the crate. Looks perfect to me. Is there a reason you're nearly naked? I heard the washing machine, but I'd chucked some stuff in one of the bags for you. Not the height of fashion, but easier on the eye than your hairy belly. Oh, that's nice. Sharon will like that. She's got a thing about pigs."

JJ walked to the other side of the room. On another upended crate sat a miniature brass bed. The bedding was dishevelled, there were socks on the pillows, and a bra hung from the bed knob. In the centre, a brass pig was eating a pizza from a box. A wooden plaque fixed to the front declared it to be 'The Pig Sty'.

"Yep, she'd love it. I wonder if it's for sale?" JJ ran his finger down the pig's back. "Lovely."

"Oh, it's for sale. The price is on the bottom." Davie smirked. "Might need a mortgage, though."

JJ pursed his lips as he checked the price. "Seems reasonable. Would have taken a long time, the materials, the overheads. Nothing is for nothing, Davie." Patting the pig one last time, JJ turned as Davie snorted. "What?"

"Says the man who said we'll only charge if they can afford it. I'll remind you of that when we tell Teresa Burns how much."

Kevin laughed. "Do you two always bicker?"

"I don't. Davie has an unusual way of delivering his opinion. Passive aggressive is his middle name. I have to say, I don't know what I was expecting, but not this. Gary will be chuffed. You still haven't said why you are in a state of undress."

"Because my natural aroma offended Davie. So I put all my stuff in the wash, jumped in the shower, but as we were still going to be lumping stuff about, I didn't want to ruin the new stuff." Kevin sniffed his armpit. "Nah. Thought I might need another shower, but I'll do until morning. Do you want to see my quarters?"

"Oh, you have quarters, do you? Lead on."

As they neared the churning of the washing machine in the kitchenette, Kevin pushed open a door to his right. "Long time since I had a bedroom. Much appreciated, JJ. You can mow me down again."

The air bed had been pumped up, and Davie's sleeping bag lay on top, together with a pair of socks, shorts and a T-shirt. Next to the bed, a sturdy cardboard box held a mobile phone, a torch and a wristwatch.

"You got your phone back, I see. Very nice. Home for the next three weeks at least. I'll pop back in tomorrow, but now, if you don't mind, I'll drop Davie back home, because I've got to come back into town to see Sharon."

"Are you staying the night with her?" Davie asked.

"No. Why?"

"Because I can come home when visiting is over. Me and Kevin decided we'd finish what we could here and go for a pizza and a pint. He's safe to go out in public now he's clean."

"In which case, make me a cup of tea, and I'll leave you to it."

"How did you get your phone back?" JJ asked as they went to the kitchen. "They found Sharon's smashed up and binned. Sim card had gone, so it's doubtful we'll ever see that recording."

"I went to the gallery with Davie and picked it up. Wanted a look at what gear Gary had in the basement. Which reminds me, I'll need his number. If he can get it to me in the morning, I can make a start on the lighting. Oh bollocks. I told you it wouldn't work."

JJ looked past Kevin and into the kitchen. The whirring noise told him the washing machine was on a spin cycle, but it was impossible to see the drum spinning because half the kitchen was full of foam. "How much detergent did you put in?"

"There was none, so I was just going to do a hot wash. Davie convinced me that the antibacterial washing up liquid would be fine." Kevin started laughing. "Glad I never got dressed now." He waded into the foam. "I've heard people pay to have parties in this. Can't see the attraction, or how the hell they clear it up. Any suggestions?"

It took an hour for them to clear the foam from the kitchen and mop up. Everything, including them, had the faint aroma of lemon. Kevin's clothes were in for another rinse, and an easy camaraderie had built up amongst the men. Sitting at the table, Davie opened a packet of biscuits to go with their tea, and told Kevin about their investigation into Amber's murder. JJ only kept half an ear on the conversation as he scrolled through the shots he had taken that morning. Some of them were good, and he couldn't wait to get home to print them. He was brought back to the conversation by being jabbed in the arm by Davie.

"Did you hear that? Are you listening, and what are you smiling about?" Davie asked.

"No, sorry, I was distracted by this morning's work, and this."

He turned the camera so the other two could see the screen. Kevin was waist high in foam, and having fashioned a hat with some of it, grinned into the lens.

Kevin held out his hand. "May I?"

"Of course. Scroll to the left." JJ passed the camera across the table and stood up. "Nice as this unexpected foam party has been, I must get back to Sharon, then

I'll have time to pop out if she needs anything. The car's not moving. I doubt I'll find parking much closer. Cheaper here too. Where are you planning on going, or shall we agree to meet back here?"

"Not far. I'm knackered already. Probably the pizza place on The Triangle. I can make that. You didn't answer my question," Davie replied.

"Which was?" JJ took the camera back and nodded thanks to Kevin, who complimented him.

"Did you hear what Kevin said about Amber?" When JJ replied in the negative, Davie rolled his eyes. "He said, as you have already concluded, that it was someone she knew, and that being the case, if we've cleared all her male friends, it must be a woman. Which is what I've said all along. But we haven't, have we?"

"Haven't what?" JJ asked.

"Cleared all the men. Namely miserable Mark, and I feel bad saying it, but also Gary."

JJ and Kevin stared at Davie, who held out his hands. "It's true. When you were on the force and something like this happened, who did you always look at first? I'll tell you: the boyfriend, the husband, the ex. Why would he have done it? I'll tell you why. Because he wanted her back, but she was having a whale of a time playing the field. I'm not saying he did it, but I am saying we haven't got his alibi. Surely Evans has checked him out? Might save you an embarrassing conversation."

"It wasn't Gary." JJ sounded assertive, but added, "I'll call Rach and ask on the way to the hospital. See you later."

JJ was making the call before he'd reached the street.

Chapter Nineteen

JJ LEFT A MESSAGE for Rachel on her phone. He considered calling Gary but dismissed that idea. Even if the police had been tardy in their work, now he was giving them a nudge, they'd get on with it. He worried about it all the way to the hospital. Had he missed something? Was Gary that good an actor? He always tried to see the best in people, so had he missed the bad? He was frowning as he entered Sharon's room.

"What's the matter? You don't look very happy?" Sharon pushed the control to raise the bed so she was more or less sitting up.

"I'm okay, I think. More importantly, how are you feeling? Has the headache gone?" JJ sat in the chair next to the bed and took Sharon's hand.

"Pretty much. I keep telling the nurses to get a doctor in here. I could come home tonight and free this bed up for someone else. Now, my condition is out of the way, why the frown? It's still there."

"I've been looking at the organisation of the exhibition with Davie and Kevin. We had a foam party, but that's another story, and Davie pointed out that whilst he and Kev both think it's most likely to be a woman who killed Amber, we haven't verified the alibis of either Mark Baxter or Gary."

"Very remiss of you, but why the...no, JJ? It's not Gary. He wouldn't, would he?" Sharon grimaced.

"I hope not, Sharon. I really do."

For the next hour, they discussed everything from Amber's murder to whether or not they'd get a holiday in the sun during the school holidays. A nurse bustled in, and their musings were interrupted while she took Sharon's vitals, giving brief nods or smiles as she logged the results. When she'd finished, she tapped the end of the bed.

"Your wish might just have been granted. Doctor is doing his rounds, if he thinks you're anywhere near good to go, he'll send you down for a scan. All your readings are the right side of wrong. But don't get too excited, there's a backlog, so keep your fingers crossed."

"What time will he be here?" Sharon asked.

"Ah, and now we're back to a piece of string, but I should think in the next hour."

"Do you think I can insist?" Sharon asked as the nurse departed.

"No. I think you need to listen to the doctor. They'd have you out of here in a flash if they thought it was safe to do so, so don't push your luck. Anyway, if Connie knows you're home, she'll expect you to work tomorrow. Staying in is another crisis averted. You're not going back to work," JJ told her.

"Don't be mean to Connie. She saved me, remember? Although I agree, she'll be on the phone as soon as she hears. She'll be taking classes herself, too near the end of the year to blow any more of the budget on a supply teacher. My kids will never forgive me, just as well they're going up a year." Sharon pursed her lips. "But I'll always be grateful that she came and checked on me. Those extra minutes might have been vital."

"Okay, conceded. I am mean and horrible. But did you notice you said check on you, not help you? I bet she wanted to give you something else to do before the bell went. When I get out of here, I'll send her some flowers as a thank you. I'm not heartless."

"So, before the doctor comes, let's go back to Gary and Amber. What are you going to do?" Sharon asked.

"I'll catch up with Mark Baxter first, and speak to Rach about Gary. If they've not checked, they can do it. I'm offended even thinking about it."

"God, I hope he's been cleared. Can you imagine how awkward it will be if his alibi doesn't check out? I won't be able to look at him without wondering if he did it. If he's going to effectively make poor Luke an orphan. It would destroy that poor little boy."

"I'm sure it will all be fine. Let's change the subject and keep your blood pressure down. The doctor might appear any moment. Talking of which, Evans was having trouble pinning down Sandy Bentley, so I don't know what's what there either."

"I thought we were changing the subject! Tell me about Kevin."

They spent the next thirty minutes talking about Davie and Kevin and how much would be fair to charge for any of the prints JJ was showing. The nurse appeared again.

"Doctor's here. Would you step outside, Mr Elliott?" she asked.

"Jenson, but yes, of course." JJ got to his feet, as a deep voice called to him.

"JJ, is that you? I think it is. How the devil are you?" Coat flapping behind him, Simon Redding strode towards Sharon's bedside, his hand held forth. "It's been what? Ten, fifteen years? Closer to the latter, I reckon. You look...how should I put this? Um. Casually healthy." He poked a finger in JJ's stomach. "No real paunch, a few more wrinkles, but what is that around your mouth?" Not waiting for a response, he turned to Sharon. "Apologies. We went to school together. Simon Redding at your service. I've had a look at your chart. Everything is moving in the right direction, so I've warned them to expect you in radiology. Not sure how long it will take, but if all is well, we'll have you home by midnight." He shook Sharon's hand.

"I'm happy to take my chances and come back tomorrow for the scan, if it helps. JJ will keep an eye on me," Sharon replied.

"I'm sure he would do little else, but it's not going to happen unless that swelling has reduced significantly. How's the headache now?"

Redding asked her several more questions, reminisced a little with JJ, before ending the consultation.

"JJ, this could take hours. They'll take Sharon down in the next twenty minutes, then it's anyone's guess. And then I'll have to sign off the results, etcetera. You get the picture. If I were you, I'd go about whatever it is you're up to these days and call in a couple of hours to see if you need to bring more grapes, or pick Sharon up. Lovely to see you. We must get together sometime soon." He pumped JJ's hand again, saluted Sharon, and was gone.

JJ dropped back into his chair. "A couple of hours will be the end of visiting, but I'll get in here somehow if it's not to pick you...uh oh. Not expecting any calls. Hope Davie and Kevin aren't in any trouble." JJ pulled out his phone, looked at the screen and thrust it towards Sharon. "Connie. Tell her you're here for a week." JJ settled back in his chair and listened to the one-sided conversation.

"Hi, Connie, it's Sharon. Yes, he's with me. Yes, I heard about my phone. Totally knackered, apparently. Of course. Not too bad, although they won't let me out until the brain swelling has gone down." Sharon winked at JJ. "No, he is not! Thank you, yes, of course. I don't know. I'm guessing once I'm out of here. Yes, sure. 'Bye." Sharon hung up and handed the phone back to JJ. "Just checking to make sure all is well. Never even mentioned me going back. Told me to take it easy."

"Good. I have to say, her actions today have made me see her in a different light. If she could but change her superior attitude, she'd be more palatable. I'll order those flowers now while we await your departure."

JJ selected what he thought was appropriate and placed the order, updating Sharon as he went.

"You didn't ask for my approval. I might not like them," Sharon told him.

"They're flowers. They're pretty. Hopefully, they'll smell nice. Oh, stand by your beds. The wheelchair has arrived."

JJ kissed her goodbye, and telling her he'd see her later, one way or another, he left her being wheeled towards the service lift. Once out of the hospital, he headed back towards his car, and called Davie who sounded very cheerful, and insisted JJ join them for a pizza.

Once more, the three men settled comfortably into each other's company. They talked about everything and anything, but nothing important. At six thirty, JJ yawned, his arms raised above his head.

"This day has gone on forever. Sorry, Davie, have another pudding or something. There's no way I'm driving back to Frampton, only to turn round again. I'll give the hospital a ring and see if Sharon has had her scan yet."

Leaving them at the table, JJ wandered out into the street and paced up and down, while the nurse tried to find out what was happening. When she returned, the news wasn't good. Sharon had had her scan, wasn't yet back on the ward because a few emergencies had come in, and the doctor had been called away. It was unlikely she'd be discharged. Back in the restaurant, he updated the others.

"So, all is not lost, but I think I'm going to head for home now. Try to get some sleep in, just in case they let her out later. Would you mind?"

"Never thought we'd get there. I might fall asleep in the car on the way home. You fit, Kev?"

Kevin finished his drink and the three men headed back to the bank building. JJ had only seen Kevin from the waist up, and laughed as he came down the steps to the street.

"Kev, I'm sorry. I never thought about shoes. What size are you? I'll see if I can dig some out. You can't wear those boots with shorts. Even I wouldn't do that. Did the staff in the restaurant not say anything?"

"Already sorted. We've ordered some online. Should be at your place tomorrow," Davie told him. "I've ordered a few other bits, too. We'll talk money tomorrow."

They settled a very contented Kevin back in his building and drove home. The traffic was light, and both were quiet. It was Davie who broke the silence as they drove up the hill towards High View Terrace.

"I don't think we've ever been this quiet for so long. What's on your mind? You can't be worrying about Sharon. She's in the right place."

"Indirectly. Something is niggling at me, and I don't know what. Until we catch whoever it is, she's in danger. We're missing something. I reckon we know it, but haven't realised it, or something like that. I'm rusty."

"Once you know what's happening with Sharon, we can track down miserable Mark and speak to Gary. We'll have to ask, unless the police have sorted it. Did you speak to Rach?"

"No. Left a message. Who knows, I might dream the answer., We need to set that camera on our phones but not tonight, my brain won't cope. Might take a while to sort Sharon a new one." JJ pointed at the camera on his front door as he pulled up outside.

As they walked up the path, Gary called across to them as he walked down his path.

"I've been waiting to catch you. How did it go? I was hoping to pop back in, but I've loaded the car with Amber's exhibits, and I'll work with Kevin on sorting out the where and how tomorrow. I have to say, he was a turn up, truth be told, I was concerned when I first saw him in the gallery. How rude, how's Sharon? Not home I see."

"Sharon's fine, still in, but that's a long story. Kevin is great, isn't he? Everything is under control. Davie and Kevin have made a good start for you. I'll pop in myself once Sharon's sorted and home. How did you get on at the undertakers?"

"It's booked. Need to meet with the vicar now. Not looking forward to that. Never expected to be doing this at my age." Gary seemed to deflate. "How's the investigation going? Do I owe you anything?"

Davie put his arm around Gary's shoulder before JJ opened his mouth. "Don't worry about money at the moment. We can sort that out another day, but I do have a question for you. It's delicate, but it's got to be asked." Davie held up his hand to silence JJ. "No, JJ, Gary won't mind."

"I'm sure I won't but can't imagine what it is. I'm braced. Fire away."

"With the exception of Sandy Bentley, we've confirmed the alibi of everyone who might be considered a suspect, except miserable Mark, and...you. JJ here is finding it hard to phrase it correctly, so I'll just shoot from the hip and hit you between the eyes." Davie gave Gary's shoulder a squeeze and removed his arm. "Where were you when Amber died, Gary? And can anyone confirm it?"

Gary deflated a little more. "Was murdered, Davie. She died, yes, but only because someone pushed her off that bridge. I was with a friend, female. All totally innocent. She left me at about eight thirty but I stayed in the restaurant talking with the owner until a little after nine thirty. The police have confirmed that."

Gary gave JJ's arm a half-hearted punch. "You could have asked, you know. No offence taken. I'd better get back. It's Luke's bedtime. He might be with me tomorrow, by the way. School was upsetting for him today. Sharon is a favourite, as you know. He asked me why the bad man was hurting all the ladies he loved and told Emma she had to stay the night because we have a security camera. She'll go home once he's asleep. I'm not a violent man, but when you catch him, and I have every faith in you, I'm going to do him some serious damage and sod the consequences." With a nod and a half wave, Gary headed for home.

"Told you." JJ said as he opened the door. "Should have waited until Rach confirmed it. He was happy...ish, when he got here. He's not now."

"Yes, but you'll sleep a little easier, I hope. Look, JJ, his wife's dead, he's arranged her funeral, his kid won't go to school because he's scared, and he's got to work with you. He wasn't happy, he was putting on a brave face. I wonder who his lady friend was? Cup of tea?"

"Nope, shower and feet up in front of some pointless telly. I need a nap. Hopefully, if I call the ward, I'll get to speak to Sharon."

When JJ came back from his shower, Davie was asleep in the armchair, his feet resting on the coffee table. He hadn't needed mindless television to send him off. JJ lay out on the couch, and had been asleep for about twenty minutes when the phone rang. Davie didn't stir, but JJ whispered into the phone to avoid waking him, while he himself regained full consciousness. There was a pen on the table, and JJ opened the drawer beneath to find something to scribble a note on.

Note written, JJ placed it on Davie's lap, collected his camera and keys, and headed back to the hospital with a smile. He would definitely sleep well tonight with Sharon next to him. To stop him from thinking, he turned up the radio, and made up the words for lyrics he only half knew. With minimal traffic, he made it in record time. Sharon was sitting in the family room reading her book, and smiled as he entered.

"Told you I was coming home tonight. I said I'd wait in here, so they could get the bed ready. Wasn't expecting you this soon. I thought I'd finish my chapter." Placing a folded sheet into the book to mark her page, she dropped it into the carrier. "And I still have some chocolate left. If I can't sleep because I have been sleeping most of the day, I can watch a movie and stuff my face, as I've been good today and eaten half my body weight of fruit. Oh yes, and before you nag, I've got a list of dos and don'ts from the doctor and I have to have another scan the day after tomorrow. So, your wish is granted because I won't be going back to school this week. You may carry my bag to the car."

The journey home was as quick, and Sharon read the precautionary warnings from the list to JJ.

"I won't be doing any strenuous exercise, drinking alcohol, or driving. If I start vomiting, I will allow you to take me back to the hospital and I will also expect you to do that should I faint, lose consciousness, or black out. Have you got all that?"

"I have. Underlined, and highlighted in my brain. Quiet as we go in, it was a long old day for Davie, he's been doing physical stuff. Oh, that's a thought. You can come and give your opinion on the exhibition tomorrow. You'll get to meet Kevin and can help Gary decide how he wants Amber's work displayed."

"I'll look forward to it. Shh. He's still asleep."

Sharon walked into the living room and looked at Davie. "Is it me, or does he look a bit healthier than when he arrived?"

"He does. Probably coming off a diet of burgers and crisps helps. And he's clean, of course. I'll show you the shots I took of Kevin when you're settled. You won't recognise him as the same man when you meet him. Sit down, I'll put the kettle on."

Sharon walked to the coffee table and pushed the drawer shut. "You've been pilfering my already pilfered stationery. Oh, sorry, Davie, did we wake you?"

"No, I was resting my...they let you out then? I must have dozed off. How are you feeling?" Davie stretched and yawned. "You look okay."

Half an hour later, the house was locked to Sharon's satisfaction, and they headed for bed. As she had threatened, Sharon found a romcom on television and propped up, she ate her way through a bag of chocolate buttons.

JJ drifted off to sleep. He was woken up in the early hours by Sharon shaking him.

"JJ wake up. You're dreaming and I don't want another injury."

JJ blinked against the light and sat up. "I'm sorry, love. I don't know what brought that on, and I'm supposed to be looking after you."

"It wasn't your usual. It was about a woman. Have a drink of water, go and have a pee, and let's get back to sleep."

JJ grinned at her. "A woman? What was I saying?"

"I don't know. Stop grinning. It wasn't spicy. I don't think so, anyway. You were mumbling something about someone being right, over and over again. Then you shouted it's her, threw your arms out and hit me in the chest. We're going to have separate beds if you're making a collection of nightmares. Pee. Now."

JJ swung his legs off the bed and drained his glass of water. He took it with him to the bathroom to refill. When he came back, the bedroom was in darkness and Sharon was feigning sleep. He kissed her forehead and snuggled down, believing that sleep would now evade him. JJ was wrong. He was snoring within minutes. Sharon nudged him, grunted and turned her back on him.

When he woke, daylight filtered around the edge of the curtains, and Sharon's breathing was calm and even. Unlike his own. He placed a hand on his chest. His heart was pounding. Moving slowly, he got out of bed and waited to make sure he was safe to walk. He felt fine, so he tiptoed down to the kitchen. He might not be having a seizure, but something was wrong with him.

Filling the kettle, he unlocked the back door and walked to the top of the garden. It was going to be another scorcher. The slight breeze lifting his hair was already warm. Leaning against the top fence, he looked back at the house to assess his condition. He felt nervous. Not ill. Nervous. His heart was beating a little faster, his stomach was fizzing, and...no. Not nervous. Excited. That's how he felt when he tied up a case. This was how he felt when he found the last piece of the puzzle.

He knew who did it. He knew who had killed Amber.

Except he didn't.

JJ ran back to the house and looked at the sheets tacked to the wall. Davie was right. He needed a board, because this wasn't working. It was too difficult to note, edit, add. Something was missing and he couldn't see it. What? He pulled the sheets down and scribbled notes on them. The whys, the connections, and put them back up in a different order. Nothing.

"Morning. How long have you been up?" Sharon put her head around the door.

"Morning. Don't know. What's the time?" JJ gave her a smile and returned to his wall of paper.

"Almost six. What are you doing? Tea?"

"An hour. I know somewhere in my brain I know who did it, but I can't access it. It's driving me bloody mad. I'm getting a whiteboard ordered today. I can't work with sheets of paper. They're too...wrong. Yes, tea would be lovely, and a piece of toast wouldn't go amiss. I'll come and join you."

JJ made the breakfast, having refused to allow Sharon to help.

"You should use smaller cards. In there. If they were smaller, you could move them about easier. You could even go all retro and use red thread to join one to the other."

"Join what to what? Is there tea in that pot?" Davie walked into the kitchen. "How do you expect me to sleep when I can smell toast? Pass a clean spoon, JJ. Don't want to contaminate anything. What's the topic of conversation that you join one to the other?"

Laughing, JJ held out a teaspoon but snatched it away before Davie could take it.

"I know who did it. I bloody knew I knew, and now I know. Shit." JJ banged the spoon against his forehead. "Shit."

"JJ, mate, stop being dramatic and tell us who you think it is," Davie said as he joined Sharon at the table.

"Hush. Let me think."

Turning away, and leaving them sitting at the table, JJ walked back to the top of the garden. He ran through everything again, only this time he put his suspect in the middle of the action. Yes, yes, and yes. All he needed was motive, and he knew how to find out. But before he jumped the gun, one final check.

"Look out. He's coming back, and he looks like he means business." Davie pointed his toast at JJ who was marching down the garden.

"I'm pretty sure I'm right about who the murderer is but I just need to check something."

"How? What's happened that we don't know about?"

"The cards. But that's what I want to check. Sharon, I need you to think very carefully because you could hold the key to all this."

JJ asked Sharon several questions. She confirmed what he thought was the case. Davie and Sharon exchanged a glance.

"But you can't think—" Sharon began but fell silent as JJ left for the garden again.

"One call and I'll tell all." Once at the top of the garden, he made his call. "Hello, Gary. Sorry it's so early, a question for you, who was the lady friend who supplied your alibi?"

"Connie Gerrard. But you know what she's like. It would be—"

"I think you need to get Emma to stay with Luke and come here. I'm calling the police."

Chapter Twenty

RACHEL SAMPSON TOOK A seat at the kitchen table. Davie had decided today was the day he'd smoke his last cigarette and was hovering just outside the back door. Gary held his head in his hands, and Sharon was comforting him. JJ stood stony-faced, leaning against the sink.

"Come on, JJ, I'm going to miss the briefing and get a bollocking. I can see something's happened. Tell me."

"I wanted you to make the arrest, and I didn't want Evans to take the credit. I'm going to tell you who did it and why, and when you get back to the station, you can spin that whichever way you please. It'll look good on your record and might secure you a place in CID."

"Bloody hell. Go on then. Tell me."

"Gary and Amber separated because Gary, chair of the Parent Teacher Association, had a fling with Connie Gerrard. It was brief, and it was mutually...I don't know use your imagination. Anyway, Gary realised it was sex for sex's sake, finished it, and came clean with Amber. Neither woman took it well. Amber kicked him out. Connie was the woman scorned, but she held onto the hope that she could make it right again. Then Gary started dating Amber, hoping they could reconcile."

Gary gave a groan, and Sharon patted him on the back. "He's okay. Carry on."

"On the night Amber was killed, Connie saw Amber while she was locking up after the exercise class. I don't know what they spoke about, but it seemed amicable. They parted company. Connie leaves the school to drive to Bristol to have dinner with Gary, possibly full of hope that they can rekindle their affair. Gary tells her the reconciliation with Amber is going to happen, and that in future he won't even take Connie's calls. Connie leaves him at eight thirty, having made quite a scene. She's 'fighting mad' was Gary's description, and he stays in the restaurant to drown his sorrows. Connie has plenty of time to get back to Frampton Down, meet up with Amber, and push her off that bridge."

"But why? Why would Amber go with her?" Gary asked. "Why would she be so stupid?"

"Why stupid? Amber didn't know about your emotional showdown. She only knew the headteacher, Connie, the one who had been very pleasant as she saw them out. Amber had had a few flings herself since your separation. Most meant little to her, apart from one. Perhaps she thought it would be for the better. Who knows what Connie said to convince her? Perhaps Amber did know, there are few secrets in this village, and wanted to talk to make sure it was all over. Perhaps Connie told her what she wanted to hear. Who knows? Did Amber know your lady friend was still bothering you, even if she didn't know it was Connie?"

"No." Gary covered his face with his hands. "I didn't want her to get jumpy and think I might get tempted again."

"So, Amber had no reason to believe that Connie was a threat to her for any reason. I doubt Connie met with her with murder in mind. Although, what possessed Amber to clamber up onto that parapet escapes me. Perhaps Connie will tell you that, Rach, with enough coaxing."

"Okay, I'm with you so far, but how did you get there? Connie wasn't even on the radar." Rachel asked.

JJ held up the card he'd left on Davie's lap the night before. "Stationery, or lack of. I'd like to think I'd have worked it out, anyway. But Sharon pilfered these cards from school. If you check, the card that was sent here yesterday is similar, if not identical. I realised that connection this morning, so I asked myself who worked at the school or would use these cards, especially when something they hadn't planned happened."

"Keep going, JJ. That makes no sense, and I know the rest." Davie came back into the kitchen.

"Okay, in the adding up. One, Connie comes bearing gifts when news of Amber's death gets out. Gary is taking calls from someone he doesn't want to talk to. Connie openly told me to leave it alone. Connie knew Sharon would be at the school alone, and I believe she might even have put the card through the door before she attacked Sharon. That or she did it before she went to the hospital. I suppose that's more likely. I also don't think she meant to hurt her so severely and was genuinely remorseful. She also knew about the door cam. Gary told her he was helping Davie fit theirs and why, when she called him. So she took Sharon's phone and smashed it up. Connie called while I was at the hospital to speak to Sharon. Do you know what she asked her?" JJ shook his head that he hadn't cottoned on earlier.

"Go on," Rachel encouraged.

"Had Sharon heard about the phone being found? Had the police managed to get anything from it? Would JJ stop interfering now Sharon had been injured?"

"I hadn't told anyone about the threat to me, and certainly not the card Davie found." Sharon joined the conversation. "I can barely believe it, but it makes sense."

"Okay, I'm sold. But we have no proof. No fingerprints on anything. No one saw her, and unless our chaps can get something from that phone, she might just deny it." Rachel shrugged. "I'm not saying we won't bring her in, but the CPS wouldn't go to court on that, would they?" She looked at JJ. "You know better than me."

"She wouldn't deny it, how could she?" Gary demanded. "I'll make her bloody tell you."

Gary jumped to his feet and grabbing his arm, Sharon pulled him back down.

"No, you won't, I will. JJ, give me your phone. Silence now. I'm putting this on speaker. Rach, record it."

Connie snapped a greeting as she answered the call. "JJ, what do you want? In case you've forgotten, I'm short staffed and—"

"It's me, Connie. I'm home. Where are you?" Sharon asked.

"Hello, Sharon, sorry I was short. I'm run off my feet. I've been here since seven trying to do my job before I do yours. You wouldn't believe...haven't got time. We'll catch up later. What did you want?"

Sharon sighed. “I don’t know how to say this, so I’m just going to come out with it. Why shouldn’t I go to the police?”

There was silence while Connie considered this. “Sorry, Sharon, about what?”

“Connie, don’t mess about. I’m in pieces here. Why did you do it? What have I done wrong?” Sharon managed to sob. “I’m your friend. The one person who always has your back. Why?”

“Sharon, calm down. I don’t know what you’re talking about.”

JJ could tell from Sharon’s face that she was beginning to doubt their theory, and he wound his finger, encouraging her to continue.

“I’m talking about you hitting me over the head, then pretending to be my saviour. I saw you, so I know what I’m talking about, and I’m asking you why? Or should I just go to the police?”

Connie started crying. “I’m sorry. So sorry. I had no intention of hitting you so hard, but I had to stop JJ. I...”

Rachel left her phone on the table, pointed at JJ, and jerked her thumb towards the front door. She then turned to Sharon and mouthed, ‘Keep her talking.’ They left silently as Connie continued.

“Please don’t go to the police. I can explain. But not now. People are arriving. I need to clean myself up. I’ll be with you as soon as I’ve sorted the class out. Probably get them to double up in the hall or something. Promise me, Sharon, you won’t do anything until we speak. Make sure JJ’s not there. I can’t do it with him there. I know he hates me.”

“JJ doesn’t hate anyone. You know that. He won’t be here, anyway. He’s going to Bristol to sort the exhibition out with Gary. Gary’s going to include some of Amber’s work, which I think is nice, fitting, don’t you? Gary’s organised the funeral, by the way, but I don’t know the date yet.”

“Nice. Yes. Good old Gary, what a man. Look, promise me you’ll wait until I get there before you do anything. I must go, the kids are starting to arrive. Promise me.”

“I promise I won’t speak to JJ or the police until we meet. But Connie, I—”

“Thank you. See you later.”

Connie hung up, and Davie stopped Rachel’s phone recording.

"Do you want to drive down and see what happens? Because I do."

Sharon and Gary were on their feet before he'd picked up his keys.

Connie Gerrard looked around her office. Had she lost it all? What now? Hold her head up and lie. That's what. She knew her makeup would be ruined, but she couldn't halt the tears.

Bloody Amber Wilton. All she'd wanted to do was explain to Amber that she and Gary were in love. It might have been a little one-sided, but it was love. So, she'd apologised about the affair, but before she could get to the punch line, Amber told her she was forgiven, and Connie wanted to slap her. But Connie had to get it sorted and thanked her. She'd invited Amber to walk with her. Connie could convince her to let Gary go. Connie could convince most people she was right, whatever the subject. And if all else failed, she would put a spoke in the wheel to stop any reunion.

But Amber wouldn't shut up.

"I know what it's like now. The thrill of something new. The excitement of the first time. But I'm glad it's over. I'm a homebody at heart. Don't get me wrong, I like a laugh, and things can never be the same, but he loves me, and I love him. I forgive you. I forgive him. We'll turn the page and start afresh. I'm going to tell him tonight. I'll call him, tell him to pack a bag and get his arse home. Can't wait to see him." Amber giggled. "I feel like a bloody teenager, and I want to shout at the top of my voice, and I want to dance. I want everyone to know how happy I feel."

Connie had swallowed back her chosen response. She wanted to slap the stupid woman senseless. She couldn't, though, could she? "You should do something wild, then. You're certainly wired tonight. Get up on the bridge, shout into this bloody wind. It can carry your message to the world."

Amber stopped walking and looked at Connie. "Wow. I would never have expected that from you. So poetic. So real. I've always thought you were very strait-laced. Thought that might have been what the attraction was. Winning over the ice queen. You know, the opposite of me. Bugger it, I will. Get your phone out, take a picture so I can paint it."

And there she stood. Amber bloody Wilton, calling out her happiness into the wind while Connie's world crumbled around her. Connie would have to move. She couldn't put up with this day in and day out. How long before everyone knew he'd chosen Amber over her? Distracted, Connie realised Amber was still speaking, the woman never stopped, and she lowered the phone.

"One photo will do. Help me down before I go off the edge. I can jump down if you hold my hand." Amber giggled as Connie grunted disbelief and stepped closer. "Don't doubt me, I can do it. But brace yourself because I might make the earth move. I'm good at that."

Connie wanted to slap her, and she stepped forward to tell Amber Wilton exactly what she thought of her, but as she raised her hand, an anger, the like of which she'd never felt before, took hold, and pulling back her arm she punched Amber's fat, wobbly leg.

Amber's scream had brought Connie back to her senses. She shouldn't have done that, but the stupid woman could sort herself out. She was going home. Home to work out how she could leave Frampton Down without everyone knowing why. Without everyone knowing he chose Amber over her. Could she even go into work the next day? What if Amber came into school to have a showdown?

Connie turned and ran.

Connie had been running one way or another ever since, and she needed to run now. Snatching her bag and keys from her desk, she headed for the carpark. Ignoring whoever had called her in the lobby, ignoring the caretaker's wave, she headed for her car.

Shit. There was JJ. Flipping off her shoes, Connie sprinted to her car. The woman with JJ ran the opposite way. JJ was running towards her.

Stay calm. Shut the door. Start the engine. Swerve past JJ. See, she could drive. Now accelerate.

Three seconds later, she screeched to a halt as someone jumped in front of the car.

Sara Dent. Stupid bloody bitch.

Opening the door, Connie sprinted towards the field. She only got a few yards before she was brought to the ground. Her face hit the gravel. Connie still had some fight in her and flipped over, expecting to see Dent. Her mouth fell open as the woman who'd been with JJ flipped her back over.

"Connie Gerrard, I am arresting you for the murder of Amber Wilton."

Connie heard a collective gasp from the few gathered to watch the spectacle as the handcuffs went on. The woman carried on.

"And for causing grievous bodily harm to Sharon Elliott. You do not have..."

Connie opened her mouth and screamed; she didn't hear the rest of the caution. As the woman helped her into the back of her car, Connie was sobbing. As the gathered crowd inched closer still, and Sara Dent applauded, she passed out.

Chapter Twenty-One

JJ TOOK LUKE'S HAND and walked up to the Three Bells. Old Sam limped along on the other side.

"Are you happy with that, young 'un?" Sam asked.

"Yes. Daddy said I could plant some flowers there, and we can keep coming back for a chat. It doesn't matter that she's not there, you know, she can still hear. Did you know that?"

"I did. I talk to my missus all the time. She still argues with me, up here." Sam tapped the side of his head. "What's it going to be today? You brave enough to try them pork scratchings yet?"

"No! Disgusting!" Luke turned to JJ. "Race you to the bench. Last one there has got to pay."

"What? Have you got money to pay? I'm feeling fit today."

"Yep." Luke pulled a five-pound note from his pocket. "The lady from the café gave me it. She was saying hello to her mum, too. GO." Luke took off at speed, and shouting after him, JJ followed at a leisurely jog.

It was three days until Amber's funeral, and Gary had decided that it would be too much for Luke to cope with, so he'd purchased a bench, and with permission from the vicar had installed it, complete with a brass plaque, at the rear of the churchyard near the water pipe. A suitable location for the bereaved to sit and have a silent word. It had been installed the night before, and Luke had insisted that JJ and Sam go to see it with him as soon as he got home from school.

Luke won the race, and by the time Old Sam had reached them, JJ and Luke were sitting on a bench with their drinks. A beer was waiting for him. He perched next to Luke and took a draft.

"Just what the doctor ordered. So are you going to this exhibition? Jemma is." Sam asked Luke.

"Yep. I'm going with Miss Elliott because she's better now. Daddy will already be there, and JJ. Are you coming?"

"I'd love to, but someone has got to stay and run this place."

"I'm on holiday from school now, so I can go when I want. I could go with you tomorrow."

"What if it's rubbish and you don't want to go again?" Sam asked with a wink for JJ.

"It won't be rubbish. My mum's paintings are there. I'm going to buy one with this." The five-pound note appeared again. "So, do you want to?"

As they agreed that JJ would take them, Davie and Sharon arrived.

"We thought we'd find you here. I convinced Sharon to come for a quick one. We're all dolled up, but you JJ cannot go to the opening night of your exhibition dressed like that? Can he, Zed?" Davie asked.

Luke looked JJ up and down. "He looks like he always does. I'm not putting a shirt on. Daddy never said we had to wear shirts. He always does, but we don't." He then looked Davie up and down. "You look the same, even with a shirt."

"Thanks." Davie turned back to JJ. "Did Teresa get hold of you? She came to the house."

"Yep, we're going to Liverpool after the...after Monday. The exhibition will be well underway, so I won't be needed. We'll talk later. Right now me and Zed are going to get spruced up. He's got a fiver, he's going to buy one of his mum's paintings."

When they arrived at the exhibition, Gary hadn't let them down. Huge plastic banners let passersby and invitees know there was an exhibition on. Large posters of some of the exhibits had been pasted onto the boarded windows. Inside there were a dozen visitors milling around, drinks in hand, looking at the artwork. By seven, there was a constant stream of people coming in and out, and Kevin, with his new haircut and black trainers, handed out the last drink on his tray and beckoned JJ to one side.

"It's going well. You've sold half your exhibits. Candice must be rolling in it. She's sold quite a few of her sculptures too. Haven't checked on Amber's."

"They'll all go. Amber's paintings always did. You look very smart, I must say. Not sure how much use a white shirt will be to you in the future though."

"That's what I wanted to tell you. You need to buy some more frames and get your printer sorted. I showed Gary that collage you gave me. He wants you to show them. He's extended this for another week. So I've agreed to stay on. Three weeks. Who knows, if the next lot sells well, maybe longer. How much stock have you got? I'm getting used to a comfortable bed."

Teresa Burns walked over and put her empty glass on the tray.

"Oh, JJ, how amazing that they could make this old bank look like this? There are some lovely things here. I've bought one of yours and one of Amber's. Couldn't make myself pay for any of the sculptures. Sharon's disappointed. She wanted one of them, but it's gone. When we looked for the price, it had a sold sticker on it. I can see why you didn't want to start my job until next week now, that and the funeral, of course." Teresa tutted and shook her head. "Glad you caught her. Who'd have thought? You couldn't make this stuff up. Oh look, that bloke is taking photos. Is that allowed?"

"Can't see why not, but I'd better have a word. Teresa, this is my friend Kevin. He made the bank look like this. With a little help from Davie, of course."

JJ wandered over to the man with the camera. He was a reporter. The second one they'd had in. JJ glanced at Davie, who grinned and gave him the thumbs up. As he approached, the man took several photos of JJ.

"JJ Jenson. Nice work. I understand there are many strings to your bow. Police officer, missionary, artist, and now, I'm told, private detective. We'd like to interview you. This will make a great story for the Sunday mag. An excellent feature." The man pulled a card from his top pocket. "Terry Johnstone. Give me a ring. I'd have sorted that bit first, but only heard from Davie this morning."

"Will do. Now, if you'll excuse me, I need a word with Davie." JJ jerked his head towards the door, and Davie followed him to the carpark.

JJ leaned against the bonnet of Sharon's car.

Davie perched next to him. "Good news that, JJ. Terry tells me they'll do a spread. You see, I can spread the love. It's not all about me."

"Thanks, done in good faith, I know, but I don't want the attention. I won't be speaking to them, and I don't want you to."

"Why not? Are you mad? You'll either flog more photos or get more PI jobs. And you know how it is, JJ, if you don't speak to them, they'll speak to everyone else and print their version of you."

"Then that's what will happen. I've got no secrets, Davie, but I'd like to keep my head down. I—"

"But why? Come on, JJ, forget the PI stuff. Think about your art."

"If you shut up long enough, I'd tell you."

Davie pretended to zip his mouth shut. "Fire away."

JJ had just finished giving Davie his reasons, as Sharon came out to find them. Neither man noticed her approaching.

"You can't be serious. JJ, get a grip. Think about what happened last time."

"I have, and that's what's driving me."

Sharon slowed to a stop several feet behind her car.

"But it nearly killed you."

"I'm different now. The world has moved on. I'm doing it, Davie, might take years, but that's what I'm doing. I don't expect you to help but felt it only fair to tell you."

"Tell him what? What are you discussing? Look at his face. He's gone white, he looks like he's in shock." Sharon stepped forward and peered at Davie. "Are you okay?" When he nodded, she turned to JJ. "What are you going to do?"

"It's a job. Detecting. Nothing to worry about."

"Nothing to worry about?" Davie slid off the bonnet and faced JJ. "I'd say there was plenty to worry about. Do you know what he wants to do?"

"No. I'm waiting for someone to tell me." Sharon looked from one to the other. "Either of you will do. But no one is going anywhere until I know."

"He's only going after Bryn Jenkins. No word of a lie. Bryn Jenkins."

"The man who killed Daniel Boyd?" Sharon stepped forward and took JJ's face in her hands. "Is this true?"

"Yep. Sorry, love, you won't stop me. I have to do this."

"I never said I'd stop you, but before I give you my blessing, I want the full story. Not just the bits I can pick up from the internet. That case changed your life, JJ. If that happens again, I think it's only fair I know why. Don't you?"

"Probably. But not here, not now. Come on, we'd better get back. I think there's a pig with your name on."

"I saw it. It's sold." Sharon let her shoulders sag.

JJ put his arm around them. "Now I wonder who bought it?"

Davie snorted. "If I'm allowed a guess, I'd say the idiot who's going to hunt for Bryn bloody Jenkins. That's who."

Author's Note

Thank you for reading An Ill Wind. I hope you enjoyed meeting JJ Jenson & co, as much as I did. If you did, I'd be grateful if you would be kind enough to leave a review on Amazon when you have a moment. Constructive reviews are invaluable to authors. If you would rather contact me personally, the details are below. If you want to read more of my work, you can grab a free ebook copy of The Making of Meredith, the prequel to the Meredith & Hodge series, if you sign up for my mailing list at mkturnerbooks.co.uk

ABOUT THE AUTHOR

Having worked in the property industry for most of my adult life, latterly at a senior level, I finally escaped in 2010. I now work as a consultant for several independent agencies, but I dedicate the bulk of my time to writing and, of course, reading, although there are still not enough hours in the day.

For more detail visit my website: https://www.mkturnerbooks.co.uk/about

I am married with two children, two grandchildren, and two German Shepherds. We live in Bristol, UK.

I would love to hear from you, and can be contacted here:

https://www.mkturnerbooks.co.uk

Printed in Great Britain
by Amazon

40287832R00139